THE RAVEN

ALSO BY JEREMY BISHOP:

JANE HARPER HORROR NOVELS
The Sentinel
The Raven

Torment: A Novel of Dark Horror

WRITING AS JEREMY ROBINSON:

THE JACK SIGLER THRILLERS
Prime
Pulse
Instinct
Threshold
Ragnarok
Omega

THE CHESS TEAM NOVELLAS
Callsign: Queen—Book 1
Callsign: Rook—Book 1
Callsign: Bishop—Book 1
Callsign: Knight—Book 1
Callsign: Deep Blue—Book 1
Callsign: King—Book 1
Callsign: King—Book 2—Underworld
Callsign: King—Book 3—Blackout

THE ANTARKTOS SAGA
The Last Hunter: Descent
The Last Hunter: Pursuit
The Last Hunter: Ascent
The Last Hunter: Lament
The Last Hunter: Onslaught

MILOS VESELY NOVELLAS
I Am Cowboy

STAND-ALONE NOVELS
Kronos
Antarkos Rising
Beneath
Raising the Past
The Didymus Contingency
SecondWorld
Project Nemesis
Island 731

THE RAVEN

Jeremy Bishop

47N❂RTH

The characters and events portrayed in this book are fictitious. Any similarity to real persons, living or dead, is coincidental and not intended by the author.

Text copyright © 2013 Jeremy Bishop
All rights reserved.
Printed in the United States of America.
No part of this book may be reproduced, or stored in a retrieval system, or transmitted in any form or by any means, electronic, mechanical, photocopying, recording, or otherwise, without express written permission of the publisher.

Published by 47North
PO Box 400818
Las Vegas, NV 89140

ISBN-13: 9781611099157
ISBN-10: 1611099153
Library of Congress Control Number: 2012951475

DEDICATION

For Hilaree Robinson, my wife, who taught me how to write like a sarcastic woman.

1

The fist headed toward the side of my head is roughly the size of a sledgehammer. I doubt it carries the same weight or density, but the arm propelling it forward resembles José Canseco's, after he shrunk his manhood with steroids. The point is, if it hits me dead-on, I'm out for the count. Maybe worse. Even a glancing blow is going to hurt.

Lucky for me, I'm quick. And a small target. I lean back on my bar stool, locking my feet under my surly neighbor's chair to keep myself from spilling ass over teakettle.

The missed swing whirls the drunken fisherman around on his stool. When his body stops spinning, he cants away from me and falls. The man lands on an empty stool, taking the blow to his stomach with an "Oof!" Then he slips off the side of the three-foot-tall stool and lands on his back, driving out whatever air is left in his lungs.

I've somehow managed to pummel the man without lifting a finger. I sit up, polish off my third twenty-ounce beer, and guffaw along with the bar's four other regulars. I know it's not nice, but the big Greenlander had it coming. Granted, he only asked me to dance, but (A) there's no music playing, (B) his breath smells like boiled mutton left in the sun too long, and (C)—well, there isn't a (C).

And sure, I could have just said, "No, thank you." I didn't need to mention his mother.

Or sister.

Of course, it wasn't until I brought the goat into my retelling of his unfortunate birth that he drove his fist into the bar and demanded an apology. At which point I took a mouthful of lager and squeezed it out between my teeth, arcing the amber liquid onto the man's gray sweater, which I quickly learned had been handknit by his recently deceased grandmother. I'd managed to insult three generations of his family inside of thirty seconds, and here in the dock district of Nuuk, Greenland, that's cause for a fight. Even against a girl.

Family is kind of a big deal here, and familial honor, loyalty, respect, and fealty stretch back generations to the Vikings who first settled this frigid nation and told the world's most monumental lie by naming it Greenland. So I don't think he's wrong for taking a swing. I had it coming. But I've got my own set of excuses for instigating the scuffle, even if it's somewhat of a flaccid affair.

To start, I was raised by a man I call "the Colonel." My father. A hard-ass if there ever was one. He taught me how to fight. How to survive. And how to run off at the mouth. Some people get freckles, or red hair, or apelike brow lines. I inherited a proclivity for four-letter words and a knack for sarcasm that makes them sting. I'm an army brat. Blame the military. Hell, blame the president. That seems to work for most things.

But that's not really the reason for this row, or the handful of others I've sparked over the past three months. My court-appointed psychologist calls it survivor's guilt with a dash of psychosis brought on by hypothermia and starvation. I'd like to say that's what I asked her to say, but she really believes it. After all, who would believe a story like mine without seeing it firsthand? I joined the radical crew of the *Sentinel*, an antiwhaling vessel, as an undercover investigator for the WSPA (World Society for the Protection of Animals). During a confrontation with the whaling ship *Bliksem*, the *Sentinel*'s captain used C4 explosives and sank both ships. The survivors wound up on an island where an ancient clan of Vikings had been buried. Not only were these Vikings the ancestors of the *Bliksem*'s captain, Jakob Olavson, and his son, Willem, but they were also turning into zombies. Fucking *zombies*. But these weren't your run-of-the-mill shambling Romero-style undead. They were Draugar—the ancient inspiration for modern zombie *and* vampire stories. To make things worse, they were controlled by some kind of parasite that slowed decay, imprisoned their minds, and controlled their bodies.

Most of us died on that island. Only three of us survived. And we've been telling the same story since, despite being labeled insane, at least temporarily, which was our lawyer's plea. If there weren't bodies strewn all over the island, the judge might've agreed. But the "ongoing investigation" has been ongoing for two and a half months, which means they found something.

Meanwhile, I've got a GPS tracker strapped to my left leg and my name on every no-fly and no-sail list. I'd love to leave, but I'm not going anywhere. So, like a little kid coming down from a sugar high, I've decided to make myself a nuisance instead. It's not really going to help my case, but it makes me feel better, and I've yet to meet a beefy Greenlander willing to tell the police a five-foot-five-inch woman with apple cheeks and black pixie-cut hair put him in a world of hurt. His ancestors would turn over in their graves, which I now know is actually possible.

I'd like to say I'm making the Colonel proud by beating up men twice my size, but I'm also wasting my life. "Make the best of every situation," he'd say. It sounds Zen, but for him that meant something closer to, "If you run out of ammo, stab your enemy in the eye with a ballpoint pen." Or a chopstick. Your finger. Really, whatever is handy. But however you look at my past three months, I'm not making the best of anything.

I don't have a job. I'm living off the meager inheritance I discovered I had when they released me from the hospital (the Colonel died just before I set sail on the *Sentinel*). And I've distanced myself from the only two people who don't think I'm cuckoo for Cocoa Puffs. Seeing them doesn't just remind me that I survived a nightmare. It reminds me that I don't think it's over. Willem, Jakob, and I weren't the only survivors. The parasites, which can inhabit any warm-blooded mammal, escaped the island, too, carried to safety inside a herd of walruses and a pod of orcas.

So I'm alone, afraid, and, most of the time, fairly pissed off that no one will listen to me. Worse, I understand why. I do sound nuts. And I won't be surprised if I get locked up when all is said and done. Hell, if things play out the way I fear, a cell behind the walls of a mental institution might be one of the safest places to be.

The Greenlander groans as he sucks in a fresh breath. His face burns red from lack of air, but probably just as much from embarrassment. "Ilisiippoq!" he hisses.

I've acquainted myself with as many colorful Greenlandic phrases as I can retain, but this word sounds unfamiliar. "What did you call me?" I get down off my stool and find myself wobbly on my feet. I hold on to the stool with one hand and try to steady myself.

"Witch!" he says, pushing himself up.

"Stay down," I warn.

He's not going to listen, which isn't surprising, since he's drunk. Of course, he's had the same amount to drink as me, and I'm still on my feet. I'm a regular—what's her name? from *Raiders of the Lost Ark*. Margo? Maggie? Marion? That's it—Marion. Man, I'm drunk.

The giant gets to his feet and nearly careens over again. He finds his balance and raises his clenched hands as if he's about to engage in some old-timey fisticuffs. I brace myself and get ready to kick him in the nuts.

But then the TV distracts me. Something about whales.

I thrust my open palms at the man, but not as the prelude to an attack. "Wait, wait!" I say.

My moment of supplication confuses the man. He lowers his fists for a moment and glances at the TV. He's heard the whale footage and grows interested, too. "I can wait," he says.

"Turn it up," I say to the barman, who's been watching the altercation with a smile on his face. Most of my scuffles have taken place in and outside this bar. I think he likes to watch. Maybe he's simply admiring the action, as his Viking ancestors might have. Maybe he's getting his rocks off. I don't care. Whatever the reason, he doesn't call the police.

I turn my attention to the TV. I can't understand most of what's being said, but the bartender keeps the closed captions on and set to English at my request. I read the text on the screen, ignoring the stock footage and talking head.

Whales have not been seen in the waters off Greenland in the past two months, and the small whaling industry has ground to a halt. Scientists speculate that environmental factors may be the cause, but local fishermen disagree.

The image changes to a Greenlander in a bright yellow slicker and winter cap. But it's the image in the background that catches my attention. Two figures wheel supplies down a dock toward a waiting stark black ship. They're distant, so I can't really make out details, but I recognize the pair. Willem and Jakob Olavson.

What are you two up to? I wonder. I notice a label at the top of the screen that reads "Recorded Earlier," so it's not a live feed. Not that that changes anything. None of us are supposed to get near a plane or a boat.

Orange closed-captioned text covers the pair, translating what the fisherman is saying.

The whales are gone, but the fishing is better than ever. The waters are thick with krill. There is no good reason for the whales to have moved on so early in the season. It makes no sense.

"The hell it doesn't," I say to the TV.

When the report ends, I turn to leave and find the way blocked by the big man I'd quickly forgotten. He's raised his fists again.

"While I'd love to teach you a lesson about the fine art of hand-to-hand combat, I don't have time for this."

"Make time," he says in passable English, which isn't surprising, since most Greenlanders speak my native tongue. Then he goes and tacks on a "bitch."

I sigh. "This could have ended differently."

I'm not sure if it's the alcohol thinning his blood or if he's just slow, but the man looks shocked when I quickly reach into my pocket and step up close to him. A moment later, his wide eyes scrunch tight as a sharp crack fills the air. His body convulses for just a moment before he falls to the floor as though freed from a noose, crumpling in on himself.

When he falls, the bar's open door is revealed. Two people stand in the doorway, looking at me with disapproving eyes: Jakob Olavson and, half hidden behind him, son Willem.

Jakob, whose gray beard and hair frame his aging, weatherworn face, motions to me. "Raven. Come with me."

I hesitate.

"Now," he says. Even on land he's still a ship's captain.

Willem steps into the room. His golden locks and neatly trimmed beard, not to mention his wide shoulders and tall stature, make him look like the honest-to-goodness living embodiment of the Norse god Thor. As much as I'd like to channel my inner Destiny's Child and break into a musical rendition of "Independent Women," I still care what Willem thinks of me. Under his gaze, I see my current disheveled state for what it is and feel a little ashamed.

Jakob waves his hand toward my toppled adversary. "Pick up Malik."

"You *know* this guy?" I ask as I step around him.

Willem offers me a consoling but halfhearted grin. "He's our cook."

"And soon to be yours," Jakob says. "The ocean beckons us once more." He fixes his eyes on me. "All of us."

2

Despite being dubious about Willem and Jakob's presence and the demand that I join them, I can't deny I'm happy to see them. Knowing that these two men, without a doubt, don't think I'm insane is a relief. And when Willem opens the rear driver's-side door to an aged Chevy Tahoe, smiles, and says, "It's good to see you, Jane," I return the smile, wink, and say, "Right back at you, big guy."

The sentiment is true—I *am* glad to see him—but the message is filtered through sixty ounces of beer. My slurred, silly words shrink the smile on his face.

He nods to the open door. "We have something to show you."

I climb into the vehicle, which smells of oil and fish, a concoction so vile it almost brings some of those sixty ounces back to the surface. I keep the fluid down, but my face must reflect my discomfort.

Willem keeps the door open and asks, "Can I close this? Or do you need to puke?"

I groan and lean my head back, breathing through my mouth rather than my nose. It's not quite a "no," but he closes the door. As my stomach churns, I roll down the window. When Willem casts a nervous glance in my direction, I say, "Just in case." When he doesn't budge, I add, "What? It's not like I could make this dead fish on wheels smell any worse."

His smile returns before he climbs into the driver's seat. I turn my head to the right and find Malik's unconscious face lolling toward me. I shout in surprise, pushing the big man away. If Jakob hadn't quickly closed the door, Malik would have been flung outside. Instead, his head thunks hard against the window.

Willem looks back at me. "He's a nice guy. A rough sort, but kind."

"And loyal," Jakob says when he slides into the front passenger's seat. "He's a lot like you, Raven."

"You think I've been loyal?" I ask, knowing I've been anything but. I've basically abandoned them. I let out a drunken "Pfft."

Jakob turns around in his seat as Willem steers the car onto the road. "You could have changed your story at any time. You could have fled to the American embassy. You have friends in the antiwhaling community."

"Not anymore," I say with a wave of my hand.

"Had you changed your story, I'm sure one of your colleagues would have ferried you back to the United States."

I say nothing. He's right. I could have left if I really wanted to. I've got money. And with the right cover story, a number of people, including military types who owe my father, would have helped me back to the States. Even if that weren't true, I'm resourceful. Leaving Greenland *would* have been fairly easy. But I can't say that. Can't admit it. It would mean revealing that I care.

And that scares me. If the world goes to hell, or, more likely, we go to jail for the massacre on that hellish island, it will be easier to endure if I'm not also close to Willem and Jakob. Not because I'll feel responsible for *their* fates, but because the overprotective Norsemen will feel responsible for *mine*. And I don't want that to happen. Of course, the fact that they're here now, after months of me dodging them, means it's a futile effort. So I resign myself to whatever it is they've got planned and turn my attention to the view.

Nuuk's streets are lined with simple but colorful homes painted red, green, blue, and yellow, as if God ate too many Skittles and puked them up on the city. There are some industrial-looking apartment buildings, and the downtown area has some taller modern structures, but nothing over twelve stories. All of it is absolutely dwarfed by the tall, stony mountains farther inland. It's the largest city in Greenland, but in a country with a total population of fifty-eight thousand, Nuuk is closer to an average-size seaside New England town than a booming metropolis. It's quaint. And the people are kind. But it's cold. It's October, and the days are getting short. And dark. In two months we'll have just four hours of daylight per day.

But it beats a cell.

And it sure as shit beats being on an island full of Draugar.

The memory of that place turns my attention back to Willem and Jakob. I wouldn't have survived that island without them. I should trust them implicitly. But they're up to something. "Where are we going?"

No reply.

They know this will irk me, and knowing they know irks me even more. "*Guys.*"

Still nothing. I note our general direction. "We're going to the docks, right?"

Willem's quick glance at Jakob confirms it, but neither says a word.

"I saw you there, you know. On TV."

That gets a reaction. Jakob spins around. "On *TV?*"

"Just before I dropped Captain Fish-Breath over here." I hitch a thumb toward Malik. "You were in the background. Loading something onto a ship."

Jakob is mortified. Speechless.

Willem turns toward his father. "If the authorities saw…"

"Don't sweat it," I say. "I don't think anyone else would have recognized you." It wasn't necessarily true. Their pictures had been shown on the news more than a few times, along with mine, and Nuuk had a tight fishing community. As the only survivors of the *Bliksem*'s sinking, the pair was well known around the docks.

Willem steps on the gas, speeding through the winding streets. My head spins from the motion, and a wave of nausea passes through my body.

"We're going to have to move faster," Willem says.

I groan as we round a corner and I'm pressed up against Malik's body. "You're moving fast enough." My vision blurs.

"We'll leave today," Jakob replies. "We have everything we need."

"What about her?" Willem asks.

I see Jakob turn back to look at me, but his features are lost as my vision fades. "If she wakes in time, we'll give her a choice," he says.

My eyes close.

"And if she doesn't?" I hear Willem ask.

I feel myself fade as Jakob replies, "I would rather give her a choice, but in her current state, she won't be able to think clearly. No one should be forced to face the Draugar, but I think it's for the best."

Draugar? *Draugar!* The small part of my mind still awake tries to scream a string of curses at the old captain, but I fade into unconsciousness with nothing more than a drunken sigh.

3

I wake and open my eyes, but I don't see a thing before someone punches my skull from the inside. My hands go to my clenched eyes as if they can stem the stabbing pain. With a groan I let loose a string of whispered curses. I'd like to scream the words, but anything louder than a dog fart is going to make me vomit.

Among the great hangovers of my life, this isn't quite the worst, but it's compounded by a dizzying undulation that's making me queasy. *Where am I?* I wonder, and then remember who I was with when I passed out.

I stand but am sucker punched again and sent back down. I sit still, take several deep breaths, and slowly open my eyes. The floor is smooth. Painted dull gray. But a colorful braided rug covers most of it. A circle of light on the rug draws my eyes up. Through squinted eyes, I see a porthole, which confirms my fears.

I'm on a ship.

The light sends a fresh wave of pain through my head, and I turn away. The rest of the room is decorated…nicely, which seems strange. The dull gray floor and subtle scent of rust hint that this is a working vessel, not some cruise liner. So why are there flowers on the desk? Why is the blanket on the bed beneath me soft and colorful? And why is there a frikken bowl of fruit sitting atop the night table?

When I see the glass of water and antacid beside the bowl, I understand. Hangovers are caused by dehydration. A lot of people drink coffee to defeat a hangover, but it's actually counterproductive, since caffeine and alcohol are both diuretics, which dehydrate you further. Water hydrates. Antacid makes the road to recovery more gentle. And the fruit replaces sugar and nutrients flushed from the system by the alcohol.

They're taking good care of me, and for a moment, I don't question it. I pop the antacid into the water, let it dissolve, and then chug the sixteen ounces of Greenland's remarkably clean H2O. A banana chases the drink, and I'm actually starting to feel more human than tenderized beef.

As the pain subsides, I stand, let my equilibrium return, and step slowly to the portal. The light still hurts, but I push past it. The urge to know whether or not we're at sea is overpowering. Beams of sunlight reflect off the placid waters, striking my eyes like laser beams, but aren't enough to squelch my relief. We're still docked.

Which means there is still time to get the hell off this boat. I head for the door and spot my keys, wallet, and Taser resting on the dresser. I pick them up, stuff them in my pocket, and reach for the door handle. It turns before I reach it and swings open.

Willem stands on the other side, holding a fresh glass of water. We stare at each other in silence for a moment. Then his eyes drift toward the dresser and then my jeans, where the lump of keys is easy to see.

"You're leaving?" he asks.

No shit, I think, but I keep the quip to myself. Not because I'm afraid of hurting his feelings, but because I really want that glass of water he's holding. Without answering, I reach for the glass. He hands it to me, and then offers me two painkillers. I swallow the pills and drain the glass.

The silence between us grows uncomfortable, and then he grins. I'm about to smack the grin off his face when he says, "The head is right here." He raps his knuckles on a door to his right.

"The head?" I say, wondering why he'd bring it up, but then it hits me. I have to pee. Bad. "Damn your Viking voodoo," I say as the urge becomes unbearable. I open the door, slip inside, and quickly perch myself on the toilet bowl like a doting mother hen warming her eggs. I didn't bother looking for a light switch, so I sit in perfect darkness.

"Why the hell did you bring me here?" I ask, knowing Willem hasn't abandoned his post by the door.

When he doesn't answer immediately, I shout, "Well?" but regret it when my voice echoes in the small metal-walled room, exacerbating my headache.

"I'm trying to think of a way to explain that won't result in you slugging me," he says.

"Good luck with that," I mutter.

When he laughs, I know he heard me. Which means he can probably hear me peeing, too. "How about some privacy? Or do you have some weird fetishes I don't know about?"

"I'll be in your room," he says, and I hear his heavy, booted feet clomp away.

My room. Ugh.

I finish up and return to the bedroom.

"It was my father's idea," he says when I enter.

"Bringing me here?"

"The decorations," he replies. "Bringing you here was my idea."

"I thought you were trying *not* to get punched?"

He only half grins at this, probably because I'm only half joking.

"You've seen the news," he says. "You know what's going on. With the whales."

In fact, I do know. Whales have been disappearing from northern Atlantic waters, not just around Greenland, but in all Atlantic waters from the Arctic Circle to the 45th parallel, an imaginary line stretching between New Hampshire and France. That's a lot of water. And a lot of whales. "I know about the whales. The seals. The porpoises. And the fucking walruses. I've been telling your thick-headed Norse kinsmen the same thing for the past three months."

"I know," he says. "Can you blame them for not believing you? Or me? Or my father?"

He knows I don't. If someone came to me with the same story, I'd have shipped them off to the loony bin. And maybe that's where I belong.

"We can make them listen," he says. "We can show them the truth."

"How?" I demand. "Get video of whales acting weird? That won't change a thing. At best, people will just argue about the cause. Probably blame pollution. Or navy sonar. You know Occam's razor, right?"

"Lex parsimoniae," he says. "I was a history professor, remember? The simplest explanation is usually the correct explanation."

"That's how most people think, Willem. We're not going to be able to change that with a video."

"You forgot the second part of Occam's razor," he says. "The simplest explanation is usually correct, until new evidence proves it false."

I roll my eyes. "Video is *not* new evidence."

"We're going to get a sample," he says. "A parasite."

I react as though he's just slapped me in the face. After a few moments of shocked silence, I say, "*What?*"

"If we can collect a parasite, maybe let it infect a rat, show how it spreads and controls mammals, someone might take us seriously."

"You're insane," I say.

Willem gets to his feet, nearly hitting his head on the low ceiling. "You know what's coming as much as we do! How can we not try?"

I don't have a good answer for this. I understand what he's saying, but if I could go back in time and tell myself, "Hey, if you set foot on the *Sentinel*, you're going to be shipwrecked on an island populated by Viking zombies that will eat your friends, unleash a parasitic plague on the planet, and generally fuck up your life," I would. My reasoning is entirely selfish, and I'm okay with that.

"I have nightmares," I confess. "They start out simple. Like I'm brushing my teeth. But then my eyes are white and full of little white worms. Sometimes I claw my eyes out. Sometimes I try to wash it away with soap. In one dream, I jumped out the window. But each dream ends the same—I wake up screaming."

After a moment of staring at the floor, Willem says, "I have similar dreams. But they end differently."

"How?" I ask.

"With you," he says.

"Please don't say I save you or something ridiculous like that," I say. "It won't matter. You can't guilt me into coming."

He smiles, but it's sad. "You don't save me," he says. "You kill me. In a strange way, I guess that means you are saving me. From becoming one of them. A Draugr."

"That's screwed up," I say.

He laughs gently. "I know. But you'd do it, wouldn't you?"

I don't answer. Can't. Who would want to confess something like that?

"That's not really why we want you here," he says. "You were an investigator. It's what you do. You understand collecting evidence, proving things to a court. My father is a whaler, and I'm a professor. We're kind of out of our element here."

I step toward the door. "You're fast learners."

"Do you know the ships?" he asks quickly, stopping me before I leave the room.

I turn back slowly, asking, "*What* ships?"

4

After saying that he thought it better if his father explained, Willem leads me through the bowels of the ship. We're on the second deck, which is the lowest deck on the ship and mostly below the waterline. In rough or even choppy water, the portal in "my" room might be submerged. Fourteen crew quarters large enough to hold two people each line the hall at the core of the ship, seven to each side, each with its own small head—bathroom, to the nonseafaring. The quarters are sandwiched between the engine room at the ship's bow and the propeller at the ship's aft, which means that it's loud as hell down here when the ship is under way.

We follow the hallway until we reach a stairwell leading up. We take the stairs past the main deck and onto deck one. I follow Willem around a corner to another staircase that takes us to deck two. Why the second deck at the bottom of the ship and deck two are identified so similarly, I'll never know. Most people chalk it up to the strange habits of captains or ship designers, but I think they're just being lazy. When we follow two more staircases to reach the bridge, I know we're on a sizable ship, which begs the question, What ship are we on?

Willem pauses at the door to the bridge and looks back at me. "The *Bliksem* was insured," he explains. "And since the whaling industry has gone belly-up…" He shrugs. "We picked up the *Ra*—the ship—with money left to spare."

Before I can comment on his cheesy "belly-up" pun, he opens the door. "C'mon."

The bridge is laid out a lot like the bridge of the *Sentinel*. In fact, where I am now is about where I was standing when the C4 that sank both ships exploded. The people who died from the concussive force of the blast or flying metal shrapnel or who drowned as the ship sank got off easy compared to Jenny and Peach, who escaped the bridge with me. I wouldn't wish their fates on anyone. Yet here stands Willem, ready to buy a ticket for a chance to win that unholy lottery.

I see workstations—radar, sonar, communications—all the stuff you need to pilot a ship this size. The long line of oversize windows provides a view of Nuuk Bay, full of islands that dull the brunt of the Arctic Ocean's wrath. But I don't see a single person. "Do you have a crew, or am I it?"

"There are eight of us," he says, but then he corrects himself. "Seven, if we're not counting you."

"We're not," I say.

"I'm in here," Jakob calls out.

I follow his voice to port, where I find a chart room off the back of the bridge. A long table dominates the space. It's covered with maps of the North Atlantic, rulers, protractors, and compasses for course plotting. All very old-school, and exactly what I'd expect from an old Viking like Jakob.

"I'm surprised you're not sailing by the stars," I say.

He looks up at the sound of my voice and smiles so wide I can't help but return it.

"Raven!" he says and then rushes around the table to give me a bear hug. "I'm glad to see you're feeling more like yourself."

I'm not sure if that's a compliment, but I let it slide, partly because if I let the air out of my lungs, he's liable to snap my ribs. When he puts me down, I see they've actually got a laptop at the back of the room. So not entirely a Middle Ages operation. But still suicidal.

I decide to let Jakob down quick. "I can't come with you."

His smile wavers for only a moment. "But you must."

"I'm sorry, Jakob, you—"

Willem interrupts. "Tell her about the ships."

Right, I think, *the ships*.

"If we're talking about a party ship in the Caribbean with a conga line of Chippendale dancers, sign me up. Otherwise, I'm heading home."

"Raven," Jakob says, sounding serious.

"Please stop calling me that," I say. The nickname came about because of my black hair and black clothing, and the black hooded cloak I wore when I'd first met Willem and Jakob. The raven has been the Olavson family crest going back to the Norse, so Jakob saw my appearance as a good omen. But the raven was also one of Odin's pets, a creature called Muninn, later revealed to be Áshildr, a sixteen-year-old girl, an Olavson ancestor, and host to a Draugr Queen parasite capable of controlling the others. If not for the strong will of Torstein, Áshildr's father-turned-Draugr, she would have killed them all. So I'm not the biggest fan of the name.

Jakob waves off my request. "The strength of the Olavson crest is why we stand here today. The name is an honor."

It's a fight I can't win, so I drop it. "Get to the ships, so I can leave."

With a sigh, Jakob takes a seat and clasps his hands over his belly. "You know about the whales?"

"God. Yes," I say, getting exasperated. "We've been over this."

"Well, the ocean's mammals aren't the only things disappearing," he says. Seeing he's caught my attention already, he continues. "There have been an increasing number of ships lost at sea. No Maydays or distress beacons. No wreckage. They leave port and never return."

"How come I haven't seen this on the news?" I ask.

"The ships are from all over the world," he says.

"The only people putting the pieces together are online conspiracy theorists," Willem adds.

"We've tracked down news reports of twenty-three missing ships from around the world whose course took them through the North Atlantic."

"Twenty-three isn't that many," I say.

"These waters haven't been this dangerous to sail since World War Two," he says. "The ocean might as well be teeming with U-boats!"

"And yet you two are prepared to charge headlong like blind tap-dancing monkeys into a lion's den."

Jakob looks confused. "Blind tap-dancing monkeys?"

"Forget it," I say. "The point is, you're both idiots. And I want nothing to do with it."

"Jane," Willem says in a pleading voice, his hand resting on my shoulder.

It's been a long time since I've felt his touch. I *like* his touch. But right now it only serves to exacerbate my annoyance. I shrug away. "Look, I get why you're doing this. You feel some kind of ancestral responsibility. It was your ancestors who inadvertently set this plague loose, wiped out the original Norse settlements. And in a way, it was us who let that same plague escape the island. But it's not just some mindless plague. It's a parasite. An intelligent parasite. With a will of its own. It would have happened eventually, with or without the Sons of Olav. It's not your fault. It's not your responsibility."

Jakob's face turns a few shades of red darker. "Jane, it's our responsibility simply because we know and no one else does."

I read between the lines. He's saying it's *my* responsibility. I lean forward, planting my hands on the table. "I know that, Jakob. While you two have been at the docks playing Popeye the Sailor Man, I've been telling everyone who will listen. I've destroyed my life and any chance of a future outside of jail. And I really don't need *you* reminding me about that."

"What would your father think?" Jakob says.

Somewhere deep in my mind, a countdown commences. I'm about to go nuclear on Jakob. Bringing the Colonel into this argument is a low blow. I haven't even been able to return to the States to say good-bye at his grave. Jakob should have known better than to pick at that fresh scab.

It takes all of my effort to walk away, and I'm sure Willem is calling after me. But I'm not really hearing him. I yank open the bridge door and step out into the frigid October air. The sun is low on the horizon, casting the distant islands and line of docks in a striking orange glow. But I hardly notice as I storm down the exterior steps to the main deck. I don't see a ramp bridging the ship and dock, so I head for the rail.

A large man turns at my approach. His eyes go wide when he sees me. It's Malik. He's talking to me. By the look on his face, he's probably apologizing, even though he had every reason to want my head bashed in. Rather than listen to his apology, I climb the rail and hop onto the dock. When he looks over the rail at me, I flip him the bird and say, "Fuck off."

I'm not only the queen of bad first impressions. I'm the dark overlord of even worse second impressions, mostly because the first could be chalked up to alcohol consumption. This one's all me.

Not that it matters. Malik, like the rest of them, will be just another dead seaman at the bottom of the ocean soon enough.

"Idiots," I mutter as I charge up the dock, my feet stomping over the old wooden beams. "Stupid Viking macho idiots." I don't look back as I walk away, not because I don't care, but because I might change my mind. I'm sure they're standing there, watching me leave like a bunch of pitiful sad puppies. The thought is too much, and I can't help but look back.

There are no puppy-dog eyes beckoning me back. No one is watching. Part of me is grateful—it means I can go without an extra layer of guilt—but part of me is hurt by how easily they let me go. It's a stupid girlie thing to do. The Colonel would call it "acting nancy," but I am a girl.

I'm about to turn forward again when I catch the bright white name stenciled on the back of the jet-black ship. *Raven.* I shake my head. *Are they inviting ironic deaths?* "Idiots," I say again, and then start the two-mile walk back to my apartment.

5

My apartment is a two-room gem on the tenth floor of the second Jagtvej tower. Together, the twelve-story buildings are the tallest in the country, which means I nearly have the best view in Greenland. While the people on the two floors above have slightly higher elevation, it's really the people on the other side of the building—the ocean side—who got the best view. The view from my side is all mountain. Beautiful, but stark and unmoving. When the sunset reflects off the snowy peaks, it's quite striking, but I'd prefer a view of the ocean, especially now that I'm wondering if Willem and Jakob really did set sail without me.

I haven't changed my mind. Hell, I'm eating a freshly nuked Hungry-Man dinner—Salisbury steak, though how much cow is really in this thing is debatable—with slippered feet propped up on the cardboard box serving as my coffee table.

I've only been here for two months and haven't bothered properly furnishing the place. My bedroom has a mattress on the floor and stacks of cardboard boxes for shelves. The kitchenette has a frying pan, a single pot, and a few utensils for cooking, left behind by the previous tenant. But I mostly use the microwave for cooking or order out. The flat-screen TV is my nicest possession, but I didn't buy it. I found it in the trash and fixed it by replacing a five-dollar fuse. I've used it primarily for watching *Star Trek* reruns and movies.

The reruns play on TV quite frequently, but the DVDs are pirated copies from a guy on the third floor.

It's not that I'm a spendthrift or have bad taste—I just don't think I'll be staying here long, whether I'm allowed to head home to the States or carted off in the paddy wagon. That's not entirely true. I've toyed with the idea of staying, mostly because of Willem, but I'm not sure what, if anything, is really between us. And after the way I've acted these past few months, I'm not sure he'd want there to be anything between us, except maybe the Atlantic Ocean. Which is likely now the case.

My stomach churns, but it might be from the still half-frozen corn I just swallowed or from my growing fear that I'll never see Willem, or Jakob, again. Should I have gone? Should I have embraced my inner Viking and sailed to battle a mythical creature in search of a glorious death or even more glorious victory? Despite what most people think of me, I'm still sane and logical, and that Spock-like part of me says no. Going in search of Draugar, whether on land or on the ocean, is idiotic. But the part of me that listened to the Colonel tell tales of standing by his brothers, of dragging their dying or dead bodies to safety, of taking a bullet to save a comrade—that part of me feels ashamed for staying behind.

I drown my guilt in a greasy mouthful of Salisbury slop and turn on the TV. I don't bother changing the channel. I watch the same thing every evening—the local news—watching for signs. But mostly I see stories about art fairs, prize-winning goats, the fishing industry, and the infrequent crime. This time the top story is about fishing, with an Inuit reporter and the usual closed-caption translation to English scrolling along the bottom of the screen. Another record haul. Interviews with fishermen, fish market owners, and consumers come and go as I chisel out my dessert brownie, which resembles a hunk of coal. Everyone sees the upswing in the fishing market as a boon. After all, it's the economic backbone of this nation with little else in the way of natural resources. So no one stops to think about why there are more fish.

"It's because there are no predators," I growl before taking a bite of brownie. After nearly chipping my tooth on the brownie, I lean back in my yard-sale-acquired chair and take aim for the cardboard box serving as my trash can. My throw is wide, and the stone-like confection slips beneath the small fridge to join a bevy of prior missed shots.

I turn back toward the TV and see a still photo of a large cruise ship. My eyes flit to the closed-caption translation.

The *Poseidon Adventure* was last seen picking up passengers in Ireland before embarking on an Arctic cruise with a final destination in Nuuk.

An Irish man in a suit appears on the screen. The label at the bottom of the screen identifies him as Sean O'Reilly, an executive at the company who owns the cruise ship. "We're still investigating the ship's disappearance. While it is likely a simple technical issue, we're not ruling anything out at this point."

The Inuit reporter returns, as does the translation.

That statement, given yesterday, seems to be less likely as the *Poseidon Adventure* missed a scheduled docking check-in this morning. Search crews have been dispatched to the North Atlantic between Iceland and Greenland in hope of spotting the ship carrying two thousand passengers and five hundred crew on what was to be the final Arctic voyage of the season.

I'm perched so close to the edge of my seat that I nearly fall to the floor. Had I not just heard Jakob's missing-boat theory, I might not have thought twice about a cruise ship going missing. After all, what can a whale or walrus do to a ship that size? The answer is "Nothing," but given the other ships going missing, it fits the larger pattern. I pick up my phone, hoping the *Raven* is still within cell range. I may not be going with them, but I can at least let them know about this—

"The hell?" I shout when my face appears on the screen alongside Willem and Jakob. I lock my eyes on the translated text and am so angry that I have to scan each line several times to retain the words.

Authorities are searching for the whereabouts of all three survivors of the seafaring disaster that claimed dozens of lives, including many local Greenlanders. Jakob Olavson, captain of the whaling ship *Bliksem*, and his son, Willem, along with the American Jane Harper, raised eyebrows and ignited fears of foul play when they returned with a tale of treachery and fantastical mythology. All three were treated for physical wounds and psychologically evaluated before being released with orders to not leave the country while their claims were investigated. Local police had no comment on the progress of their investigation but confirmed they were recently alerted that the trio might be attempting to flee.

"I'm right here!" I shout. "I'm not going anywhere!"

A police officer appears on the screen. His words are translated a few moments after he speaks them.

The Olavsons and Ms. Harper wore ankle monitors, which allows us to track their locations. We don't constantly monitor their positions, but if they roam to certain forbidden locations— out to sea, or to an airport—the trackers send a warning signal.

"I'm *right here!*"

But in this case, the warning signal indicated that all three individuals removed their ankle monitors, within minutes of each other, earlier today in downtown Nuuk.

My eyes go wide. I swear I can feel the thing still wrapped around my ankle, but I yank up my pant leg and look down. *Sonofabitch.* I've got an ankle bracelet all right, but I'm pretty sure the duct tape and cigarette box don't transmit my location very well.

"Assholes!" I shout, tearing the duct tape away. I can't believe they did this to me. Whether or not I'm found guilty of whatever crimes they determine to have been committed on that island, I'm going to spend some time in jail for removing the monitor. In fact, they might not let me out again until the trial. "Assholes!" I repeat.

More text rolls onto the screen.

Authorities tracked the three signals north to Holsteinsborg, where they believe the trio has gone into hiding, or perhaps continued north, where their trail will be harder to follow. At this time, the police aren't certain why the three are acting together, or what their ultimate goal is, but one thing is for certain—a nationwide manhunt is under way. If you have seen—

I turn away from the screen, head reeling. I want answers to a slew of questions, but I can't focus on them. I'm in fight-or-flight mode. On one hand, I could call the police right now. If they believe me about what happened, I might be okay, but I'd be implicating Jakob and Willem in the removal of my monitor and also in kidnapping me, at least temporarily. If they use a lie detector on me, they might even figure out I know what Jakob and Willem are up to. I may not have joined their suicide mission, but I'm not going to turn them in.

Which, I realize, they know.

"Assholes!" The word is becoming my mantra. The Olavsons have given me no choice. I have to go with them or go to jail and be forced to turn against them.

My TV dinner tumbles to the floor as I rush to the bedroom. I grab my backpack, stuff my few outfits inside, add what I call my "Draugr emergency kit"—a foldable hunting knife, an ultrabright, long-lasting LED flashlight, and a Glock 19 handgun, which I would certainly go to jail for if it were discovered. I have an aluminum baseball bat, too, but decide that might draw too much attention.

With my bag packed, I return to my closet and take the one item I retained from my encounter with the Draugar, the black hooded cloak that kept me warm and resulted in my Raven nickname. The cloak originally belonged to Greg Chase, the *Sentinel*'s D&D-loving first mate, who started out a coward and later died fighting for his friends. The memory of Chase and his sacrifice brings fresh guilt to the surface. Am I acting like he did at first?

I push the question aside. I have no choice now. Guilt be damned. Time is short. I button the cloak around my neck and raise the hood. It will hide my face nicely. I throw the backpack over my shoulder, turn to the front door, and freeze.

A shadow shifts beneath the door frame.

Someone is there. A firm double knock confirms it. "Ms. Harper," says a deep masculine voice. "Open the door."

6

My feet don't make a sound on the fluffy blue rug as I tiptoe to the door. During my silent transit, the man outside knocks again, but he doesn't call out this time.

Isn't he supposed to identify himself as police? I think, but then remember I'm not in the States. Things are no doubt different in Greenland. I really don't know. Nor do I care. Anyone standing outside shouting my name is a bad thing. Could even be a neighbor hoping to turn me in.

I slip up to the door and put my eye to the peephole. The fisheye lens stretches out the body of an already lanky man standing outside the door. He's wearing some silly, thick-rimmed hipster glasses that look too young for his fortysomething face, rough skin, and brown hair that's been combed over to disguise—or not disguise, as the case may be—his thinning hair. I've grown accustomed to the area's big, burly fishermen, so the man isn't intimidating physically, but the tan trench coat screams "detective." Of course, he could be a flasher, too, for all I know, but I'm not taking chances.

The man looks down the hallway, searching in both directions for a moment. Then he steps closer and raises his fist to knock again. His coat shifts, revealing a holstered weapon. Definitely a cop of some type, but that changes nothing. I'm committed. After his first knock, I grip the door handle. As his fist comes down again, I twist the handle and yank open the door.

The man's second knock finds nothing but air, and his fist extends into the apartment. I snatch his wrist and pull. With a surprised yelp, he stumbles forward, right into my fist. A wheeze squeaks from the man's lips. As he bends forward, I reach around his waist and free his gun from its holster.

Before the man can recover, I step back and mimic a wrestling move I've seen a thousand times. Normally the opponent would be thrown into the ropes and bounce back for a clothesline strike across the throat, but my adversary finds the room's only chair far less flexible. He catches the chair back at waist level and pitches forward.

A moment later, from the hall, I hear him spill to the floor with a groan, landing atop my cardboard coffee table and hastily discarded Salisbury steak. When I push the elevator call button down the hall and the doors slide open immediately, I know there is no way the man will catch me. Even better, I managed to keep my hood down for the duration of the attack. He won't be able to ID me, and claiming that my disheveled apartment had been burgled won't be much of a stretch. Of course, my current plan of action will either end in my death, never returning to Greenland, or my return with evidence that clears my name.

As the elevator descends ten floors, I tuck the man's small Ruger handgun, what my father would have called a "ladies' weapon," behind my back. When the doors open on the bottom floor, I exit casually and head toward the exit. I pass a couple entering the building but only see their feet as I keep my head down and face concealed.

A brisk breeze billows the cloak out behind me as I exit the building. A lot of people in Nuuk don't have cars. When it's warm enough, many people walk or bike wherever they're going, but that's just a small portion of the year, so Nuuk sports a good number of taxis, and there are always a few outside the country's largest and most populated buildings. I flag down the first one I see and slip into the backseat, never revealing my face.

"The docks," I say.

"Fishing or pleasure?" the cabbie asks in perfect English. He's a local Inuit, but Nuuk sees a lot of tourism and the best cabbies know that Americans tip well. So they learn the language in search of tips. Some even fake an accent.

"Fishing," I say. "Quickly."

I leave the cab five minutes later and hurry to the dock, my pace quickening. I'm a fugitive, after all, and the *Raven*'s hidden by a string of ships. An old coot with a thick tan mustache watches me approach, one eyebrow perched high on his forehead.

Ten seconds later, I have my answer.

"Shit!" I shout. "Son of a bitch!"

The *Raven* is gone.

They left without me.

They gave me no choice but to come with them, and then they left without me?

"Assholes!"

"'Scuse me, ma'am," says the old man from the bench.

Fuming, I keep my back to him.

"Ma'am?" the man says.

I spin around. "What!"

He's right there, just a foot away. His mustache twitches as one side of his mouth bends up in an awkward smile. "Couldn't help but overhear your filthy mouth."

I'm about to treat him to a second dose of my filthy mouth when his accent registers. I pause, confused, and ask, "You're from Texas?"

He gives a nod. "Born and raised."

The mustache fits now, but the winter cap and thick jacket seem out of place. I squint at him. "You're not a cop, are you?"

"Texas Ranger for twenty years," he says.

I take a step back.

"No offense, ma'am, but you wouldn't make it three steps." He lifts his jacket, flashing a six-shooter. "Not that I'd pop you," he says with grin.

"What do you want?" I ask.

"Friend of mine asked me to sit for a spell on this here bench." He motions to the bench. "Told me to wait on a lady who's not all that ladylike. Said I'd know it was you on account of your filthy mouth, that you'd be cussing like a fox with its tail on fire—could foxes speak. Turns out it was a perfect description." He looks me up and down. "Physical description wasn't too far off, neither. Raven indeed."

"Jakob," I say, though it's more of a grumble.

"The same," he says, then raises a finger. "Quick disclaimer. I had nothing to do with the shenanigans that brought you here. Fact is, I thought it was a bad idea."

"Doesn't really matter," I say. "I'm here now. Like it or not."

"If it's all the same to you, I'd like to be on your good side, ma'am. You've got a reputation, and I'd rather not be Tasered or thrown over your living room chair."

My defenses go up. What if the cowboy is lying? What if he's the flasher's partner? Then I realize Jakob wouldn't have totally abandoned me. Not if he wanted me to follow them. "The man at the apartment was sent to pick me up?"

A broad grin stretches across his face. "Poor old Randall Klein. He's ex-CIA, you know. Can't tell it from his reflexes, but he knows stuff."

"So, what? Jakob's putting together some kind of geriatric task force?"

His laugh becomes a wheeze and then a cough.

I smile and put my hands on my hips. "You're not inspiring much confidence here, Ranger."

He waves a hand at me, composes himself. "Haven't laughed that hard in a while. To answer your question, yeah, it's something like that. Fact is, we're the ones who believe him. Believe *you*. And we're here to help."

I turn toward the sound of an approaching car. The taxi stops and Randall Klein steps out, a hand over his stomach.

The Ranger chuckles. "You sure did a number on him, din'cha?"

While Klein makes his way down the dock, I say, "Didn't catch your name, cowboy."

"Talbot," he says. "Ed Talbot." He shakes my hand. "Pleasure to meet you, Raven."

"Call me Jane," I say.

He looks at me with one eye squinted. "Nah, Raven suits you." He turns away before I can complain and heads for what looks like a small tugboat. "Let's get a move on. I'd like to get this dark business wrapped up and get back to my horses."

I stand rigid for a moment, weighing my options for all of three seconds. I don't want to be locked in a jail cell if the Draugar make landfall, and despite my frustration with the Olavson men, they have my loyalty. I follow him to the boat. "Talbot, your horses are about to become the least of your worries."

7

It takes us an hour to catch up to the *Raven*. She's moving at a steady ten knots; slow enough for us to catch up, but far enough out to sea they'd be hard to find should someone start looking. The *Raven*'s black paint job reminds me a lot of the *Sentinel*, whose captain viewed the vessel as a modern-day eco-pirate ship. Unfortunately for him and everyone under his command, the pirate mentality and a dose of lethal hubris doomed them all.

I hope the same thing isn't happening here. I really don't want to die. But as we get closer, my fears seem to be realized.

Three—*three*—harpoon guns are mounted at the back of the ship. One is center aft, another to port, and the last is on the starboard side. And they're not the handheld kind of harpoon used for spear fishing or something. They're the big-ass kind that fire 150-pound spears with titanium flukes for gripping flesh and a cast-iron tip that explodes on contact. If one of these harpoons were aimed at a human being, well, you could jar what was left as strawberry preserves and no one would see the difference. These are whale-killers, designed to punch a hole in one-hundred-plus tons of meat and stop a heart big enough for me to swim through. I may not have been the most passionate antiwhaling crusader on the planet—hell, I've eaten whale meat—but this ship is a whale-killing machine.

Klein, who I haven't talked to since I apologized for the beat down and returned his gun, joins me on the deck of our twenty-foot vessel, the *SuzieQ*. She's a simple vessel with a small hold for fish and a basic wheelhouse. Certainly seaworthy, but I'm eager to climb aboard the much larger *Raven*.

"You don't approve?" Klein asks when he sees my dour expression.

"Actually," I say, looking up at one of the harpoons, "they're perfect."

His eyebrows rise. "Really?"

"Yup."

"Huh."

He's standing farther away than most people would. Probably remembers how his stomach felt when it was wrapped around my fist. Not exactly the kind of person I'd figure for CIA material, but what do I know?

"Don't fit the profile?"

"Not at all," he says.

"What, do you have a dossier on me?"

When he doesn't reply, I crane my head toward him, eyes widening. "You *do* have a dossier on me!"

He raises his hands in defense. "Yes, yes! But only because I was trying to determine whether or not you and the Olavsons were trustworthy. Whether or not I should believe your story."

"What did you find?" I ask.

"That you are a competent investigator trusted with sensitive information and able to adapt to undercover situations better than some of my colleagues. You would have made a good agent."

"Now you're just trying to butter me up."

He laughs lightly. It comes out as kind of a nerdy-sounding "Heh, heh!" Then he says, "Well, that's what I thought before I discovered your fiery—"

"Watch it," I say. It was meant as a joke, but the man cringes a little. I'm starting to feel like a bully, which is ironic given my size and stature.

"—temper," he finishes.

"Sorry about that," I say. And it's an honest apology. "I've been a little more fiery than usual lately."

"Understandable," he says. "If I'd survived what you had, I don't think I'd be quite the same, either."

"Thanks," I say and extend my hand. He takes it and we shake. Friends. *See, that wasn't so hard, Harper*, I think. I just need to repeat the process a few more times and I'll be hunky-dory with the *Raven*'s crew in no time. That is, if they don't mind me beating the shit out of the captain and his son first.

"So you know a lot about me," I say. "What's your story? All I know is that you used to be CIA and you've got slow reflexes." He doesn't smile. "That was a joke."

"Oh, heh, right." He pushes his thick-rimmed glasses higher on his long nose. "I was an analyst. Reviewed data. Images. My job was to look for connections. Develop leads based on numbers, troop movements, or construction. You know—spreadsheets, maps, and satellite images."

"So I don't have to worry about you going Jason Bourne on me?"

"Who's Jason Bourne?"

"Don't get out much, do you?"

"I've spent fifty percent of my life thus far in an office with no windows."

That's when I notice he hasn't really taken his eyes off the Arctic view. This must be all very foreign and new to him. Probably terrifying, too. "Why are you here?"

"Because I did my job," he says. "I put the pieces together and determined you were telling the truth."

I feel a brief moment of hope—having genuine support from the CIA could change things—but then he goes and smears my lifted spirits beneath the cold, hard boot of truth.

"I believed you," he says, "but no one believed me. Nearly lost my job arguing my case. But it's just too crazy sounding. I had months of vacation time saved up, so I came out myself."

I stammer out a confused, "W-why?"

"If you believed the planet was threatened by some kind of mind-altering parasite, wouldn't you do what you could to—oh. Right. You wouldn't. Weren't."

"Touché," I say with a frown. The man has pretty much deflated any argument I had about not being here. He doesn't know it, but he's just spared Willem from a beat down.

Our conversation is suddenly interrupted by a voice that confuses me. "Ahoy!" Not only is the voice not familiar; it's also feminine.

I look up at the aft deck of the *Raven* and see a six-foot-tall blond bombshell with wavy locks and full lips. My first impression is that she's some kind of runway model, but then I notice she's got broad shoulders and a bit of meat on her bones, mostly in the right places. I hate her, of course, but manage to give a casual wave.

She hurls a coil of rope at me. It unfurls as it crosses the distance, but I have to step to the side to avoid getting bludgeoned by the heavy cord.

"Sorry," she says. Her accent is local. A Greenlander woman.

Fall overboard and drown, I think. "Don't worry about it."

"Tie it off, will you," she says. "We'll tow the *Suze* from here. You can take the dinghy between the ships."

When she steps away, I turn to Klein. "Who is that?"

"Her name is Helena," he says. "But I haven't spent much time with her. She seems to know her way around a ship, though. And she seems close to Jakob. And Willem." He glances at me, a crafty look in his eyes. "That doesn't bother you, does it?"

"Put the pieces together on that, too, huh?" I say.

He shrugs. "Wasn't hard."

"Don't think I won't slug you now that we're BFFs." Before he can ask, I say, "Never mind."

I tie off the rope and give Talbot a thumbs-up. He eases back on the throttle, letting the slack out of the cable. The line goes taut so gently that I barely feel it. But the engine cuts a moment later, and Talbot steps out of the wheelhouse. He's so bundled up in his jacket, hood, hat, scarf, and snow pants that I'd never guess a cowboy hid beneath the layers, but when he speaks it's like looking at the Abominable John Wayne. "Less y'all are fixing to freeze to death, I suggest we git on over to the *Raven* while the sun is still shining."

"You do realize this is the Arctic, right?" I say. "It's going to be cold. Like, all the time."

"Girl," he says from the aft, where he's lifting a small dinghy over the rail. "You best paint your butt white and run with the antelope."

I turn to Klein.

He shakes his head. "I have no idea."

"Coming," I say. We pile into the dinghy, which is the last boat on the planet I'd like to be on right now. Not only is it shaky, but we're basically a convenient bite-size package right now. I stand at the center of the small dinghy and command the other two to sit. Happily they listen. The *Raven* is still moving—five knots now, which is faster than I can row—so I channel my fear into my arms and drag us up the side of the *SuzieQ* and then up the line stretched between the two ships.

Malik greets us at the other end, helping us onto the *Raven* one at a time. When he takes my hand, I pause and say, "Sorry about the Taser."

He shrugs it off.

"And when I cursed at you yesterday."

A nod.

"And what I said about your mother…and sister."

He smiles. "Thank you." As I step past him, he stops me with a hand on my shoulder. "The captain would like to see you. Now."

"Did he hear about the cruise ship?" I ask.

"Cruise ship?" he says, looking confused. "I know nothing about a cruise ship. But a whale was spotted."

"That's right," Klein says. "Diane Simmons with Greenpeace. She's a friend of yours, right?"

For a moment I wonder just how detailed that dossier of mine is, but I don't dwell on the topic. Diane *is* a friend. And if she's spotted a whale, she might be a dead friend by the time we reach her. I push past Klein and Talbot, heading for the bridge and, shortly, battle.

8

I storm into the *Raven*'s wheelhouse like I'm Jean-Luc Picard facing a fleet of Borg cubes, demanding that we throttle ahead, that we prepare for a fight, or injuries, or worse. If I hadn't noticed everyone staring at me with humorous expressions on their faces, I might have damn well sat in the captain's chair and shouted, "Engage!"

"Jane," Willem says, stopping my tirade. "We're under way."

I pause. I can hear the rumble of the ship's single large prop cutting through the ocean. We're moving fast.

"We're in contact with your Greenpeace friend," says Helena. She's standing by the windows at the front of the bridge, her shapely body silhouetted by the falling sun. If that weren't bad enough, she tinges the word *Greenpeace* with a subtle trace of disdain. "They're fine."

"The whale is dead," Jakob says. He's standing behind the wheel like a good captain, but the ship is on autopilot. I think he just likes the feel of the wheel in his hands. "And we won't reach them until morning. Even at full speed."

Well, don't I feel like an idiot. "Right. Good."

Talbot and Klein enter the bridge behind me, and I make room for them to pass. Talbot sits at a chair by the radar station. Klein sits at a workstation, where an open laptop awaits him. That's when I notice that each and every bridge station is occupied. There isn't a place for me here.

"How did you find Diane?" I ask. "Aren't we—you—supposed to be incognito?"

Klein answers. "I've been monitoring the blogs, Facebook pages, and Twitter feeds for any organization that might report whale sightings in the North Atlantic. One of the crew members aboard the, ah"—he's grinning—"*Arctic Rainbow*"—Helena snickers—"is fairly active on Twitter. GreenpeaceNate. He sent out ten tweets in half as many minutes. I sent a direct message, and Nate was fairly forthcoming with the details. I hacked into the Greenpeace system, and we're getting GPS updates every ten minutes."

"Photos, maps, and charts, huh?" I say with a grin.

"Among other things," he says, pushing his glasses up.

"But you've talked to Diane?" I ask. "She knows we're coming."

They all stare at me for a moment.

"I noticed she was registered as the *Rainbow*'s captain," Klein admits. "She was in your dossier."

I look Jakob square in the eyes. "I'm here now, Jakob. I'm not going anywhere. But I swear if you don't start being straight with me, I will find a way to turn this ship around."

A nod is all I get. It's all I need. From Jakob anyway.

"So they don't know we're coming?" I ask.

"We don't want to give away our position," Willem says. "For obvious reasons."

"Right," I say. "We're fugitives. Thanks for that, by the way."

The outside door opens, and Malik steps inside. He's brushing snowflakes from his shoulders. "Storm is nearly here."

I shake my head. *Great*, I think but don't say anything. I've made myself look like enough of a doofus for one day. But I do look to the window and see a haze of flakes speckling the sky. It doesn't look bad now, but the wall of darkness on the horizon is foreboding.

"Have you told them?" Malik says to me.

"Told them what?" I ask.

"About the cruise ship."

Urgency returns to my voice. "Right! Before Klein...came to pick me up, I saw a news report about a missing cruise liner."

Jakob looks stunned. It's news to him. "Cruise liner? How big?"

"Really big," I say. "Two thousand passengers, five hundred crew. The ship left Ireland, destined for Nuuk, and wasn't heard from again. It just disappeared without a Mayday, GPS locator, or any other call for help."

"Got it!" Klein says, hunched over his laptop. "The *Poseidon Adventure*." He reads the text on the screen. "This just says what she told us." His fingers work over the keyboard. Websites come and go. Then he pauses. "The plotted course for the ship had them traveling not far from where the *Arctic Rainbow* is now."

"Can't be a coincidence," Talbot says, stroking his mustache.

"But there is nothing to be done about it right now," Jakob says calmly. "I'll add its course to the last known coordinates we have for the other missing ships."

Jakob lets go of the wheel, and it moves back and forth slowly, under the control of the ship's automated systems. When the storm hits, Jakob or Willem will likely take manual control to more quickly adjust to the waves, but most of the time, ships can pilot themselves on the open seas.

Klein scribbles some notes on a sheet of paper and hands it off to Jakob as he walks past. On his way to the chart room, Jakob passes me and says, "Come."

Five pairs of eyes look at me like I've just been called to the principal's office. I ignore them and follow Jakob to the chart room. As we walk, I notice he still has a limp from the injuries he received three months ago. I close the door behind me, sensing I might want at least part of this conversation to be private.

Jakob leans over a large map that now covers the table at the center of the room. I recognize the southern tip of Greenland near the top of the map, but the majority of it is open ocean crisscrossed with latitude and longitude lines. A cluster of colored tacks has been pinned between the southern coast and the bottom of the map.

"What are those?" I ask as Jakob pins the end of a spool of red yarn on the left side of the map.

"The last known coordinates of the missing ships," he says while looking at Klein's handwritten notes.

I look more closely. While the tacks look close together, I know that there is actually at least a hundred miles between some of them. The total area covered by the pins is probably something close to the size of Massachusetts. Not exactly small, but a much tighter space than, say, the Bermuda Triangle.

Jakob stretches the yarn out and pins a portion to the map. He repeats the process five more times, never saying a word. When he's done, he steps back to reveal an arc of red, cutting through the middle of the cluster before turning toward Greenland's southern coast.

"Is that—"

"The plotted course for the *Poseidon Adventure*," he finishes.

"Yes."

I lean over the map, looking at all the tacks and the handwritten notes next to them detailing the ship name, size, destination, and home port. "Geez. Where is the *Arctic Rainbow*?"

He points to the tack nearest Greenland and farthest from the cluster. "Here."

"Do you think they're outside the range of attacks?" I ask.

He shrugs. "I wouldn't attempt to predict anything."

As I stare at the map, Jakob sits down. "Jane," he says. His use of my first name is so uncommon that he immediately has my attention. "I understand why you're upset about what we did, but I'm not sorry for it."

Nothing like a good ol' Norse apology.

"And I know you understand," he adds.

I start to disagree, but he cuts me off.

"Had you not understood, I would have already heard about it. Yes?"

I don't reply. We both know he's right. As much as I loathe the idea, I should be here, not because this is my fight, not because I survived the Draugar once before, but because it's the right thing to do.

"But there is another reason I couldn't leave you behind," he says, leaning forward, elbows on knees. "More than anyone—more than my son—you have proven yourself to me. Despite your size, you possess the heart and spirit of a Viking. Not only would my ancestors respect your courage, but they would also honor you for your role in defeating the Draugar. Torstein, Áshildr, and the others have found peace thanks to you. This is why I call you Raven. You have earned your place in my family."

I'm stunned. I don't know what to say. This isn't the chewing out I was expecting. After a moment, I manage, "Thank you." Embarrassment creeps up on me. I try to change the subject. "I know there isn't a place for me on the bridge, but I can make myself useful somewhere else. Swab the decks. Something."

Jakob chuckles.

"What?" I say, getting a little defensive. "I've served on my fair share of ships, you know. I'm good for *something*."

"You misunderstand my intentions," he says. "The bridge is occupied at the moment, but I'm human. And an old man. I can't always be present."

I'm not sure what he's trying to tell me.

He laughs at my confusion. "Raven, I would like you to fill my position when I'm not on the bridge."

"Wait, what?" My confusion mushroom-clouds up my neck and fills my skull. "What are you saying?"

Jakob leans back with a satisfied grin. He plants his hands on his belly and says, "What I'm saying, Raven, is that you are my first mate."

I lean against the map table. *Holy shit.* "Do the others know? Does Willem?"

"He does, and they do," he says. "Not everyone was pleased, but no one will question my decision or your orders, unless they are contrary to mine. And right now, your orders are to get some rest. The storm will not be kind to you."

He's right about that. The first few days at sea can make some people queasy, even if they're accustomed to life at sea. But a storm on the first day is basically a guaranteed puke-fest.

I step toward the door and pause with my hand on the knob. "Thank you, Jakob—er, Captain."

He tilts his head forward, and I feel a new kinship with the man. More than ever before, I feel respected. That's one trick the Colonel never pulled off.

"Have Talbot or Klein ridden out a storm before?"

He just smiles.

"Right," I say and open the door. I step back onto the bridge and decide to test my newfound position. "Klein, Talbot, come with me." After just a moment's pause, both men gather their things and stand. I share a glance with Willem and find his expression impossible to read. I'd like to talk to him. About everything. And the blond she-Hulk. But now's not the time.

"Where are we going?" Klein asks.

"The head," I say. "It's going to be a *long* night."

9

I wake to a knock on my door. For a moment I forget where I am, but then I recognize the braided rug beneath my toes. "Coming," I say, but I don't need to get dressed. I never undressed. I just want a moment to wake up.

The storm was merciful. I had spent just ten minutes in the head, and that was a false alarm, more nerves than seasickness. It had only been three months since I'd been at sea for more than a month and weathered a fair share of storms, and my body had little trouble readjusting. Talbot never even showed a moment of discomfort. Said the storm was "akin to breaking in a rowdy stallion." Klein, on the other hand, spent the first half hour heaving up his supper and the following three hours dry-heaving. He eventually fell asleep clutching the toilet bowl with his head leaned on the seat.

My hands feel cool on my eyes as I rub them, so I linger a moment longer.

"Jane?" Willem says from the other side of the door.

I cringe, feeling unprepared for this conversation. Do I apologize? Do I go on the attack? Do I bring up the Viking princess? I quickly grow annoyed with myself and sigh. *I'll apologize*, I decide. My feet pad across the cold floor beyond the rug. I'm moving fast by the time I pull open the door. "Good morning, my Norse—"

She's standing with him.

Right behind him.

Smiling at me.

"What do you want?" I say, all of the peace, love, and harmony gone from my voice. I'd have made a shitty hippie. Too much of the Colonel in my blood and not enough LSD.

Willem seems bewildered by my rapid-fire manic depression. He glances back at Helena, seems to think nothing of her presence, and then turns back to me. "We're almost there."

I close the door in their faces, eager to get dressed and head to the bridge. Then I remember I'm already dressed.

Damnit.

I open the door again, just seconds after I closed it. "Ready," I say.

"Are you…feeling okay?" Willem asks.

"Fine." I push past him and head for the stairs.

I step onto the bridge feeling refreshed and find Jakob, Talbot, and Malik already present. Willem and Helena enter behind me, followed by a deflated-looking Klein.

"You're going to hate me for saying this," I say to Klein, "but you need to go eat something. And drink. You're not going to be any good to anyone if you don't."

He nods and continues toward his workstation. I take hold of his shoulder. "Now, Klein."

He looks back at me, lacking the energy to argue, even if he wants to. "Fine."

As Klein shuffles back out of the bridge, Jakob gives me a wink.

"Where are we?" I ask.

"We're at the last known coordinates of the *Arctic Rainbow*," Willem says.

"Last *known* coordinates?" I ask.

"The GPS coordinates stopped updating last night," Jakob says.

I scan the horizon, which is about three miles out. I see nothing.

"We've been looking for a while," Talbot says. "She ain't out there."

I put my hands on the sides of the window and stare at the endless ocean. "Radar?"

"Nothing," Helena answers. "There isn't another ship within eleven miles."

The news is disconcerting, but there are a number of possible explanations, the first being that Klein's breach of the Greenpeace network was discovered or severed somehow. Could be as simple as the storm knocking out the satellite connection. Of course, it's also possible that we're floating over a ship full of whale-loving corpses.

But none of that interests me as much as the object I see about a mile out.

I reach my hand out to no one in particular. "Binoculars."

I close my hand when I feel the cool metal of the binoculars on my finger.

"I'm telling you," Talbot says, right next to me. "She ain't out there."

The binoculars magnify everything so much that I'm immediately lost. Can't do anything about the bend of the earth, so three miles is still the limit. But it feels like I can reach out and touch the distant waves. I scan back and forth, looking for the aberration.

"What do you want to do?" Willem asks.

I nearly shush him, but then Jakob replies, "Course-correct twenty degrees to port. Let's find those—"

"Actually," I say, "take us ten degrees starboard." I lower the binoculars and look back. Helena looks ready to tear my head off. Jakob doesn't look too pleased, either. "Oh, right," I add, then point in the direction I'd like us to go. "Thar she blows. Or doesn't blow, in this case."

Talbot takes the binoculars. "Give me those." He looks through the lenses, adjusting the focus. "Well, there's something out there."

"It's a whale," I assure him.

"How can you tell from here?" he asks.

"I've seen a lot of whales," I say. "Dead and alive." I motion to Willem, who's looking through his own pair of binoculars. "Just ask him."

Willem lowers the binoculars. "It's a whale."

The ship tilts as Jakob quickly changes course and throttles forward. It's been two months since anyone has seen a whale off Greenland, and Jakob pursues the prize as though he means to harpoon the beast and bring its corpse to the fish market. Of course, he's after so much more. If there is any evidence to be found on this specimen, our journey might end here today. And if that's the case, there might yet be hope.

We close the distance quickly. Five hundred feet from the flat gray bulge in the water, Jakob throttles back. "Willem, Helena, man the forward and starboard harpoons. Talbot, help them load. Be ready to reload if necessary."

The trio exits quickly, heading for the forward deck.

Klein reenters the bridge at that moment, a mostly eaten granola bar clutched in his hand. "Why are we slowing?"

"Get both cameras," Jakob says to the man. "Get on deck with yours. Give the submersible to Raven."

Klein grips the granola bar between his teeth and rushes into the chart room.

The captain—unusually for him—is speaking so fast and animated that I nearly miss a key word.

Submersible.

"Did you just say 'submersible'?" I ask. "Why do I need a submersible camera?"

Jakob turns to Malik. "Get the wet suit, air tanks, and collection kit. We'll meet you at the stern."

Malik looks from Jakob to me, then disappears into the bowels of the ship.

"Jakob," I say, putting every ounce of my inherited Harper hellfire into his name. "What the hell do you think I'm going to do?"

He looks apologetic for just a moment, but then he says, "We need to collect samples. We can't do that from the ship. Someone has to get in the water."

"We're in a whaling ship," I point out. "Can't we just drag the thing back to port?"

"Not only would we risk infecting the mainland—"

"The mainland is already at risk," I say.

"—but we could also be wrong. If we return to port with a whale in tow, every news reporter in Greenland will be there to greet us. And if this is just a dead whale, how long do you think it will be before all of us are in jail?"

"Okay. Fine. But why *me*? And don't you dare give me any chest-thumping 'you're the Raven' bullcrap."

"You're the only one on board with dive experience," he says.

I look to the ceiling. Of course I am. "Was that in my dossier, too?"

"Sorry," Klein says from the chart room.

"You know, if I become a Draugr," I say to Jakob. "I'm coming for you first."

"And I'll do what needs to be done when you do," he says.

A thousand different sarcastic remarks flit through my mind, but his comment sinks in and sobers me. "I know you will."

"As would you," he adds.

I'm not so sure about that, but I don't mention it. He'll just disagree anyway.

Klein returns from the chart room holding two cameras. The one with the clear plastic casing is obviously mine. I reach out, take it, and head for the door. "Let's get this over with."

10

"Could be a little more subtle there, Malik." The wet suit fits like a glove, and while I may not be an Amazonian bombshell like Helena, I've got a nice figure, which right now is smoothed out and accentuated. Given the way Malik's eyes linger on my lady curves, you'd think it was a sheer body stocking. Of course, we're the only two people standing on the dive deck off the back of the ship, so there isn't really anyone else to look at, and he might just be checking over my gear. But I don't think so.

The big man turns away, embarrassed. "Sorry," he says. "I've been at sea too long."

I laugh but then realize he might not have been joking.

Then he adds, "Sometimes even the fish start to look good," and I laugh harder for just a moment before stopping cold.

"Wait, are you comparing me to a fish?"

Malik pulls my face mask down. The gear is fancy, and I'm not sure where it came from. Maybe Jakob bought it with his insurance claim. Maybe they stole it. Whatever the case may be, the ends justify the means. And I'm just glad we have it. The full face mask will let me breathe freely and communicate with the bridge. The rebreather strapped to my back mixes trimix—oxygen, helium, and nitrogen—with my exhaled carbon dioxide. The rebreather is percent more efficient than an air tank and can last for up to eight hours. It's smaller and lighter than a traditional air tank, too, which means I can move more quickly, especially with the wonky DPV (diver propulsion vehicle) I've been given. It weighs nearly a hundred pounds, but will carry me through the water at 4.3 knots—about five miles per hour—which is faster than Michael Phelps, or anyone else, can swim. What makes this DPV different is that instead of held out in front of me with my hands, it will be attached to my feet. Speed is controlled by a pedal, and I steer just like I would if I were swimming. I'll be an honest-to-goodness human torpedo. But the best thing about it is that my hands will be free to collect samples, which is pretty much a nightmare made real, so I'm focusing on the cool gear and Malik's wandering eyes.

Malik, on the other hand, is back to business. "Check your mic."

"*Raven*, this is Raven. Jakob, do you realize how redundant and confusing that is? You need some originality in your names."

"We hear you, *Jane*," he says. "Iluatitsilluarina."

I recognize the Greenlandic phrase for "Good luck."

"Qujan," I reply. *Thanks.* "Good to go?" I ask Malik.

He hands me a mesh bag containing a glass jar for samples and a variety of blades for acquiring them. "I'll toss in the DPV when you're ready. *Iluatitsilluarina.*"

I look down at the water. Its bright blue surface is speckled white from the clouds above. While I can't see anything below, I feel like I'm looking into the eyes of a thousand hungry Draugar. As much as I love the ocean, and diving, this is where the enemy now resides. And I'm about to jump in.

Idiot, I think to myself.

Without another word, I step back and fall into the water. I feel the frigid water wrap around my body, even through the wet suit, but it will be a while before it becomes unbearable. The DPV's battery life is just one hour, and I don't plan on being in the water a second longer. In fact, I'd like to be back on board inside thirty minutes.

I spin around in a tight circle, looking for an attack I'm sure is coming. But there is nothing around me except for endless blue. Water sheets from my mask as I surface.

"Move back," Malik says. When I kick away, he pushes the DPV into the water. The white device, which is shaped like a blender with two large propellers at the end, splashes into the water and bobs to the surface. "I've already turned it on. Just put your feet where I showed you and accelerate with the pedal on the right side. To stop, just lift your foot."

I straddle the tubular top that contains the DPV's engine and batteries and carefully slip my feet into the slots on either side. I can feel the pedal beneath my right foot. I give the pedal a tap and am propelled through the water. I turn in an arc, getting used to how the thing moves. As I finish my arc, I give Malik a thumbs-up, angle myself down, and push the pedal hard.

Before I can blink, I'm fifteen feet beneath the surface. I arch my back and level out, correcting my course so I'm just beneath the *Raven*'s hull, headed toward the bow, beyond which I'll find the corpse of a whale and maybe something more. I feel safe and hidden inside the shadow of the *Raven*'s black hull, but it lasts for just a moment. As I pass out of the ship's shadow and into the morning light, I get my first glimpse of my target. It's just a dark blue shape a hundred feet ahead, but as I'm propelled closer, the form resolves.

The wide barnacle-encrusted fluke tells me I'm approaching from behind. So I angle out and away, hoping to identify the species. "Almost there," I say.

"What do you see?" Jakob asks.

"Not much yet. Hold on."

The DPV slows as I pull my foot away and turn back toward the whale. Then I see it. All of it. "Holy shit." It's just a whisper, but Jakob hears me.

"What is it?" he asks. "Are you all right?"

"Fine," I reply. "But I can't say the same for the whale."

The front half of the whale—a fifty-foot humpback—is intact, but the rest of it is in ruin. The whale has been torn open from just behind the pectoral fins, up and back to the dorsal fin. Nearly all of the meat and muscle between this area and the whale's fluke is gone, though much of the gap has been filled in by giant tendrils of intestine, organs, and stringy veins. Several feet of spine, which is nearly all that's holding the fluke to the body, have been exposed.

"Looks like something, or several somethings, made a snack of the whale."

"Orca?" Jakob asks.

It's a good guess. Even when not possessed by parasites, killer whales are known to attack and consume their larger cousins. It's not exactly cannibalism, since orcas are really porpoises—big dolphins—not whales. While orcas don't normally kill people outside of captivity, there were a few reported attacks around Greenland two months ago, just before all the sea mammals started going AWOL.

I take a look around and see only the whale and the *Raven*'s hull. That doesn't mean there isn't a pod of Draugar orca circling out of view, but I trust Jakob would let me know if something appeared on the sonar.

Ignoring the tendrils of gore wriggling in the current, I aim toward the humpback's head and accelerate.

Whales have always made me feel small, even though I've only seen them from the deck of a ship. Being this close to a fifty-foot giant makes me feel absolutely insignificant. And blue whales can be twice this size!

Moving slowly, I head toward the creature's massive mouth. Humpback whales are filter feeders. They suck in vast amounts of seawater and then use their giant tongues to force the water back out through their sieve-like baleen, filtering out the tiny krill. Normally they're not a threat to people, though I suppose this one could easily suck me in, filter me out, and swallow me whole. I have no intention of being a modern-day Jonah, though, so I keep my distance.

I'd hoped to find its tongue hanging out of its mouth, but no such luck. The Draugar are the basis of not only modern zombie stories but also the vampire legend. Young generations of parasites reside in the gut, driving their host to consume flesh. Brain matter is a delicacy. Once the parasites have matured, they move to the tongue, covering it in a layer of wriggling white worms. The parasites on the tongue easily invade new hosts via simple bites and start the cycle anew. Victims decay to a point, but everything essential is preserved by some kind of secretion. This gives the Draugar the look of a zombie, but the eternal life of a vampire. And since they've got some kind of hive intelligence, controlled by a much larger Queen, they're capable of strategizing in ways I have yet to comprehend.

All of this flits through my mind as I swim back toward the eye. If there is one other place the parasites are guaranteed to be found, it's the eyes. They fill the host's eyes, wriggling inside the juices and using the clear membrane as a window on the world. A single human eye might hold fifty parasites, each of which has two black specks for eyes and a tiny but powerful mouth. I doubt they can see well individually, but together, who knows?

I pause in front of the closed eye, knife in hand, sample jar ready. My plan is simple—jab the eye and position the jar to catch anything that spews out. I aim the knife tip over the navel-orange-size eye but don't strike. My pondering on the inner workings of a Draugr has me concerned.

"Jakob," I say. "How do we know this whale is dead? Like really dead, not Draugr dead."

"It's not breathing," he replies. "Did it move?"

"No...but do Draugr even need to breathe?"

His answer is not what I was hoping for. "I—I don't know."

Damnit, I think. I should have thought of this before I jumped in the water. But I'm here now, and the whale hasn't shown any sign of life. *Just do it and get the hell out*, I tell myself.

I take one last look around, searching for some imagined danger, and then turn back toward the eye.

The white, wriggling, *open* eye.

11

I have no idea if they can hear my rapid-fire string of curses up on the bridge of the *Raven* or not, but I'm pretty sure even the Colonel would have winced at some of what I've just shouted.

"Jane, what happened?" Jakob says. He may not have understood what I've just said, but he clearly understood the abject horror that fueled my words.

"It's a Draugr!" I shout. "A fucking Draugr whale!"

I jam the DPV pedal down as far as it can go, surging up through the water. A sound gives chase, deep and resonating. I recognize the whale call instantly. The ten-second blast vibrates my insides and makes my head spin. But it's not the sound that bothers me; it's the knowledge that sound travels faster and farther in water. Whales can hear each other's calls hundreds of miles away. This means that every Draugr whale inside a several-hundred-mile radius might now know exactly where to find the *Raven*.

The DPV launches me out of the water, but not completely. After catching a glimpse of the *Raven*, I fall back to the sea. I manage to arc my body and reenter smoothly, but feel like a doofus—first for leaping out of the water like some kid pretending to be a dolphin, and second for not keeping my wits about me. Fleeing up? Where the hell is *up* going to get me?

As I surge beneath the water again, I'm pummeled by a strong current that spins me around.

The whale isn't just alive. It's mobile. The fluke pounds at the water, pushing the whale away from me.

I take the chance to flee. Horizontally. Toward the *Raven*.

"Jakob!" I shout. "Make sure Malik is waiting for me on the dive deck!"

The old captain either doesn't hear me or just ignores me. Seems he's got plans of his own. "Try to keep track of your distance to the whale," he says. "Willem will try to harpoon the monster, but he can't if you're too close."

Feeling a small measure of security knowing Willem is watching over me with a weapon that can destroy the Draugr whale's brain, or remove its fluke, I look back so I can give a report.

But I see nothing.

"I don't see it!"

That a creature so big, so close, could already be out of view seems impossible. "Jakob, I—"

"Beneath you!" Jakob shouts. "It's beneath you!"

I glance down into the dark deep and see a vague circular shape rising up to swallow me whole. The shape emerges from the gloom as the whale's wide-open maw. Capable of pulling in eighteen thousand gallons of seawater, the humpback has no trouble sucking me in.

Darkness surrounds me. The circle of sunlight above me begins to close. Near hysterics, I scream, "It swallowed me! Jakob! Oh my God!" I continue to scream as I slide deeper, thrust inward by water pressure. My body is jolted and beaten. My mask is nearly pulled from my face, but I manage to get a hand over it. I'm not sure why I bother. Drowning would be preferable to being digested or, more likely, turned into a human Draugr. I may also find the belly full of parasite larvae, hungry for sustenance.

For a moment I'm stuck, clogged in the whale's esophagus. But the water pressure behind me builds. I'm squeezed so tight I can't breathe. I can hear Jakob shouting in my ear, but I can't reply. *I'm going to die here. I'm going to die in the throat of a whale like a hunk of mozzarella in the throat of a fat man who doesn't chew!*

My chest feels like it's going to implode. The pressure becomes unbearable. My mouth opens to scream, but without airflow, I can't make a sound. Then I'm free, launched like a torpedo by the water pressure pushing from behind. I tumble through the water, limbs flailing for a moment before I'm snagged by what feels like soft, squishy ropes. But I'm not in its stomach. I can feel the water pushing past me.

While gulping in air, I twist and turn, trying to free myself. At first, I'm not sure why I'm struggling. It doesn't really matter what part of the whale I'm lodged in. Sooner or later, the parasites will find me, if they haven't already, or I'll be melted by stomach acid or drowned. Then I see a flash of blue.

I turn toward the color again. Beams of sunlight ripple through the water.

I passed straight through the ruined, stomachless whale! But I'm still stuck. As I fight to free myself, I realize where I am—tangled in the beast's intestines. I look for the knife in my hands. It's gone. As is the sample jar. But the mesh bag of sheathed blades is still attached to my weight belt. Fighting against the loop of bowels wrapped around my arm, I reach for the pouch and dig inside. I can't feel much with my gloved hands, but I find what I think is the thickest handle and pull it out.

After shaking the knife free of its sheath, I see the glint of a five-inch blade.

Ignoring the undulations of the gore in front of me, I twist the knife downward, against the pink intestines. The flesh resists the blade for a moment, but then gives in to the steel. The blade passes through the viscera, and it quickly unravels from around my arm. But in slicing the digestive organ, I've also provided an exit for the ton of shit—literally—held in the humpback's gut.

A brown cloud explodes around me, blocking my view. I gag at the sight despite the wet suit protecting my body from the sludge and the mask keeping me from smelling it. But as disgusting as being showered in whale feces is, it's the worm-shaped flecks of white wriggling past that turn my stomach. If the parasites hadn't found my body before, they have now.

"Jane!" Jakob shouts. "Are you okay?"

Never better, I think, but I don't say a word. I'm too focused on freeing myself and getting clear of the shit storm. I'm being dragged by my feet now, and the current has knocked me back, keeping me horizontal. I crouch my legs and stretch my arms down. The first tendril of intestine I find gets knifed a moment later.

The cloud of filth around me thickens for a moment, but then I'm free and the whale is moving beyond me. I kick away from the cloud billowing out from the backside of the Draugr like a jet contrail. I lose the creature in the cloud.

"Jane!" Jakob sounds horrified.

"I'm here," I say. "I made it out."

There's no "Thank God" or "Are you okay?" though. He's all business. "Jane, it's coming back around. We're coming for you, but it's going to be close. You'll have to come to us."

I start swimming toward the distant black hull. The whale must have fled after swallowing me. I'm swimming as hard as I can, but it feels like I'm barely moving. That's when it dawns on me that I've lost the DPV. Not only that, but since the DPV is controlled by feet, I'm not wearing swim fins. I might as well be standing still for how fast I can swim. But I try anyway. I'm not about to quit after passing through the gut of a humpback.

As the *Raven* gets closer, I realize they're backing up to me, which will help me get onto the dive deck faster, but the spinning prop will pull me in. The end result will be something like a frog in a blender. Well, not something like. Exactly like.

"Jakob, cut the engines!" I shout. "I'm almost there."

The rumble emanating from the *Raven* dies down, and I see the prop slow to a stop. The ship is still drifting toward me, but now that it has slowed, it feels impossibly far away. I surface for the first time since my retarded dolphin leap and see Malik standing on the dive deck, waving me on. Behind and above him is Willem. He looks like a noble Viking hero, with his blond hair caught up by the wind, a look of fury carved into his face, and a powerful harpoon gun gripped in both hands—a harpoon gun that seems to be aimed directly at my face.

When I hear him shout, "Dive," I understand why.

The whale is upon me.

Without looking back, I dive beneath the surface and kick as hard as I can.

I hear a muffled crack, followed by an impact, a high-pitched squeal, and then—oblivion.

A concussive force hits me hard at the same time I hear its deafening roar. I feel pain on every bit of my body. And then, nothing.

If I weren't wearing the mask, I'm sure I would have drowned. But I just kind of float limply like one of the many hunks of whale meat bobbing around me. I'm only partly aware of this. I'm flickering in and out of consciousness, severely dazed. I'm so far gone that when something wraps around me from behind, I don't fight against it.

What happens next is a blur. I'm moving—being pulled, really. Then I feel heavy. The weightlessness of water is gone. I'm lying on my back. I hear voices. Shouting. My name.

Despite the volume and intensity of the voices around me, I feel comforted by the knowledge that I'm on the *Raven*. Someone came in to get me. But then some of the words filter in: "get it off," "parasites," "careful," "everywhere." I finally register what's happening to my body. I'm being manhandled. I'm yanked, pushed, and pulled like I'm the last piece of candy that spilled out of Hansel and Gretel's birthday piñata.

My eyes snap open with a surge of adrenaline. The first thing I see is Jakob, Helena, and Malik standing over me. Reaching toward me. Hurting me. Then I look down, following their eyes. The top of my wet suit is missing, as is everything I wore beneath it. But the sight of my bare breasts doesn't even faze me. I've already seen what's below them.

Malik, wearing rubber fishing gloves, has his hands wrapped around the waist of my wet suit and is forcibly removing it. I scream at the sight, but not because I think Malik is trying to harm me. In fact, he's trying to save me. Either during my passage through the whale's body or when I was coated in waste, or both, thousands of maggot-like parasites began gnawing their way through my wet suit. Had it not been the extra-thick variant designed for cold water, they might have reached my skin.

They still might, which is why the crew is tearing away my clothes with wild abandon. I kick with my feet, aiding Malik's efforts. Jakob lifts me from under the armpits and pulls. The wet suit rolls in on itself, concealing the parasites as it slips free. Malik gathers up the freed clothing, bunches it up, and tosses it overboard, which I presume is where the rest of my clothes went.

Still, I feel no shame as I get my feet beneath me and start rubbing my hands over my body, inspecting every inch for a wound.

"Nothing on your back," Helena says.

When I look at her, I notice that Jakob and Malik have both turned away. So I think nothing of it when I drop my panties and give my feminine parts a once-over.

"Clear in the back," Helena says. For a moment I'm surprised and a little shocked that she's inspected my ass, but ultimately I appreciate it. That is, until she says, "Hold on."

"What!" I say.

"On the side of your right calf."

I yank up my underwear and twist my leg to look. There's a white spot surrounded by red, irritated skin on the side of my leg halfway between my knee and ankle. I fall to the deck, twisting my leg back for a closer look. Three-quarters of the inch-long parasite is still sticking out of my leg. My instinct is to reach down and yank the thing out, but I have no idea if these things are like worms. If it breaks on the way out, the half inside my body might grow to become a fully functional adult.

I pinch my skin and try to squeeze it out like an oversize whitehead. But it doesn't budge. Instead, it wiggles frantically back and forth, and I can feel its tiny jaws chewing at my flesh.

"Keep it pinched," Helena says as she crouches beside me.

I do as she says, but then I see a knife in her hand.

"Don't cut it in half," I say.

I can't see what she's doing as she leans in close, but I feel the flat side of the blade touch my finger for a moment. "I'm going to get the whole thing."

I'm about to ask for some clarification, but then her arm whips to the side. For a moment, I feel nothing. Then a burning sting rises up through my leg, eliciting a pain-filled cry from my mouth. When she stands I see the chunk of leg flesh I'd pinched together between her fingers. The parasite, whole and living, had yet to pass through.

As she stands with the chunk of meat in her hands, I see what she's about to do and try to stop her, but my voice is stopped by an involuntary gasp from the pain.

With a flick of her wrist, she tosses the sheet of skin—and the parasite sample we needed—overboard. I don't bother mentioning it. It's too late now.

Suddenly, Willem is by my side, first aid kit in hand. Like Helena, he's unfazed by my nakedness. He should be, after all. He's seen me more naked than this three times before—after getting out of the hospital and before I started picking bar fights. Without a word, he sets to work on my leg, cleaning it and then attempting to wrap it in gauze. But he's struggling. His hands are shaking.

That's when I notice his pale blue lips, shaking hands, and drenched hair. "You came in after me," I say. It's more of an observation than a question.

He nods, but it looks more like a seizure.

"Willem," Helena says, taking the gauze from his hands and shoving him to the side. "Go change and warm yourself."

After just a moment's pause, he glances at me. When our eyes meet, I see relief in his face. He might be glad I'm alive, but I'm not the one telling him to go take care of himself, am I?

Willem obeys and disappears from the deck.

Helena attends to my wound, quickly and tightly wrapping it. The dressing will have to be changed soon—blood is already threatening to seep through, but it's no longer flowing from my body like a mountain spring.

I'm about to thank her when I hear Talbot shout, "Captain! Klein says we've got a GPS distress call coming from four miles away. But the radar screen shows a large target eleven miles out and closing at thirty knots. The GPS signal is dead smack between us. I reckon we can beat the incoming target to the distress beacon if we go full steam ahead."

While I just sit there wondering, *Now what?* Jakob rattles out a string of commands. "Ahead, full throttle! Get us there first! Helena, get back to the bow. Man the harpoons. Malik, stay here and be ready to take on survivors." He turns to me. "And you. Go take care of yourself. But do it quickly. The fight isn't over yet."

12

I limp my way through the ship, clutching the first aid kit and wrapped in a blanket. By the time I reach the second deck, I'm trailing drops of blood. My leg is throbbing, but the pain is bearable. Maybe because of adrenaline. Maybe because of elation at not being in the stomach of a zombie-whale. Maybe because I'm in shock. Who knows? I can't complain.

Of course, when I sit on my bedside and peel off the wound's dressing, I complain. A lot. The gauze pulls away small dollops of coagulated blood, reopening the wound. I watch the blood rolling over my leg. It's dripping all over the braided rug. I'm not freaked out by the blood. I just don't want to do what comes next.

Man up, I tell myself. When I was a kid, the Colonel did this part. He was merciless about it. "Just grit your teeth and take it. Next time be smart enough to not get injured." I never pointed out the number of scars crisscrossing his body. I was smart enough to know that wouldn't go well. But his advice got me through a number of childhood gashes. It would get me through this.

I unscrew the rubbing alcohol. It was included with the first aid kit for sterilization, not wound cleaning. And I know it's going to destroy good and bad cells alike. My father should have never used the stuff on my scrapes. But there's no way in hell I'm going to risk leaving behind even a tiny fragment of that parasite.

As I move the bottle over my leg, the ship takes a wave hard, slamming through the water. The impact jars my arm and spills a few drops of alcohol. The drops strike my wound like little bombs, exploding pain beyond that of the original injury. I scream for a moment but swallow it down, grit my teeth like Daddy taught me, and douse the leg in liquid fire.

I growl at the pain, waiting for it to subside. The alcohol scours the dried blood from my leg. Pink fluid drips onto the blood-soaked rug. My nose twitches at the strong scent of rubbing alcohol that's made my room smell like a doctor's office. I feel the skin of my leg tighten as the liquid quickly evaporates. Then it's over. The alcohol and pain are gone. But the freshly rinsed wound is now bleeding. Helena sliced off a chunk of skin half an inch wide and about an inch long. That it needs stitches is a no-brainer, but it's not going to get any. Not unless Jakob thought to bring along a medic, which I assume he didn't, since I'm sitting here on my bed, buck nekkid, tending to my own damn wound.

Using a few fresh sheets of gauze, I put pressure on the wound. A lot of pressure. Hurts like hell, but the flow of blood stops for the moment. I'm sure it will start leaking again when I start walking around.

Moving slowly and carefully, I take away the fresh gauze. It hasn't bonded with coagulating or drying blood yet, so it comes away without aggravating the wound. After letting it air out for a minute, I place an antibiotic gauze pad against the wound, cover it with two absorbent bandage pads, wrap the whole thing in a thick layer of gauze, and then tape the shit out of it. It looks like a giant white tumor when I'm done, but I doubt I'll bleed through it.

There's a knock at my door. I turn to say, "One minute," but the door is already swinging inward. Willem steps in, and his eyes go wide when he sees me, still naked on the bed.

"Sorry," he says, spinning around. He doesn't leave, though.

"Nothing you haven't seen before," I say. "Though some of me is missing."

"Are you all right?" he asks.

I stand, putting just a little weight on my leg, and grunt. "I'll live."

A chill grips my body, covering every square inch of me with goose bumps and making my hair stand at attention. As I open my backpack and root around for fresh clothes, I glance at Willem. He's got on fresh jeans, likely fleece-lined, and a few layers up top covered by his trademark sweater. He'd been wearing similar clothes when I saw him, soaking wet on deck. He's lucky all those wet layers didn't pull us both to the bottom. That we're both standing here is a testament to his strength and strong will.

"Thanks, by the way," I say as I slip into some tight boxer-briefs and pull on my loosest pair of pants. The black cargos aren't exactly stylish, but they fit over my wrapped wound.

I don't see him shrug, but I know he did. "You would have done the same for me."

"I would have tried," I confess. But I'm not sure I could have dragged his two-hundred-plus-pound body out of the water. I slip into a formfitting, moisture-wicking black long-sleeve shirt and then follow it up with an equally tight black wool shirt. I catch my reflection in the room's mirror. My hair is matted against my head, weighed down with sea salt. Luckily, my go-to hairstyle is easy. I put both hands in my still damp hair and shake. The resulting mess is just about perfect. My damp hair chills my hands and sends another wave of goose bumps over my skin. Without thinking, I grab my black cloak, throw it around my shoulders, and button it at the top. Warmth envelops me.

"You can turn around now. I'm decent," I say.

"I doubt that very much," he says, turning toward me. When he sees me, a smile spreads across his face. "Dressed for battle?"

"What?" I ask, looking in the mirror. I immediately see what he's talking about. I'm dressed from head to toe in black and wearing the cloak that helped earn my Raven nickname.

"My father will be pleased," he says.

I roll my eyes and let out an "Ugh." The clothes are the warmest I have with me, and I'm not about to change again. I look down at the brown boots I was wearing before. They'll screw up the whole Raven thing nicely. But then I think how pleased Jakob really will be. He's the kind of guy who sees omens and takes pride in connections to his ancestors. "Fuck it," I say, reaching into my backpack and taking out my steel-toed black shit-kicker boots. While I'm working on the laces, cinching them tight, I ask, "So what's the deal with Helena?"

"What do you mean?" he asks. He sounds casual. Not at all defensive. And I'm not sure what to make of that.

"Why is she here?"

"She volunteered," Willem said. "My father was opposed to it, of course."

"Because she's a girl?" I ask. "You'd think I put that stereotype to bed for him."

"Because Helena is the one person my father adores more than you," he says.

I pause tying my boot mid-loop. *How much more do you adore her?* is the question I want to ask but don't. When it comes to Draugar, man-eating polar bears, and undead whales, I'm all spit and venom. When it comes to Willem, I'm kind of a pansy. If he's with Helena, it's my fault. I'm the one who pulled away. And I really don't want to hear that right now, so I clamp my mouth shut and finish tying my laces.

Willem, on the other hand, decides I need to hear all of Helena's finer qualities. "I'm actually the one who talked him into allowing her to come. She's been around ships more than I have. Knows how to pilot, can repair an engine, and can fire a harpoon better than most whalers. Her father was a whaler. Died at sea when she was sixteen. She's been working the sea since."

Boo hoo, I think.

"At the time we had a crew of just five, two of whom hadn't spent any time on the water. She really is essential."

I finish on the boots and sit up. "If I'm the person your father adores second in the world, why was he not just willing but determined to have me on board? Is there room for just one person at the top of his list of people to protect?" Willem looks confused by my line of questioning. "I suppose that's better than you, though, right? You wanted both of us here."

"Jane," he says, sounding all caring. He puts a hand on my shoulder, but I yank it away. The act makes me feel like a bitchy teenage girlfriend, but I'm not about to reverse course.

He sighs. "Jane, you're here because you've proven yourself to my father. He's seen you in action. You're not just a survivor—you're a fighter. He didn't think we could do this without you. And I agree with him. You proved it again today. No one else could have gone head-to-head with fifty feet of Draugr and come out alive."

I hate being buttered up, and it takes all of my self-control to not cuss him out. The only thing that stops me is that I think he's actually telling the truth. In fact, Willem rarely ever lies. But he's also wrong. "Willem, I'm not as strong as you think. I drowned myself in alcohol. I picked fights. I've been a total mess for the past two months."

He sits down next to me. "My father has been on Prozac since the hospital."

This is news to me. I can't picture the old sea dog taking prescription drugs or admitting that something like depression exists.

"We all have ways of coping with horrible things," he says.

"What was yours?" I ask.

"At first, it was you." He squirms uncomfortably, and I think I know what's coming. "Then you left."

"And Helena took my place," I conclude.

"I wouldn't say she took your place," he says. "But she—"

I stand and limp toward the door. I've suspected their relationship all along, but confirmation fills me with a jealous rage. And right now isn't the time or place for a love spat.

"What—where are you going?" he asks.

"Last I heard, we had a distress call to answer and an incoming target."

Willem's blue eyes widen. He'd already left the deck when Talbot delivered the news. "Distress call? Target?" He stands. "Are you okay to walk?"

In answer, I hobble out into the hall and make my way toward the stairs without looking back. I move with purpose, like I'm storming the beaches of Normandy, but my mind is still on the conversation. I'd like to move past it, but I find my thoughts focused on the man behind me. Then I step onto the bridge and forget all about Willem.

13

"Target is four miles out and closing!" Talbot shouts out as I step onto the bridge. He's standing at the radar display. "But it's popping in and out like a dang woodchuck!"

"GPS signal is just a half mile out," Klein says, staring at his laptop screen.

"I reckon we'll have about twelve minutes before it reaches us," Talbot adds.

"Does anyone see a ship?" Jakob asks.

A quick glance out the window reveals there's no ship within a half mile. Even a small boat would be easy to spot. But something even smaller might not be. "Look for something small and orange," I say.

All eyes turn back toward me and linger for a silent moment. I don't know if they're surprised that I'm here at all or confused by my darkly clad appearance. Maybe they've heard stories of Jakob's mythical Raven and are in awe of my glory. Whatever the case, Helena snaps them back to reality.

She steps through the exterior door and onto the bridge. "Off the port bow!" I might not like Helena for catty reasons, but she's earned my respect. She's all business and rarely not focused on the task at hand, including hacking off part of my leg.

"Show me," I say, stepping up to the window. When she joins me, I feel dwarfed. She points, but I've already seen the life raft. It's similar to the one I used to escape the sinking *Sentinel* a few months back; it bobs in and out of view as it rolls up and over wave crests before disappearing in the troughs.

"Can we turn around and back up to it?" Klein asks.

When the captain doesn't answer, I glance back. He nods at me, giving me the go-ahead. Apparently I've earned the lead on this. "Take us alongside the raft, and park us in front. Keep us between it and whatever's coming our way." Speaking of which... "Talbot, where is it?"

"Should be in visual range any second now," Talbot says, looking up from the radar screen like he can eyeball an object three miles away. "But it's still erratic. Appears for just a few moments at a time, then it's gone again."

I turn to Helena. "Keep watch with the harpoons. We're going to be vulnerable when we stop to pick up the people on board that raft." As she turns to leave, I take her arm. Whatever issues Willem and I have, they're not her fault. When she turns to me, I say, "Thanks. For the leg."

She smiles and sings—yeah, sings—"Let me take a part of you." She does a little jig, too, which is one part adorable and one part freakish, mostly because it's so out of character. She's forever destroyed the standoffish Viking warrior-maiden aura. She's also created a conundrum for me. By not only singing Devo but altering the lyrics to suit the situation, she's (A) revealed us to be about the same age, (B) exposed a previously hidden sense of humor that I appreciate, and (C) made me not hate her guts. *Bitch.*

My laugh sends Helena on her way. I turn to Willem, who's still at the back of the bridge. "Go with her."

As Willem heads out, I look at Jakob and ask, "Malik is ready at the dive deck?"

He nods, steering the ship closer to the orange life raft.

"You won't have any trouble steering us into position?"

He gives me a look that says *Please*, like I've just asked him if he can breathe air.

Klein joins me at the bridge window. With us being nearly on top of the GPS signal, he doesn't need to be at the laptop. He hands me a pair of binoculars and raises a second pair to his eyes.

"Talbot?" I say. The unsaid question is obvious.

"Two point five miles. Dead ahead."

I stand at the center of the bridge, line up the binoculars with the tip of the forward bow where Willem mans a harpoon gun, and slowly raise them toward the horizon. All I see is an endless, empty stretch of ocean. "I don't see anything."

"Neither do I," Klein adds.

"It's not on the radar, either," Talbot says. "But it's been like that the whole ti—wait, there it is."

I turn my attention back to the binoculars in time to see a gray blur fall into the distant ocean, casting up white froth as it drops out of sight.

"The hell was that?" Klein says. Apparently he saw the same thing I did but couldn't identify it either. "Looked like a surfacing submarine."

"Wasn't a sub," I say. I suspect the truth but don't want to say anything until I'm sure. I adjust the focus on my binoculars until the waves surrounding the object's appearance come into focus.

It returns thirty seconds later, and a good deal closer. As it rises from the deep, I adjust the focus and see it clearly as it reaches the apex of its breach.

"Oh my God," Klein says. "It's a whale."

I watch the giant bend forward and plunge back into the water. When it's gone I turn back to Jakob, my face ashen. "It's a sperm whale. A bull."

I don't need to say anything more. Jakob knows everything there is to know about whales. Bull sperm whales can grow up to sixty feet long and weigh fifty-six tons. They've got the largest head in the history of all living things, which can be, and has been, used to ram and sink ships. Sperm whales also have the largest brains of all animals, weighing up to twenty pounds, which means they're also quite smart. For a whale. Unlike the humpback whale, the sperm whale doesn't use baleen to filter out its food. Its powerful jaws sport sixty conical teeth that are eight inches long and weigh two pounds each. That's a tooth bigger, heavier, and denser than Malik's hand. Basically, you don't want to be in the water with a sperm whale if it's grumpy. And given the speed and course of this whale, I'd say it's beyond grumpy.

It's Draugr.

Probably summoned by the humpback's call.

How many more are on the way? I wonder, but I force my thoughts back to the situation at hand.

"Why is it jumping out of the water like that?" Klein asks.

"It's spotting," I say. Whales breach for a number of reasons, but I think the one barreling toward us is jumping out of the water for the same reason we're peering through binoculars. While sound travels great distances through water, visibility is the same for a whale as it is for a person. It's not going to see us underwater until it's quite close. But with each leap, it gets a glimpse of its target—an easy-to-spot black splotch marring the blue sky and ocean.

"Coming up on the raft," Jakob says.

I see the orange life raft pass by on the starboard side. The cover is up, and the hatch is zipped shut. Not unusual, but I don't see any movement, which is uncommon for people about to be rescued. It's not a good sign.

"Klein, come with me," I say, heading for the exit. "Malik might need a hand."

As I leave with Klein in tow, I glance at Jakob, and he gives me a nod. If it was a test, it seems I've passed. I'm not sure why he's so willing to let me take charge, but I appreciate it. I don't think I'd have admitted it before—hell, I could barely think about it—but this is my fight. The Draugar killed my friends and tried to kill me. Same as Jakob. And now we're in this together. A regular pair of Captain Ahabs.

The Arctic wind blasts me as I leave the bridge and hobble my way down to the aft main deck.

"Should you be walking on that leg?" Klein asks me.

I ignore him and move faster, arriving at the ladder that leads to the dive deck a moment later. Malik is there, reaching out to the raft with a long wooden rod with a hook on the end, usually used to move whale meat. I wonder if the Greenpeace people aboard will have a moral quandary about being rescued by a device used in the slaughter of the creatures they're sworn to protect. That is, if anyone on board is still alive. For a second it looks like Malik is going to pop the raft, but he raises the hook and snags the top of the rubber covering. With one hand gripping the cable running from the *Raven* to the *SuzieQ*, he pulls the raft in until the zippered hatch is resting against the dive deck. He lowers the pole, squats by the raft, and says a gruff "Hello. Is anyone there?"

"Just open it," I say, making the big man flinch.

He looks up at me. "I nearly fell in!"

"Sorry," I say. "We've got about five minutes before a bull sperm whale with a grudge gets here."

This news sobers him up. Like Jakob, Malik has spent a lot of time on the ocean. He understands the power of a sperm whale, and I doubt he's read *Moby Dick*. It's boring as shit.

Malik unzips the hatch and pushes it open. I can't see what's inside, but he hauls the raft farther up on deck and leans inside. When he comes back out, he's got a young man in his arms. The kid looks young, barely drinking age if that. And he's passed out cold. Maybe dead. I don't think Malik has checked, and I don't ask. I just reach down with Klein and take the kid's flaccid arms. Together, we haul him up onto the main deck and lay him flat.

Malik climbs the ladder. He's got a metal bucket in one hand.

"Just the one?" I ask.

Malik nods. "He was alone."

I kneel by the kid and gently slap his face. "Hey. Wake up." When there's no response, I check his pulse. "Well, he's alive."

A column of ice-cold Arctic water pours from Malik's bucket and strikes the kid square in the face. The reaction is immediate. He coughs. Sputters. Flails. His eyes dart around, seeing Malik, Klein, and then me. And then he starts screaming like we're playing jump rope with his intestines.

14

The kid's really shrieking like a banshee. His eyes are wide with horror, but I don't think he's really seeing anything at all. Or maybe everything he's seeing coupled with Malik's ice-cold rude awakening has him supremely confused. Whatever the case may be, he needs to get a grip. And soon. I've got him by the shoulders and am shouting in his face, but it's not helping, so I do the only other thing I can think of.

The slap knocks the scream right out of him. His hand goes to his face, and his eyes slowly rise to meet mine. Relief melts the tension in his face and body when our eyes meet. He's really just seeing me now.

"Where—where am I?" he asks.

"You're on board the *Raven*," I say.

"The *Raven*…" He looks around the ship and sees one of the harpoon guns mounted on the aft deck. "A whaling ship?"

I know the kid is a Greenpeacer, so this could go bad, but there's no hiding the fact that the *Raven* was outfitted for the sole purpose of slaughtering whales. "Yeah, you could say that."

He looks even more relieved now, which surprises me until I remember what he's probably endured.

"Thank God," he says. He turns and sees the second and third harpoon guns. "Probably still not enough, though."

I ignore the comment. "What's your name, kid?"

"Nathan. You can call me Nate."

"GreenpeaceNate?" I ask.

His eyes light up. "You follow me?"

"I do," Klein says. "I'm SpooKlein."

"Seriously? *SpooKlein?*" I say, looking at Klein. "Do you *want* your bosses to figure out it's you?"

"You DM'd me," Nate says. "About the...whale." His eyes go distant for a moment.

"We found the whale," I say. "The dead one."

His head snaps toward me. "It's not dead!"

I place a gentle hand on his shoulder. "It is now. It's chum."

"What about the others?" he asks.

"What others?" Malik asks.

"There were at least ten," Nate says. "I think a few of them killed themselves ramming the ship. But I'm not sure if they can even die."

"What happened to the *Rainbow*?" I ask. I'm not sure I want the answer, but I need it.

"I—I'm not sure." He scratches his matted brown hair. "I remember the attack. The hull was in serious trouble. I was getting the life rafts ready, but it seemed like a really stupid idea, you know? If the *Rainbow* was in trouble, what good would an inflatable raft be?"

"What kind of whales?" Malik asks.

"Humpbacks mostly," Nate says. "Two female sperm whales. And a big bull. They came when the dead—not dead—humpback called out. We thought it was dying and didn't think anything of it when the others arrived. But then..." His eyes flick back and forth like he's trying to remember something. "I don't know how I got in the raft. I remember holding the case. Being ready to toss it overboard. But that's it. My next memory is here."

"Jane," Malik says. "I'm going to warn Jakob about the whales. There might be more than just the one."

I nod and Malik leaves. When I look back at Nate, he's wide-eyed, but not from fear this time. In fact, with all the stupid resilience of the young, he seems to be perking up. "Your name is Jane?"

"Yeah."

"And the captain is Jakob?"

"Yeah, kid, why?"

"You're Jane Harper!"

I stand up. "How do you know my name?"

At this confirmation of my identity, he grins and chuckles. "Hashtag, awesome. You were trending the Twitterverse a few months back. At least in the circles I follow. I know all about what happened to you. Or what you say happened. I didn't believe it."

A shiver runs through his body, and I swear the kid is about to burst into tears, but he sniffs hard, crushes his hands into fists, and pulls himself together. He might not have believed my story before, but he sure as shit does now.

"No one did," he says. "You were a traitor to the cause. But, man, your investigative videos went viral on YouTube. Your picture was everywhere, too, mostly because you're kind of a hottie. Um, I mean. I didn't recognize you because of the cloak—" His eyes appear a little less haunted as he looks me up and down. "OMG. It's true! They said people were calling you the Raven. That you wore a cloak. I thought it was like that stuff. What's it called? Legend or something. But it's for real, right? The Raven. Awesome. BT-dubs, I never really believed you did it. Killed all those people."

That's enough of that, I think. "First, never say OMG in my presence again, or you might be the first living person I actually kill. Second, BT-dubs?"

"Uh—by the way. Dubs is—"

"Yeah, I get it." I sigh. "Never say that again, either. Even the Greenlanders speak English on this ship."

"'Kay," he says.

"Jane!" It's Malik, shouting down from the exterior bridge door. "It will be here in a minute!"

The engines fire up, and the prop starts chewing water.

"Coming!" I reply before yanking the kid to his feet. He's wet, and cold, but he's going to have to deal with that for a bit.

"What's coming?" he asks, looking a little squirrelly.

I want to joke with the kid, but I can't think of any funny way to put it. "The bull."

Nate lets out an involuntary yelp that sounds something like a panicked zebra. Klein claps him on the shoulder. "BT-dubs, this ship can handle a single whale. And then some."

I don't know if it's the use of the forbidden phrase or Klein's confidence in our ability to slay whales, but the kid gives him a shaky grin, so I let it slide.

My leg starts to throb as I climb the exterior stairs to the bridge. My instinct is to stop and look at the bandage. See if it's bleeding through. But I ignore it and limp back onto the bridge.

Jakob is still behind the wheel, his eyes locked on the empty ocean in front of us. The only other person on the bridge is Talbot. Malik now mans the third forward harpoon gun. I move to the windows, looking in all directions. "I don't see it."

"You will," Talbot says. "It's clo—"

The leviathan rises, shedding sheets of water as it arcs into the air. The bull sperm whale is a giant. It exudes power and ferocity. And for a moment I feel it is looking straight at me. Sunlight glimmers off its wet gray flesh, creating a surreal aura around the beast. It's no wonder these creatures spawned legends of sea monsters.

The whale, just a football field away, descends with a mighty splash. I can feel the *whump* of its body striking the ocean through the metal of the ship.

"It's going to ram us!" Nate shouts.

For a moment I think he's being paranoid, but he has experience with these things that none of us do.

"He might be right," I say to Jakob.

The captain is nonplussed. In fact, I'd say he's in some kind of Viking berserker rage. His eyes are full of fire when he replies. "The *Raven* is a double-hulled icebreaker, and the bull's head is little more than an oil-filled balloon." He shoves the throttle to full. "We're going to split him open like a melon!" He toggles a handheld radio. "Hold your fire down there, we're going to ram the son of a bitch!"

I watch the dark shape of the whale approaching quickly. If the whale is still moving at thirty knots, and the ship is at its full twenty-knot speed, the fifty-knot collision is going to be jarring to say the least. Icebreakers aren't designed to strike fifty-six-ton objects moving at fifty knots. That said, despite the whale's size and power, it's even less prepared for this collision. I have no doubt we'll come out on top, I just don't want to sink afterward.

With the collision imminent, I step away from the window and grip a chair bolted to the floor. "Hold on to something!"

I instinctually close my eyes and grit my teeth, waiting for the impact. Ten seconds later, I open them again. Nothing.

"He's gone beneath us!" Jakob shouts. He picks up the radio. "Willem, Malik, move to the back! He's coming up behind us."

I see the two men leave the harpoons on the forward deck and make for the rear of the ship. I follow them, heading for the door. This isn't just any normal whale. It's controlled by an intelligence that makes it capable of strategizing on a level that's human. Maybe beyond human. They're going to need all the help they can get.

I open the door as Willem runs past below.

"How do the harpoons work?" I shout down to him.

"They're all loaded and prepped," he shouts back. "Just aim and pull the trigger. And keep your foot clear of the line." I'm not sure why we're using harpoons with lines. We're not trying to catch whales, we're trying to kill them. But there's no time to ask.

Willem takes the harpoon at the ship's stern. It's just above the cable connecting the *Raven* to the *SuzieQ*. Malik has the starboard gun ready, so I take the port. The big weapon weighs a ton, but it's so well balanced and oiled that I have no trouble maneuvering it around.

If only I had a target. "See anything?" I shout.

"Nothing," Malik replies.

"Willem?" I shout.

"Hold on..." he says. "I think I see someth—"

A sharp crack, like the snap of a felled tree, whips me around. For a moment, I think Willem's harpoon has misfired and blown up in his face, but then I see the *SuzieQ* rising out of the sea. Water clings to its sides but then slurps away, freeing the boat from the liquid's grasp. The ship splits in two as it's catapulted upward, the halves spiraling away from each other, shedding planks of wood and random debris. A surprised shout rises in my throat, but it is squelched when I see what launched the *SuzieQ* skyward.

15

I watch in slack-jawed awe as the bull sperm whale rises from the depths like a living missile, following through on the blow that reduced the *SuzieQ* to toothpicks. The whale twists as it rises forty feet into the air, which is just over half its body length and also more than enough for it to peek over our back deck. Its creamy white eye seems to lock on me despite the absence of a pupil, mocking me, saying, *You're next.* The raw power and horror of the creature immobilize me—that is, until I see the trajectory of a large chunk of hull.

It's going to crush Willem, who has steadfastly stayed on task.

I'm already in motion when I shout a warning, but my voice is lost in the din of shattering wood and crashing water.

Willem tracks the whale through the air, aiming for the prodigious head.

The debris rushes toward him.

"Willem!" I shout.

I don't know if he hears me, but if he does, I think he believes I'm ordering him to shoot. He pulls the trigger. The harpoon explodes from the cannon. A coil of white cable unfurls behind it. I see it all in a fraction of a second. After that, I'm airborne, lunging for Willem.

I strike him from the side like a half-pint linebacker. He's not expecting the blow and tumbles to the side, taking me with him.

There's a tremendous crash from behind us as we hit the deck, which is reverberating from the blow. When I roll off Willem, we get a clear look at the chunk of debris lying on the metal deck where he had been standing.

"Thanks," he says, but he doesn't linger. He stands quickly and helps me up.

My leg screams in pain. Any healing has been undone by my pell-mell sprint across the deck. *Could be worse*, I think, looking at the debris. Then Malik is there, lifting the chunk of *SuzieQ*'s bow and heaving it over the aft rail.

"You struck the whale!" Malik shouts. "Center head. He's done for sure."

I'm not so sure. The sperm whale's brain is located essentially in the center of its massive head. It's protected on all sides by tons of meat, muscles, and the whale's largest organ, called the case, which is full of yellowish, oily wax called spermaceti. All of that provides a nice buffer for ramming ships, or in this case, surviving a harpoon strike.

Granted, most whales would be stunned into submission with a hole blown in their head, but this isn't just a normal whale. It's Draugr, which means we can shred the case all we want, but it's not going to stop until we destroy the brain or completely immobilize the body. Even stopping the heart won't help. It's the parasites populating the whale's body that are keeping it alive and mobile now.

I look at the water behind us. All that remains of the *SuzieQ* is a debris field bobbing in the waves. The whale is gone, but it's left behind its footprint—the large area of flattened water created by surfacing sea giants—and a swirl of straw-colored goo, which confirms a head shot.

Willem starts hauling in the line, and I see the harpoon rise to the surface. For a moment I wonder why the line isn't embedded in the whale's side, but then I notice the harpoon has no flukes. These harpoons aren't made for catching whales. Armed with just the explosive tip, they're designed for killing whales. Plain and simple. The line is attached so the projectile can be retrieved, rearmed, and fired again. It makes sense, since the harpoons are quite heavy and storing a large number of them on board would be difficult. Explosive tips, on the other hand…

Malik arrives with a wooden crate the size of a computer tower. He throws open the top, revealing a container that's been divided down the middle by a wooden slat. On one side are the explosive charges that fire the harpoon. On the other side are the bomb tips.

Moving fast, Malik ejects the spent charge and replaces it with a fresh one. Willem gets the harpoon on deck, so I pick up a spear tip and hand it to him. He carefully slides it onto the end of the harpoon and secures it. Then, working together, Malik and Willem lift the harpoon and slide it into the large barrel. Total reload time is about a minute. In the heat of battle, it feels like a lifetime.

No wonder they've got so many harpoons, I think.

A splash of water draws my eyes to port. I'm confused by what I see for a moment; then my eyes focus and I realize that I'm seeing the underside of the sperm whale. It has breached on the side of the *Raven* and is falling toward us.

I'm thrown off balance as the ship turns hard to port, pulling the back end out of the monster's shadow. The whale crashes back into the ocean. While it has missed crushing the main deck, it still slams into our side, sending a vibration through the ship.

I scramble to my feet and run for my harpoon. When I reach the giant weapon, I swivel it toward the rear of the ship and catch sight of the whale. It's just off the port side, its head nearly touching the hull. Apparently even Draugr whales can be stunned. When hunting sperm whales, whalers typically aim for the sweet spot between the dorsal fin and eye. It's here that the explosive head can penetrate deep into the whale's body and cause massive damage to the heart and other vital organs. The trouble with this is that whales are designed to go long durations without taking a breath. Even with its heart stopped, the whale may still be alive and suffering, even when it's pulled up onto factory boats. Possibly while it's being disassembled for market. For me, this sweet spot won't do any good. Luckily, my target is easy to spot. The giant's gray body is marred by a five-foot hole, through which globs of spermaceti flow. The yellowish hue is easy to spot from the surface.

I focus on the yellow and place my crosshairs dead center.

What I'm about to do goes against everything I've done for my entire adult life. I haven't always been the most passionate antiwhaler in the world, but I do believe in the cause and that harpooning is a cruel and disgusting way to kill an animal. What I'm about to do is wrong, but it's unavoidable.

"It's not a whale," I say. "Not anymore."

Then I pull the trigger.

The explosive charge that fires the harpoon is louder than any handgun I've handled, and it nearly knocks me over. I keep my grip on the large cannon and watch as the harpoon, trailing its white cable, soars down toward the ocean, piercing water, then whale.

The harpoon slips through the waxy oil and strikes the hard surface of the whale's skull. The resulting explosion launches a spray of seawater, red, meaty mist, and globs of yellow. A fortunate sea breeze carries the fleshy debris away from the *Raven*, but not before

I've caught a whiff. Coppery blood, cordite, and something fishy fills my nose, amalgamating into a scent that instantly sours my stomach.

But the horrible smell doesn't stifle my excitement enough to stop the war whoop that comes unhindered from my lips. I step away from the cannon and up to the rail, looking over the side to see what's become of the bull Draugr.

Willem and Malik step up to the rail beside me.

"Did I get it?" I ask. The water swirls with gouts of red blood turned pink as it mixes with seawater. Trails of yellow spiral up from below. It must be dead. Really dead. It has to be.

Then the whale's fluke, which is like a muscular hang glider notched at the center, rises from the water and slams back down. There's enough power behind the strike to convince me that the whale is not yet out of commission.

Malik begins hauling in the harpoon line, while Willem rushes back to his post. I just stand and watch as the whale pulses its tail down into the water and slides beneath the surface.

It rises again, coming alongside. When its head—what's left of it—clears the water, I see what's become of it. The whale's brain is located at the center of the head, between the eyes. It's so well protected that even after two explosive harpoon strikes, we have yet to reach it. What we have managed to do is separate the entire upper jaw and case. The lower jaw dangles uselessly below a huge empty space from which gouts of blood pour.

One more shot should finish it, I think.

Malik retrieves the spear, but he is moving more slowly to rearm the charges without Willem's help. I really need to learn how to do this stuff, but now is not the time. I'm liable to blow off my hand, or worse.

I look back to the whale, hoping it's still in range. But it's moving away.

Not away. In a circle.

It seems we've managed to injure it after all. Or perhaps the parasites' control can't overcome the whale's nervous system's response to the catastrophic injury. *Or maybe there aren't any parasites at all,* I think. As fear grips my chest, I look out at the whale, searching for some sign that it's more than just a whale. Or less than a whale. I find my proof on the whale's lolling tongue. It's not pink, like it should be. It's white, covered in thousands of parasite larvae anxious to be passed on to the next unfortunate host.

As the whale falls behind, continuing its spiral through the waves, the *Raven* comes about, performing a tight turn that brings the ship on a collision course with the whale.

"To the bow!" Willem says, rushing toward the front of the ship, where Helena stands alone.

I follow him as quickly as I can, while Malik stays behind, rearming the harpoon. When we arrive at the bow, Helena isn't manning the harpoon, she's standing beside it, clutching the rail.

"Helena," Willem shouts, sounding annoyed. "What are you—"

She turns toward his voice, eyes wide, and shouts, "Hold on to something! Jakob's going to ram it!"

I catch sight of the whale just twenty feet out and closing fast. The *Raven* is going to strike the beast's side. Before I can react, Willem wraps an arm around my waist, lifts me off the deck, and deposits me between him and the rail. I see the muscles in his hands flex as he grips the rail and holds me tight. I'm pinned in such a way that I can look down over the rail, and my gaze casts downward just as the two titans of the sea collide.

The ruined whale doesn't stand a chance against the ice-breaking hull of the *Raven*. The sixty-foot body bends at the middle and then splits, falling away to either side. For all the violence of the collision, I barely felt the impact, though that might have been because of the human safety belt enshrouding me.

With the collision over, Willem steps away. I'm about to thank him when I feel the engines of the *Raven* kick into high gear. We turn north and haul ass away from the whale. "What the hell? Why are we leaving?"

"I'm not sure," Willem says, looking back at the whale halves we're leaving behind.

"Our sample is right there!" I shout and storm to the bridge stairs.

My leg hurts so bad that I make the climb about half as fast as I want, but my arrival on the bridge is no less dramatic because of it. "Why are we leaving!" I demand.

Jakob keeps his eyes on the sea ahead, unfazed by my outburst. Talbot, on the other hand, looks up from the radar, looking a little worse than someone who's just seen a zombie-whale split in two should. "More whales are coming," he says. "A *lot* more."

16

"How many more whales?" I ask. My blood is pumping from the confrontation with the sperm whale and I feel ready for a fight, but I'm not stupid. If the odds are stacked against us, I'll happily retreat. Even my father subscribed to the "live to fight another day" theory. "Wars are won by surviving," he'd say. "Not dying."

"Hard to say," Talbot says. "They keep popping on and off. Like the first. But the signals are spread out. Were I to guess, I'd say six. Maybe seven."

I'm not a fan of maybes. I turn to Nate and find him sitting at one of the workstations. He's got his knees pulled up to his chest and his arms wrapped around them. And, damnit, he's got tears in his eyes. But I'm not about to coddle the kid. "Nate, how many came at the *Arctic Rainbow*?"

His eyes flick toward me. Mixed with the tears is an angry fire. He twitches oddly, distorting his expression for a moment, and says, "How could you do that?"

Apparently he saw me blow the front half of Moby-Draugr's head off. I know where he's coming from, understand his passion and revulsion. But there is a single glaring flaw in the kid's logic.

"It wasn't a whale," I say.

"Certainly looked like a whale from here!"

I take a step toward him, clenching my fists. "Kid, I swear if you don't man up, like right now, I'm going to toss you overboard and let you find out firsthand if those are the nice kind of whales or the undead, man-eating, parasite-controlled sonsabitches that we're fighting on behalf of you and every other whale-loving, tree-hugging, daisy-smelling asshole on the planet."

He stares at me. His stunned expression morphs to confusion. "Did you say parasite controlled?"

"Yes," I say. "It wasn't a whale. It was a Draugr. The same thing that attacked your ship. Although somehow you didn't notice."

"I don't remember what happened to the *Rainbow*," he says. "We were attacked, but I thought maybe the whales were just finally fighting back? Maybe they wanted to take back the ocean from all ships, you know? And the *Rainbow* could be fine for all we know. Did you find a debris field? An oil slick?"

The kid makes a good point. We found neither. It's not conclusive, but it could mean the *Rainbow* didn't sink. There's just one problem with his theory. "And yet you were found in a life raft."

"I don't remember why," he says with a sigh, eyes cast downward. "Draugr…" He says the word slowly, trying it on for size.

"Draugar if there is more than one," I add.

Then I give him the whole spiel, the one I'm already getting a little sick of repeating. Not that I've had much call to. Áshildr Olavson and her relationship to the present-day Olavsons, the parasites, how they infect, preserve, and sometimes gnaw on their mammalian victims. I don't spare him the gory details; his horrified reactions to them is what gets me through the story without yawning, which probably says some awful things about me, but I also don't give a shit, so I'm good. When I finish explaining their collective hive mind and its relationship to the Queen, I jump into the worst of it.

"The worst part is that we think the host is at least partially aware of what's happening but has no control over it. Imagine watching yourself slaughtering and eating people, but not being able to stop it. Killing a Draugr is a merciful end for the host."

"But—"

"Just shut up for another minute, kid," I say. "How's your Greenlandic history? Spend much time there?"

"Yeah," he says. "About a year."

"Been to the Viking ruins?"

He nods.

"Remember what happened to them?"

He thinks for a moment. "The colony disappeared. No one knows what happened to them."

"Really?" I ask. "When did the colony disappear?"

"Umm, fourteen hundreds, I thi—" I can see the kid connecting the dots. "You think these Draugar wiped out the Norse colony?"

"I *know* they did." I give him the lowdown on Jakob's great-times-ten-grandpappy, Torstein, and his history with the Draugr. I end my tale at the Arctic island. "Torstein and his men entombed themselves behind corpse doors and stayed there until—"

"Three months ago," he says. "I remember your story. You're saying all that crazy stuff is true?"

"Kid, even pissed-off whales don't attack ships this big, definitely not after they've taken a harpoon to the head."

"I remember," he says. "I remember the dead whale we found. It called out. It wasn't dead at all."

"A Draugr."

"There were ten," he says. "Whales. Including the bull, so maybe nine now."

"Too many," I say to no one in particular. I turn to Jakob. "Where are we heading?"

"West," he says. "Then south. Our target remains the same, but we'll avoid the whales."

"What if they chase us?" I ask.

"They haven't course-corrected yet," Talbot says. "If we're gone by the time they get here, I don't think they'll—"

"If there are more sperm whales, they can echolocate us from eleven miles out," I say.

"Not to mention hear our engine from more than a hundred miles away," Nate adds. Kid knows his stuff. "You can't hide from them. This is their territory."

I sense that Nate is about to dump some antiwhaling propaganda and quickly whisper, "Not whales."

He pinches his lips together and takes a long, slow breath through his nose.

"Assuming they course-correct, how long do we have?" I ask.

Klein starts talking to himself, rattling off numbers. "They're eleven miles out?"

"Roughly," Talbot says. "Moving at thirty knots."

"And we're at twenty, tops," Klein says. "They'll catch up somewhere between seventeen and twenty hours, depending on when they course-correct."

"Is that before or after we reach our target destination?" I ask.

"Before," Jakob grumbles.

I cross my arms over my chest. "Then we have seventeen hours to eat, rest, and get ready for a hell of a fight." I share a look with Jakob, and he grins.

"Geez," says Nate. "It's like being on a Klingon Bird of Prey."

"Klingons don't have anything on the Vikings, kid," I say, putting a hand on his still-wet shoulder. "Let's go find you some clothes. I think we have a red shirt around here somewhere…" The one thing you can count on in *Star Trek* is that the away-team crew member in the red shirt will bite the dust first. They have a nearly 100 percent mortality rate.

"That's not funny," he says, understanding the reference. He looks at Talbot. "That's not funny."

Talbot shrugs. "I can't fathom why it would be, son."

My grin is hard to hide. "I don't know what you're talking about. Klein, you look about the same size. Can you find something for Nate?"

"Nothing red," Nate says.

The Trekkie banter is a welcome change from the heated battle. A little calm before the storm is always a good thing. Of course, the coming storm is going to be unlike anything any of us have ever conceived of before. Seventeen hours. Until what? A fight for sure, but the outcome is anyone's guess. The *Raven* is built for the fight, but nine whales? I'm not sure the ship's hull can take that kind of pounding. But the hull isn't the main concern. As a former antiwhaling crusader, I know that the weak spot on any vessel is the propeller. A suicidal Draugr might be able to gum it up with whale meat, or possibly even destroy it. If that happens, we're dead in the water. And if we're dead in the water, well, we're just plain dead.

17

With time to kill and Nate's needs being tended to by Klein, I retreat to my room to change the dressing on my wound. We've got about seventeen hours, give or take, before the fleet of whales—which did adjust course to pursue the *Raven*—catches up, right around sunrise. During that time, we're supposed to eat, sleep, and prepare our souls, whatever that means. But it's what Jakob requested, and no one argued; by this time tomorrow we might all be dead.

So how does one prepare one's soul? I doubt any two people on board would agree on how that's done. Hell, I don't even know what I believe. The Colonel was Catholic, born and raised, but I don't know if he truly believed or if he was just going through the motions. I have no memory of him going to confession. If he did, I imagine he spent as much time doing Hail Marys as he did fighting wars. The man's language alone was probably enough to earn him a cozy plot of beach beside the lake of fire.

Maybe I should pray for him? Catholics do that, I think. Pray for the dead.

I decide that wherever my father is now, the prayers of a nonbeliever for anything other than self-preservation won't do him a hell of a lot of good. I consider praying for myself, but the same conundrum exists: To whom do I pray, and for what? Salvation? Protection? Forgiveness?

I decide on protection simply because if it's granted, I might have time to figure the rest out before I die. Or become a Draugr. "So," I say to nobody in particular, "here's the deal. I don't know anything about you. I've never really cared. And if you're real, you know all this. But this thing we're trying to stop, it's bad, right? You're supposed to care about the people you made. And the animals. So I'm not just asking this for myself. I'm asking for everyone. Everywhere. Cut us some slack. Help us kill these things. Of course, I guess you technically created the parasites, too, which was a sucky thing to do, but still, you're supposed to love us, right? We're made in your image or something? So keep us safe. I'm not going to promise I'll be a better person or that I'll go to church. You know I won't. But I'll kill them all if you let me, and I'm pretty sure I'll save a lot of people who do believe in you."

I stop, feeling uncomfortable, but knowing it's unfinished. "Amen," I say.

"Amen," repeats a voice from the doorway.

I turn to find Helena standing there. She grins at me, blue eyes radiating kindness. Why'd she have to be nice?

"So was that a blasphemous prayer or what?" I ask.

She comes in, pulls up a chair in front of me, and motions for me to lift my leg. After a moment's hesitation, I do. I have no reason not to trust her. Personal issues aside, she's now my comrade in arms. If she's anything like Jakob and Willem, she takes that stuff seriously.

"Your words were honest." She lifts my pant leg and starts unwrapping my bandage, which is wet with blood. "I think that's what matters."

"Are you religious?" I ask.

"My father was a Baptist minister," she says.

"I don't think our fathers would have been friends," I say with a grin, remembering how my father referred to all Protestants, regardless of denomination, as "Jesus freaks." I always found that humorous, since they all believed the guy was the son of God.

"What about you?" I ask. "Do you believe in God?"

"Most of the time," she replies.

The Viking warrior-princess side of Helena fits Willem, but the conservative, wholesome side doesn't. Willem likes his women a little rough around the edges. More like—well, more like me. Of course, her rockin' body probably makes up for any personality issues. Still, I can't help but dig for answers. While she finishes unwrapping my leg, I ask, "So how long have you known Willem?"

"All my life," she says. "Though we weren't allowed to see each other for a long time."

Wha? I try to think of scenarios that fit, but nothing comes to mind. "He never told me about you," I say.

"Well, he spoke plenty about you," she says with a smile.

What. The. Hell. I'm so totally confused I don't even notice she's applied new antibiotic pads until she starts rewrapping my leg.

"It will heal," she says when she notes my attention. "Not nicely, but you'll be fine. No signs of infection, yet."

"Are you a nurse, too?"

Her smile fades. She heard the edge of annoyance in my voice. Not that I did much to hide it.

"Have I done something to you? Offended you in some way?" Her questions are so innocent and tinged with hurt that my rising defenses are laid to waste. She's just too fucking nice!

I decide to be honest. If we're going to be fighting side by side, there shouldn't be anything left unsaid. "I guess I'm jealous," I say.

She looks stunned. "Of *what*?"

"You and Willem."

She stares at me for a moment, then remembers my leg. She tapes the wrapped bandage and then meets my eyes again. "Jealous of what? I spent a lot of time with him and Jakob lately, but you could have, too. From what they said, you chose to drink away the past few months."

Okay, now she's pissing me off. "How would that have worked? Unless you're batting for both teams, I don't—"

"Batting for both teams?" She looks mystified.

Right, I think. *I'm arguing with a conservative Greenlandic blonde who spent a lot of her time at sea with her Baptist whaling father.* I'm about to explain when she lets out a "pfft," which becomes full-on laughter a moment later. I guess she figured it out, but her reaction confuses me. Rather than ask for an explanation, I wait for her laughter to subside.

It takes nearly thirty seconds. Her face is flushed from laughing. Her perfect white teeth mock me as she tries to speak. "You—you think—" More laughter. "You think Willem and I—" And more laughter.

"Spit it out," I say, as serious as a warden asking a death row inmate "Any last words?"

She puts a hand to her chest, like that's going to help, and takes several deep breaths to control her laughter. "Ahh, ha, Willem." Her smile widens, and she nearly breaks into laughter again. "Willem is my half brother."

Say what now?

"Jakob is my father," she says. "He had an affair with my mother. That's why I couldn't see Willem. My father knew about the affair. He didn't leave my mother, but he didn't let me see my brother, either. I saw them occasionally. It's a small country. An even smaller whaling community. But only in passing. It wasn't until my father died that I really got to know Willem and Jakob."

"Well," I say, "I'm the biggest idiot on the planet."

She pats my knee. "You are everything Jakob and Willem said you were."

"Short-tempered, foulmouthed, and impulsive?" I say.

"Among other things," she adds. She rolls down my pants. "That should be okay until tomorrow."

"Might not need to worry about it after tomorrow," I say.

She stands and throws my bloodied rags in the room's small trash can. "My father and brother said you were brave, that you fought with ferocity and cunning, and that you come from a family of warriors, whose memory you not only respect but also draw upon for strength. Before you arrived, I saw…fear and uncertainty in their eyes. But the moment you stepped aboard, they have been at peace. Confident. Jakob named you Raven for a reason. The title might have been a superstitious response to your appearance"—she motions to my clothing and cloak—"but it is a title you have earned since. As for Willem, well, he's just—"

There's a knock at the door.

Just what? I want to know.

But finishing the sentence is impossible. Willem appears in the doorway. He looks happy to see Helena and me together, which now makes sense. "Am I interrupting?" he asks.

Both Helena and I both offer a too-quick "No."

He squints at us for a moment, then says, "Malik made dinner. It's ready now." He looks at me. "Going to be an early morning, so we should eat quickly and get some sleep."

I want to say something about what I've learned, but he's all business.

"Let's go," he says, then steps out of the room.

Helena heads for the door and looks back at me.

"I'll be right behind you," I say.

She nods, offers a smile, and leaves.

Alone again, I turn to the ceiling and say, "One more favor. Don't let him die. If he does, I'm coming for you when I'm done with the Draugar."

Threatening God might not be the best idea, but Helena said honesty was good, and if God exists, he knows what I'm thinking anyway. "Amen," I say and head for the door.

18

The mess hall, which is basically a large square room on the main deck with three long tables and an assortment of chairs that look like yard sale finds, is full of loud voices when I arrive. In attendance are Willem, Helena, Talbot, Nate, and Malik, who is laying plates of food on the table.

"You can't really believe that," Nate says as I take a seat next to Willem.

Willem smiles at me, and I don't see any of the weirdness between us that I'd imagined before. He's just happy to see me, so I return the smile.

"I do," Talbot says. "And rightly so."

I ignore them as Malik steps up beside me and puts a plate down. It's covered in some kind of broiled fish—of course—carrots and some kind of mush that I can't identify as anything other than maybe dog shit. My grumbling stomach sours.

"You don't look pleased," Malik says.

"That pretty much sums up every dining experience I've had in Greenland," I say.

"We should have brought along some microwave diners," Willem says with a chuckle that earns him a slug in the shoulder. The physical contact feels good. Well, for me, at least. Willem rubs his shoulder.

Malik produces a ladleful of creamy yellow liquid that glistens with flecks of oil and tiny green bits. He drizzles the sauce over the carrots and fish, but leaves the brown glob alone. "Try it," he says.

I pick up my fork, scrape off a chunk of sauce-slathered fish, and pop it into my mouth. I'm not expecting much, but I have to eat. The flavor hits me two chews in. It might very well be the best food I've had in Greenland, which isn't saying much, but this is good compared to anything in the wider world, too.

"Wow," I say. Then again, "Wow."

Malik smiles wide. "I like to cook."

I now view my plate through different eyes, but I'm still suspicious of the brown slop. I point at it with my fork. "What's this?"

He looks confused that I'm even asking. "Chocolate mousse."

I take a quick forkful. The dark chocolate is like silk in my mouth. I close my eyes and savor it until—

"Raven, what's your take?"

I'm not sure who's even spoken until I see Talbot's raised eyebrows wrinkling his forehead. "It's good," I say.

"Huh?" Talbot says. He twitches his mustache twice. "What's good?"

"The food," I say.

Talbot throws his head back like he's been punched. "Dadgumit, girl, we're not talkin' 'bout the grub!" The Texan's accent is thicker than usual. I knew a guy from Massachusetts like that. He was able to curb the accent most of the time, but when he was telling a story, it came out clear as day. "Snowblowers" became "snow blowahs," "boys" became "bowies," and "that stinks" became "wicked pissah." It seemed some Texans undergo the same conversational transformation, though I reckon not many of them would believe they had much in common with a Yankee.

"He thinks they're aliens," Nate says, serious but also smiling. He's already started to make himself part of the crew, helping when he can, taking part in conversations, and generally acting like he belongs. *Kid adapts quickly*, I think. He's going to need to.

"Only thing that makes a lick of sense," Talbot says.

Nate shakes his head. I watch in amusement while eating my food.

"Look, that these things, these parasites, came from outer space is essentially impossible. First, how'd they get here?"

"Asteroid," Talbot says. "Maybe a spacecraft."

"Spacecraft," Nate says, his voice oozing disgust. "They're what? Inch-long worms?"

I give a nod, confirming the face.

"Inch-long worms capable of controlling mammals," Talbot says, thrusting his finger into the air. "And they're intelligent."

I nod again, shoveling in a mouthful.

"It's far more likely that they evolved, on Earth, which is why they are perfectly adapted to warm-blooded hosts. There are parasites, just like them, all over the planet that can control the actions of fish, reptiles, and insects. That there is also a species that is capable of controlling mammals, even people, isn't only possible, it's plausible."

"Actually," I say, licking my fork clean of mousse, "the toxoplasma parasite alters the minds of mammals." I take another lick. "Damn, this is good. It's common in cats, and the rats and other animals they eat, but it's equally common in people. Fifty percent of the world's population is host to the parasite."

Nate pumps his fist. "GreenpeaceNate FT-dubs!"

"*Kid*," I say.

"For the win!" he says, defining his "FT-dubs" comment. I was referring to his entire display, fist pump and all, but decide to let it go. I've been thinking about this argument for a long time, weighing all possibilities, and am interested to hear Talbot's and Nate's diverging points of view.

"So what's this toxojumbo do?" Talbot asks. "If it's altering the human mind of half the world's population, where's the evidence?"

I lay my fork down beside my polished-off plate. "People with the highest concentrations of toxoplasma are schizophrenic. The parasite is doing something to people's minds. We just don't know what or why. Could even be a less evolved, or even more evolved, variant of what we're dealing with."

Willem is unfazed, but both Nate and Talbot look surprised. As do Malik and Helena. I'm momentarily stunned that the crew isn't already educated on the subject, with the exception of Nate, of course. Still, it's all guesswork. Everything we've come up with so far could be wrong.

"I still say it's aliens," Talbot says, crossing his arms. He looks like a gunslinger in a saloon who has just been accused of cheating at cards. In a flash, the man could produce a pair of pistols and clear the room of the living. I don't think he's used to being so wholeheartedly disagreed with.

"Actually," I say, "I haven't written that off yet, either."

Talbot looks at me. He seems pleased but also wary, like I might be setting him up. He's got a good sense of who I am, so he knows that's a possibility, but it's not actually what I'm doing. "Never mind how they got here," I say. "If they're from some other planet, we have to assume that we might not understand how they got here even if it were explained to us."

Nate sighs. "Now you sound like him! Hashtag, crazytown."

"How do you explain their ability to preserve flesh for thousands of years?" I ask.

Nate just stares at me. He can't. I've been thinking about it for months and haven't come up with anything.

"How do they communicate with each other?" I ask.

"Bees," he says, but I cut him off before he can tell me about how bees shake their asses and transmit the location of a new pollen source.

"Bees can't speak English. Or Old Norse. They can't lay traps. Most bees live fifty days tops, not a thousand years. And they sure as shit can't take the head of my friend, stick it on a mummified girl, and then fucking speak to me. Evolution falls short when you consider all that, especially if they were trapped on Greenland for thousands or even millions of years."

"That happened?" Nate says, the wind taken out of his sails. "With your friend?"

Willem answers for me. "We left that out of our reports. Didn't think it would help anyone believe us."

"Sure enough," Talbot says, though it sounds more like "Shore 'nuff."

"Jane, look," Nate says. "Before you agree with everything the cowboy says, you should know who he is." The kid lays his smartphone on the table, swipes the screen on, turns it around, and slides it across the table to me.

The screen shows a shrunk-down version of a website. But the image at the top of the screen is easy to see. It's Talbot, wearing a cowboy hat and a cocky grin. But that's not the weird part. What catches my eye is the hokey-looking alien head rising up behind him. It's a crude CGI version of the little gray guys with big black eyes. Its little mouth is curled up in a smile, and it has a three-fingered hand resting on Talbot's shoulder. A logo to the right reads "Space Cowboy."

For shit's sake.

I turn the screen to Talbot. "Thought you were a Ranger?"

"I was," he says. "They fired me. Five years ago."

I shove the phone at him. "Because of this?"

"Yes, ma'am."

"Does Jakob know who you really are?" I ask.

To my surprise, Talbot nods. "Didn't seem to mind one bit. Like you, he's undecided on where they come from. S'pose he didn't mind having someone knowledgeable about extrawordly things on board."

I turn to Willem. "Did you know?"

He nods.

Helena leans forward so she can see me around Willem's broad shoulders. "We all know."

I let out a slow sigh. "Is there anything else I should know about our crew?"

The group looks at each other while searching their minds for an answer.

"I think Klein might be gay," Helena says. When I give her an "Are you serious?" look, she adds, "He doesn't look at me. Or you."

"Honey," I say, "that someone may or may not be gay is one of the most normal things anyone has said to me in the last three days."

She sits back, deflated.

Nate giggles and shakes his head, and I swear he says something like "rawful." I'm not sure what he's saying, but I'm pretty sure it's web speak. "Kid, you're in the middle of the North Atlantic on board a ship running away from a pod of zombie-whales. There isn't a Viking, cowboy, or me not capable of throwing your ass overboard. You're smart. You made some good points. But by God start showing some respect."

The kid shrinks but can't keep his mouth shut. "But you—"

"Being a sarcastic bitch is my job." I stand and push in my chair. "So is being the first mate. So right now, I need everyone who doesn't already have orders from the captain to go to their quarters and sleep. You're going to need your energy in the morning. Hell, you're going to need more than that. So go. Now."

I wait. One by one, they file from the room without another word to me or each other. When they're gone, only Willem remains. He puts his hand on my shoulder, and I feel all the spitfire and hardness of my words melt away.

"You're getting good at giving orders," he says.

"I've always been good at giving orders," I reply. "People just didn't have a reason to listen to me before."

He smiles but takes his hand off my shoulder. "You going to follow those orders, too?"

Before I can answer, he's out the door. I stand alone in the mess hall, surrounded by dirty dishes and my own thoughts. "Damnit," I say and start collecting dishes. Regardless of what I've just told everyone to do, I won't be sleeping anytime soon.

19

"Jane," a voice says in the darkness. "We remember you. We remember everything."

A tightness grips my arm. Half buried in the meat of my shoulder is a foot-long segmented white worm. The Queen! The skin of my shoulder bulges where the baseball-size head, which I know sports two beady black eyes and pin-like teeth, slides toward my torso. If it reaches my insides, it will control me. Turn me into Muninn, Odin's raven who hungered for blood and brains. Queen of the parasites.

Maybe I never escaped the undead whale? Maybe everything that happened after I was swallowed was some kind of parasite-induced hallucination designed to educate them about who we are and what we're up to.

I grip the tail end of the oversize maggot and pull. Pain lances through my shoulder, drawing a scream from my mouth.

"You can't have me!" I scream.

"You promised," the voice says, and I realize it's not a sound at all. It's in my head! "You offered yourself to us. We remember. We remember you, Jane!"

I scream and squeeze hard. Too hard. The crushed parasite body snaps in half, allowing the front portion to slip fully inside my body.

The pain in my shoulder is intense. I clench my eyes shut, pushing tears over my cheeks.

I gasp, opening my eyes. Everything is different. It's still dark, but I feel free. Then the tightness on my shoulder returns.

"Jane."

I flinch away from the sound and slap at my shoulder. I strike warm flesh but quickly recognize the shape and feel of a human hand.

"Raven," Jakob says. "You are safe."

I sit up in bed. My confusion is fading with the dream. "Next time turn on the light."

There's a click, and the room fills with yellow light. I turn away from the lamp and cover my eyes. "Damnit."

Jakob sits on the side of the bed. "I have nightmares almost every night. About Torstein. The Draugar. And Willem. Mostly Willem."

"I feel left out," I say, forcing a half smile.

"My dreams of you are rarely nightmares, Raven."

I know Jakob is trying to have a Kodak moment here, but I can't resist. I smack him on the shoulder and say, "You dirty old man."

The captain chuckles. "It is good to be with you again, Jane. You lift my spirits." His smile fades quickly. "We'll face our nightmares soon enough. Then we will be free of them."

"One way or another," I say.

He nods. "One way or another."

I rub the sleep from my eyes. "So, Dr. Phil. What brings you to my bedside?"

He straightens. "Duty. Yours. It's three in the morning. Time for your shift on the bridge."

"Wonderful," I say, sliding to the edge of the bed beside Jakob. I'm still dressed from the day before, so I'm already good to go. Well, almost. I'll have to grab about a pint of coffee on my way to the bridge.

"The whales," he says. "They will reach us close to eight thirty. Wake me at seven thirty. Wake everyone."

I nod but ask, "Is that enough sleep for you?"

"It's more than I get most nights."

His statement makes me notice the dark rings below his eyes. He looks tired. He looks beat.

I stand and do my best to look ready and competent. I've never been a captain, but I can imagine how much every detail and every life under Jakob's care must weigh on his shoulders. I try to put him at ease. "Don't worry about anything. I'll take care of the ship. Just get some sleep."

He lies down on my bed. "I'll stay here, if you don't mind."

"Knock yourself out," I say, heading for the door. I stop before leaving. "Who's on the bridge with me?" I'm fairly competent with navigating a ship, but I'm far from an expert, and if things go wonky while I'm up there, I'll need some help.

I see a slight smile form on Jakob's lips as he closes his eyes.

"Who do you think, Raven?"

Willem. I know it's Willem. There's no doubt. Jakob would probably plan our wedding if he could.

I reach out to the lamp and shut it off. "Good night, Sleeping Beauty."

A snore is his only reply.

I rush for the stairs, eager to see Willem again, but by the time I reach the top step I'm feeling tired again, not to mention annoyed with myself. I've had boyfriends before. Lovers, too. But I've never had that giddy kind of schoolgirl crush that makes my stomach flip-flop. Not even with Willem. So what's different now? Maybe it's because I'm fairly certain I'm going to die? Can certain death crumble emotional defenses? Probably. But maybe it's just that I've spent so much time away from him when I really didn't want to. Maybe this is the real deal?

"Ugh," I say, a little disgusted with my thought process. I definitely need some caffeine, and not just to keep my inner monologue from sounding like an episode of *Desperate Housewives*; the countdown has begun. Five hours…

Five hours and then we'll face Jakob's and my mutual nightmare. Again. Maybe for the last time.

20

When I arrive on the bridge, it's dark and quiet. Most of the interior lights have been turned off. Only a few small LED lights, part of larger systems on standby, remain lit. The green glow of the radar screen intermittently pulses slightly brighter, signifying that it's still tracking the whales chasing us.

The sea is at that sweet spot between tides when the waves seem to just fade away. Without a breeze to speak of, the water is nearly placid. I step up to the front window and admire the moonlit scene. I used to love this view. The endlessness of it. The mystery. Say what you will about my lack of antiwhaling passion, I love the ocean. Always have.

Not so much anymore.

Even the world's most gentle giants have been turned against us. When I look at the waves now, I see death, for hundreds of miles in every direction—death.

Fuck, I'm a buzzkill.

"Hey."

The phrase is simple, nonthreatening, and from the one person I was hoping to see right now, but he's caught me in the midst of a doom-and-gloom-a-thon. I flinch away from the window and let out a yelp. My fear turns to amusement when Willem steps out of the shadows. "Asshole."

"Didn't mean to scare you," he says, stepping closer.

"Yeah, well, I'm feeling a little more jumpy than us—"

He closes the distance between us with one long stride, wraps an arm around my back, and pulls me against him. His lips find mine a moment later. I resist for a moment—aren't we supposed to have some kind of heart-to-heart first? Aren't I supposed to say something like, "Sorry I screwed up our relationship," "Sorry I drowned myself in booze while you plotted to save the world," or even just a simple "Sorry for being a douche"?

When his tongue finds mine, I give in. *Fuck it.* This is the Viking way after all, right? Quick to fight. Quick to forgive. Do everything with passion—something Willem is excelling at right now, his hands exploring my body.

Good God, I've spent too much time alone.

If we were in my bedroom and not the bridge, I'd have shed my clothes like they were on fire. Since we're on the bridge, we'll have to do this a little more discreetly and creatively.

The captain's chair? Doesn't feel right.

The floor? Too cold.

The map room? I open my eyes and glance at the room. I can see that the dimly lit table is empty. *That will work.*

Willem lifts me up, and I wrap my legs around his waist. I look down into his eyes and wonder why I ever stayed away.

Then everything changes.

The glow from the radar screen casts his face in green light, beckoning me to look. I try not to turn but can't resist. My glance is quick. Just a fraction of a second. But long enough to register the green blobs that seem impossibly close to the center of the screen.

I do a double take. There are five splotches of green on the lower portion of the screen, maybe two inches from the center, still a few miles away but closer than I would prefer.

Willem sees what I see. His embrace loosens. When I unwrap my legs, he places me down gently. We watch the radar circle the screen. When it glows green again, there are just four spots, but not one of them is the same as before. Each of the nine different pings is a separate whale.

"Sorry," I say.

"It was probably a bad idea, anyway," he says.

"About everything, I mean."

He turns toward me. "Jane…"

"Just say it's okay and let's be done with it," I say. "I think I've had to apologize to nearly everyone on this boat at one point or another. I'm getting sick of it."

He smiles at me. "Jane, I'm sorry."

I cross my arms and nearly bust out a Nell Carter–like "Gimme a break." But instead I say, "What the hell for?"

"For letting you go," he says.

"You couldn't have stopped me," I say, feeling annoyed by his subtle arrogance and our little heart-to-heart.

"Sure about that?" he asks.

"I preferred the make-out version of making up," I say. "If I agree that everything was your fault, can we move on?"

He laughs, pulls me toward him, and kisses my forehead.

Then it's like nothing happened. He moves to the radar screen, watching the pulsating targets. *The hell?* If I survive this mess I think I'll write a book, *Men Are from Mars, Women Are from Venus, and Norsemen Are from Effing Alpha Centauri*. Guaranteed to be a best seller north of the Arctic Circle. Still, it's better than the alternative.

I step up next to him at the radar screen. "Well, now that I'm squared away with the crew, I'm ready to die. How about you? Did you prepare your soul and all that?"

"Not funny, Jane," he says with a glance in my direction.

"Wasn't totally a joke."

He turns to me. "We're *not* going to die."

I don't really have any quips about the subject, mostly because I wholeheartedly disagree. I don't see how we can survive. We barely survived an island of human Draugar, never mind the fifty-six-ton variety.

"We're not," Willem repeats.

We fall silent after that and make ourselves busy. Willem checks the course and makes occasional adjustments that probably aren't even necessary. I keep watch on the radar and on the ocean ahead. When we're not busy, we stand next to each other, shoulders rubbing, sometimes hands. It's like I'm with Peter Jacoby again, my thirteen-year-old summertime crush, except I'm pretty sure this relationship won't end with the Colonel laying his pistol on the tabletop and counting backward from ten. Peter was a fast runner.

The sky to our left lightens to a dark purple. The sun will rise soon. I inhale a sharp breath. In this part of the world, in October, the sun rises at seven thirty. "Time to wake up the crew," I say.

Saying this makes me realize that I haven't looked at the radar screen in a little while. Nothing changed during the night, except that the splotches representing the whales slowly encroached on our position.

Willem stands from the captain's chair. "I'll wake the others."

I wander to the radar screen. "Your father is in my room." I grin.

"Already planning our appearance on Maury Povich, are you?"

I laugh. "Did you just make a Jane Harper joke? I didn't think you were capa—" I turn to the radar screen and never finish my sentence. The first thing I see is expected—several splotches still an hour out. But when the radar sweeps around again, I see two of the targets are just about on top of us. "Willem."

I hear him stop at the door, but I can't speak. I watch the screen as the radar sweeps around again. The two targets are gone on this revolution. Was it a glitch? Did they dive?

My thought process is cut off by the appearance of five new targets. Directly ahead of us, and much closer. "Willem!"

He rushes to my side. I point at the screen. "Please tell me I'm seeing things."

We watch. The first radar revolution shows some of the far-off whales. The second reveals a few more of them, but there are still two unaccounted for. The third revolution reveals the five new targets ahead of us and elicits an "Oh shit" from Willem, which is so uncommon it's akin to a normal person throwing themselves on the floor while wailing like a banshee. What he doesn't know is that the five new targets are much closer than they were when I first noticed them. The combined speed of the *Raven* and the new targets is something around forty-five knots. They'll reach us quickly.

The radar screen performs one more revolution, this time revealing several distant targets, but also the two that somehow closed the distance. "They're only a quarter mile out!" Willem says. "They must have made a long dive. Stayed off the radar."

I nearly complain that whales don't know about radar, but then I remember these aren't just whales. Willem rushes toward the back of the bridge, but not toward the stairs.

"What are you doing?" I ask.

"Waking up the crew," he says as he places his hand on a red lever marked Fire. He yanks it down, and the whole ship fills with a high-pitched siren and blinking white lights. He leaves it on for just thirty seconds, then shuts it off. If the noise didn't wake anyone up, chances are they're already dead.

But it might be too little too late. The ship shakes from a hard strike to the port side before the first crew member arrives. A second blow rattles the ship on the starboard side a moment later. "Willem," I say, pointing to the front deck. "Go! Shoot those sonsabitches out of the water."

He pauses just a moment, looking at me like he's trying to say something. Maybe good-bye. Then he's gone. Out the door and charging off to wage war. I've just sent him to his death, I think, but am distracted from the thought when the ship rumbles like it was struck by a missile.

21

"What's happening?" Jakob shouts as he barges into the wheelhouse. "Why wasn't I woken earl—" He stops his question short when he looks at his watch. The attack is earlier than expected.

"A few of them dove deep and caught up underwater," I explain.

"But that's not—"

"We don't really know what's possible," I remind him.

Klein and Talbot step onto the bridge.

"Where are Malik and Helena?" I ask.

"Already outside," Talbot says.

I glance out the front windows and see Malik manning the port gun, Willem on the starboard, and Helena charging for the forward gun. We could have used a few more people with their instincts.

"You two know how to fire the harpoons?" I ask.

"Malik took me through the steps," Klein says, "but I haven't actually fired one yet."

"Ain't a gun I can't shoot, ma'am," Talbot says with a grin, no doubt looking forward to firing one of the cannons.

"Then move your asses," I say. "Take the aft guns. Aim for the center of the head. You want to destroy the brain. I'll join you in a moment."

As they head for the exit, I ask, "Have either of you seen Nate?" I don't think the kid could bring himself to actually shoot a whale, infected or not, but it would have been nice to have someone running ammunition.

Klein shakes his head no.

Talbot just shrugs. "Neither hide nor hair."

I wave them away and turn my attention to Jakob, who's behind the wheel. "Can you manage up here on your own?"

"Not much else to do from here except try to run them over," he says. "If I need you, I'll use the intercom."

The ship shakes from an impact. I grip the radar screen to keep from spilling over.

"One more thing," I say, motioning to the radar screen. "There are five more targets coming straight at us. I think they're smaller, but they'll be here in just a few minutes."

"It was a trap," he says. "The whole time. A trap."

The discouragement in his eyes pisses me off. I head for the rear exit, saying, "That might be true, but the Olavsons don't back down from a fight, do they?"

Fire returns to his eyes.

"And neither does the Raven," I say. I'm not sure whether I'm talking about the ship or me, and I have no idea how Jakob takes the statement, but I feel the engine roar deep in the ship as the captain throttles forward, intent on bludgeoning some zombie-whales.

I find Talbot manning the aft gun and Klein at the port. Both are swinging their harpoons back and forth, searching for a target. I run to the starboard gun and nearly stumble overboard when the ship cuts into a tight turn. After catching myself, I take hold of the harpoon gun, switch off the safety, and look for something to shoot. But like Klein and Talbot, I see nothing. I look to my left and see Willem at the front of the ship, also looking for a target.

They're not surfacing, I think. Unlike normal whales, the Draugar whales don't need to breathe. So they don't need to surface. And that makes our harpoons useless. They might be able to beat the hull to a pulp without *ever* surfacing.

Willem catches my eye. At first I think he's waving at me, but then I notice he's pointing. Behind me.

I turn toward the back of the ship and see them right away. Whales. A mile out. Rising and falling as they breach. The first is a humpback. And not a big one. But then a giant rises from the ocean. A blue whale. Perhaps a hundred feet long. Then a second. And a third. Their combined size and tonnage dwarfs the *Raven*. Three more behemoths—all sperm whales—rise, these just a quarter mile off. They'll be on us in minutes.

I turn to the bow, looking for the other targets, but see nothing. They're either still out of eyeshot or not breaching.

The ship rocks to the side as we're struck from below. I see a flash of white several feet below the surface that I recognize as the pectoral fin of a humpback whale. "C'mon, baby, show me some skin," I say, but it's clear the whale won't be coming any closer to the surface.

This might be the best chance I have.

So I take it.

I swivel the harpoon gun down toward the water, sight the fading fin, and pull the trigger. The harpoon explodes into the water, slipping through the waves with ease. I don't see it strike the target, but a moment later, I know it did.

A geyser of water plumes into the air combined with a muffled *whump*. The impact-sensitive explosive head has detonated. Roiling water brings liquid red to the surface. Blood. But did I do any real damage?

I see the white fin again, shimmering pink as the morning light filters through the blood. When it reaches the surface, I see that it's still connected to a large piece of meat that has been separated from the creature.

The whale surfaces twenty feet out. It's moving quickly as its fluke pounds the water, but a large chunk of its right side, including the fin, is missing. The thing spins in erratic circles, unable to control its direction.

We don't need to kill them, I realize. *Just remove their ability to swim, or at least swim straight.*

The whale spirals away from us, trailing a path of blood. It seems any fin will do, though the fluke would probably be best.

"Aim for the fins if you can," I shout. "They're not a threat if they can't move!"

The *Raven* turns hard to port, bringing the wounded whale in line with the ice-breaking forward hull. Jakob is on the warpath.

Invigorated by drawing first blood, I begin to reel my harpoon. The line is slick with water and quite heavy. My shoulders burn after pulling in just one hundred feet of line, which I have to coil neatly next to the harpoon gun. *Why didn't Jakob find something with a winch attached?* I think in frustration. Not only would it have been less work, but it would also go faster. I answer the question for myself. The newer, fancy harpoon guns not only cost a lot more; they also would need to be bought through a dealer, and the transaction would have been easily tracked.

I hear another harpoon fire, possibly Malik's or Helena's, but no secondary explosion. A miss.

The harpoon clears the water and feels heavier than ever. When pulling it hand over hand proves impossible, I just tighten my grip, lean back, and walk backward until the spear is lying on the deck.

"Klein!" I shout, looking back to see if the man is engaging a target. He's not, and he turns to face me. "I don't know how to rearm this thing!"

He runs to my side. "I'll take care of it. Take my gun."

While Klein heads for the watertight supply closet against deck one's rear wall, I take up his position. I grasp the harpoon with both hands and quickly twist it forward and back, looking for something to shoot. There's nothing in sight, but experience has taught me that shooting straight down is sometimes a viable option.

And it is. Rising from below is the distinct shape of a humpback whale. My finger goes for the trigger, but I don't get a chance to fire. The ship shakes, front to back, as she strikes the immobilized whale. The humpback I shot looked to be in much better condition than the first, very decomposed, whale we ran down, and the impact is much harder. I'm knocked to the side and unable to fire.

But I don't fall. I keep my grip on the harpoon gun, fully intent on reacquiring my target. So I'm still standing when it happens.

The whale breaches.

It rises from the ocean as though in slow motion. I see its striped underbelly, which can expand large enough to suck in thousands of gallons of seawater and food, rise ten, twenty, thirty feet above me.

And then—*fuck*—it arcs.

Toward me.

Twenty-five tons of whale flesh blots out the sun and comes crashing down toward me.

22

My mind switches off. I don't see my life flash before my eyes. In fact, I don't see anything because my eyes are clenched shut. I can't hear anything because my adrenaline-fueled blood is rushing past my ears like a freight train. And let's face it, smelling, tasting, and feeling are low-priority senses when you're about to be smeared against the deck of a ship by a humpback whale.

An instinct for survival fuels my last-second attempt at escape. With my back to the descending whale, I run. But just two steps in, the whale lands with a boom that reverberates through the ship's frame.

My first thought is, *How am I not dead?* Which is quickly followed by, *Where did the deck go?*

Under the weight of the whale, the *Raven* has dropped several feet and canted sharply to the side, leaving me airborne and sprawling. With a shout, I collide headfirst with the harpoon gun's solid metal base. The pain is intense, but I quickly realize that the impact may have saved my life.

I hear a distant splash and a shouted, "Man overboard." Who was on the forward port gun? Malik. I'm flooded with relief and then guilt. I'm glad it's not Willem, but there isn't a person on the planet that I'd wish to be in these waters, certainly not a man I now consider a friend.

He must have been knocked over the rail when the ship canted. Speaking of that…I grip the harpoon gun, climb to my feet, and turn to my left. The whale is there. Right there. Just ten feet away.

How did it miss?

A breeze tickles my wild hair. *We're moving*, I think. Had the *Raven* been idle, I would have been crushed. Twenty knots of forward momentum saved my life. We've slowed considerably now that we're supporting more than a few thousand extra tons, but we're still floating. That's something.

A shift of movement catches my attention. The whale's eye. It's staring at me.

Though it's not really a whale's eye anymore. Humpbacks' softball-size eyes are largely black and kind looking. This monstrosity is white. And wriggling. The orb is full of parasites, some larger than I've seen before, maybe several inches long. Their beady pinhead-size eyes stare at me. They're hard to see, but I can feel them.

The whale writhes back and forth, sliding the top half of its massive body over the crushed rail, back toward the water, where it will be able to strike again. The ship tips as the whale's thick skin is gouged by the broken rail. It's a slow and messy retreat, but the whale will be back in the water, ready to strike again, in seconds.

"Oh, I don't think so!" I shout at the whale. I get a hold of the harpoon gun and swivel it around so the pointy end is aimed directly at the whale's worm-filled eye.

My finger finds the trigger.

I hear somebody shouting. I can't distinguish the words, but it sounds like a warning.

I ignore it. This whale needs to die. Here and now.

When the whale's movements become frantic, I can't help but grin. The Draugar parasites know what's about to happen. *Do they fear for their lives?* I wonder. *Do they fear being separated from the collective consciousness? Or are they just committed to the mission, whatever that might be?*

I decide I don't give a shit and pull the trigger.

The resulting twin explosions take place in just over two seconds. My mind registers the first as the harpoon leaves the cannon and punches through the whale's eye, slipping inside its skull. When the explosive head tears through the Draugr's parasite-laden mind and strikes the inner skull, it detonates. But the explosion, deep inside the colossal skull, doesn't just punch out the other side, it bursts, in every direction, including back at me.

The concussive force hits me like an ocean wave, lifting me off my feet and carrying me high into the air. Slabs of dark red meat, slippery globs of fat larger than me, and thousands of small, toasted white worms soar through the air beside me. I see the boat spin away below. The damage to the hull is significant but above the waterline. And the whale, now a headless, ragged throat and body, slides back into the water, leaving a slick of lumpy, long-since-coagulated blood across the deck. Something hard, like a skull fragment still coated in flesh, or maybe whale brain, collides with my head and knocks me out cold.

My trip to never-never land lasts only a second. I'm awakened first by an impact and second by the frigid North Atlantic. The water quickly seeps through my clothing and burns my skin like I'm being cooked over a rotisserie flame. I'll be dead in a few minutes. Less if something decides to swallow me.

There's one whale left in the advance group. Then five more coming from ahead and six more from behind.

As the *Raven* comes about to pull me from the water, I remember Malik and look for him. He's just twenty feet away, floating on his back. He's unconscious, but he had the presence of mind to wear a life jacket. It saved him from drowning, but it won't do anything against the cold. He's been in the water at least thirty seconds longer than me. Thirty seconds closer to death.

"Malik," I shout, but the sound comes out all funny. My teeth are chattering.

I try to swim to him, but my muscles are twitching and hard to control. I manage a pitiful doggy paddle, but by the time I reach him, we'll both be dead.

"Malik!" I scream it this time and manage to say it right.

The man twitches. Then wakes. Then screams as the cold that grips his body finally registers. Leaving him unconscious might have been a mercy. But we need to get him moving. "Try to move! Stay warm. They're coming back for us!"

I look past Malik. The *Raven* has completed her turn and is on the way back, but they're still at least a minute away.

The best Malik can manage is a glance in my direction. "I—I hope." His teeth chatter madly. "You did not come…to save…me…"

"I wouldn't save you if you were the last person on Earth," I say with a shaky smile.

A strange huffed laugh emerges from Malik's mouth. It disappears when bubbles rise from the deep and pop to the surface. When more bubbles rise, forming a circle around Malik, our eyes widen. We both know what it means. Humpbacks use the technique when hunting herring. Working together, they corral the fish by blowing columns of bubbles the fish won't pass through. Then, as one, the pod of whales rushes to the surface, mouths agape, and consumes a massive amount of fish—up to a thousand tons a day.

"Get away!" Malik shouts. I can see he's doing everything he can to move but is as stuck in place as a fly in a web. "Don't let it get us both! Go! Now!"

But I don't need to move. I learn as much a moment later when the whale's open maw rises up and around Malik and misses me by several feet. Malik's eyes find mine as the upper mouth starts to close like a clamshell. His gaze burns with anger.

The whale begins sliding back beneath the surface. Malik's voice rises from the still closing mouth. "Kill them, Raven! Kill them a—"

The mouth closes.

The whale is gone.

Malik is dead.

But not really. He's inside the whale, sure, but he's not being eaten. He's being transformed. Even if he drowns in the whale, the parasites populating the massive tongue will flood his body, keep him alive, and take control. If I ever see Malik again, I will have to kill him.

Assuming I don't die here and now.

The *Raven* is just thirty seconds out, but she's not alone. The telltale black fin of the ocean's most deadly predator slices through the ocean surface. The killer whale is feared by walruses, great white sharks, and even blue whales, the largest creature to inhabit Earth, ever. While orcas don't normally consume people, I think this one might be an exception.

23

If I had the energy, I would cuss a blue streak. Not only is my life being slowly sapped away by the freezing water, not only is a killer whale bearing down on me, but now a circle of bubbles rising around me indicates the humpback's return.

Do the Draugar want to bite me or swallow me? I'm pretty much dead either way. I wouldn't think a collective consciousness would compete with itself, but hey, what the hell do I know, right? No assumptions.

I don't have a lot of options. Okay, I don't have any options. I can barely move. Screaming isn't going to help. Not that I could scream if I wanted to. My mouth has given up on chattering and simply locked shut, the muscles painfully paralyzed from cold. If I'm lucky, the cold will take me in the next few seconds before the whales arrive.

I hear my name being shouted like a distant howl of wind. I look up and see the black hull of the *Raven* behind the killer whale. Willem stands at the bow. If he raised his arms he'd look like a much more manly Leonardo DiCaprio in *Titanic*. I'm king of the world! My lips twitch in an attempt to smile at the thought. The pitiful grin disappears when I realize I'm about to share Leo's fate. Probably worse.

The killer rises ten feet away.

Definitely worse.

The orca exhales loudly, billowing a cloud of fish-scented steam into the air.

Something about the smell feels wrong.

Or right.

I look back to Willem. His arms aren't outstretched. He's holding the harpoon, aiming it at the orca's back. The first problem with this is that Willem is on a fast-moving vessel and he's targeting an equally fast-moving orca that's also moving vertically. He's likely to miss. The second problem is that the whale is nearly upon me. If Willem manages to strike the killer, the resulting explosion will likely do me in. Even if it doesn't, there is still the humpback rising from below. Given the amount of bubbles surrounding me, I'd say it's on the way up now.

So unless Willem can shoot the harpoon through the orca, hit the rising behemoth, and then pluck me from the resulting geyser, I'm shit out of luck.

It takes all of my strength and will, but I manage to unlock my jaw and scream, "Don't shoot!"

Willem must hear me because he doesn't pull the trigger.

The orca dives.

Moment of truth.

I dip my head beneath the water and open my eyes. I need to see this. The salt water should sting, but I really can't feel anything. I can see just fine, though. The first thing I see is a large black circle directly below me—the humpback's mouth. I'm oddly indifferent to the rising maw, that is, until I see Malik wedged at the back of the thing's mouth, covered in a shifting film of white parasites.

Still, I don't scream. But it's mostly because I can't.

The white pectoral fins glow turquoise as they near the sunlit surface. Were this a nature documentary, it would be the shot of a lifetime. Movement catches my attention. At first I'm confused by the dark blob sliding through the water. Then I see the distinctive white spot of a killer whale. But it's not headed toward me.

It's heading for the humpback.

The giants collide. The killer whale opens its mouth, enveloping the humpback's pectoral fin and driving its snout into the giant's side. Without pause, the killer thrashes its head to the side, removing the fin. Then it swims away.

The humpback's course is altered as it can no longer maintain a straight trajectory, but it's too close and its mouth too wide to save me. *Thanks, Shamu, but too little, too late.*

Just as the humpback is about to swallow me whole, its course shifts dramatically. The open mouth misses me by less than a foot. The wake of the passing giant spins me around, but I catch sight of its fluke. Or rather, what used to be its fluke. Half of the fin is now missing.

Then I see them. Five killer whales. Five killers of whales. They're dismantling the humpback, working efficiently as a team, the way they do during a hunt. But I sense this is more than a simple hunt. The orca aren't eating the fins as they bite them, they're casting them aside. Watching the killers move swiftly through the water, like guided missiles, I think I've never seen something so beautiful in my life. I decide it's an acceptable last thing to see and close my eyes.

But fate, or maybe just Willem, has other plans for me. A splash draws my eyes open again. The patchwork lines floating in front of me confuse me. Then I recognize it—a fishing net.

Live to fight another day, Jane. It's what wins most wars. If the Colonel were here, he'd be screaming it at me. So like the good daughter I never was, I listen. I reach my arms out through the netting, bring them tight to my body, and hold on tight.

Whoever is topside must have seen me move because I'm above water and rising steadily just a second later. My body, coated in saturated clothes, coupled with my weakened state, feels like I'm being reeled in with a whale gripping my ankle. But like Ripley in the air lock in *Alien*, I manage to hold on against the impossible.

Hands grab at my sodden clothing, and I'm hauled over the rail like the day's catch. I roll onto my back. Willem, Helena, Klein, and Talbot are there. It probably took all four of them to pull me in so quick.

I see their mouths moving, but can't quite make out what they're saying. I'm not sure if it's because I'm dazed or simply because they're all talking at once. Jakob arrives and his voice cuts through the others.

"Jane," he says. There's no question asked, but his voice oozes concern, which warms my heart at least. But then I see what he's carrying—my cloak, which I left on the bridge, and an electric blanket. The blanket seems like a silly idea until I see a long orange extension cord twisting across the deck.

Knowing I'm going to survive brings clarity. We're still in the middle of a battle. And we've got allies! "Jakob," I shout. "Get back to the bridge!"

He grins in response, already moving away. "She'll be fine," he says.

Willem takes the blanket and cloak when Jakob hands them to him.

"Helena, Klein, Talbot," Jakob says as he climbs the stairs to the bridge. "Man the rear guns! They'll be coming from behind now!" After a few more steps up, he pauses again and adds, "Don't fire on the orca unless you see them get bit or they act aggressively!"

The crew springs into action, all except Willem. He crouches down next to me. "Looks like I get to take off your clothes after all."

"B-b-bastard," I say while shivering.

We're not modest about it. In fact, he pretty much manhandles me in the same way the Inuit slaughter a seal on the kitchen floor. But the result is equally effective. I'm stripped naked of several soaking layers of clothing in just over a minute flat. Willem throws the cloak around my shoulders, buttoning it in place and then pulling the hood up over my head. The cloak is phenomenal at keeping the cold out and the warmth in, but right now I don't have a whole lot of body heat to trap. Willem unwraps the electric blanket next and wraps it around the cloak. I wonder why he didn't just put the electric blanket on first, but then he explains.

"Jakob has it turned up all the way," he says. "It might burn your skin, so be careful when you hold it."

The heat seeps through the cloak a moment later. It feels like I'm on fire for the first few seconds, but the cloak's muted heat never becomes unbearable. My muscles shudder as they loosen and expand. All except for my feet.

I look down at my bare feet on the metal deck. I'm about to ask for something when Willem slides out of his boots, removes two pairs of socks, and hands them to me. I slip the socks on and sigh. They retain Willem's body heat and go nearly up to my knees.

I'll be fine, I think. After maybe ten more minutes of thawing out and a quick run to my room for clothes, I can get back in this fight.

Then Talbot's voice pierces the air. "Here they come!"

Then again, maybe we'll all be dead in ten minutes. Dead like Malik.

"Malik," I say. It's just a whisper, but Willem hears me.

"I know," he says. "He died well."

I look up, tears in my eyes, and say, "He died horribly."

The subject sets a fire in my gut that warms me faster than any blanket. I shuffle for the stairway door, dragging the blanket with me.

"Where are you going?" Willem asks.

"You seen *Rocky III*?" I ask.

I can't see him with my back turned, but I'm sure he's confused. "I think so," he says. "But what's—"

I pull open the door and look back, setting my serious gaze on Willem. "It's round three, Willem. Round three. Time to hit back."

24

Round three has a very anticlimactic start. I hobble through the ship, heading for my quarters and clothes. Halfway there, my legs start to shake. I feel like I've just finished a triathlon. The cold, rust-speckled walls support me as I slide, somewhat zombie-like, toward my room. Luckily, all the doors are closed, so I just *bump-thump* down the hall, moving from wall to door, hoping that one of the doors doesn't spring open and spill me onto the floor like that old LifeCall lady. "I've fallen and I can't get up!"

The doorknob to my quarters turns slowly as I fight to turn it against my now-shaking hands. When the door swings open, I nearly fall inside but maintain my grip on the handle and stumble to the bed. The first aid kit is still on the bed. I shift closer to it and manage to pull it open, but when I try to rummage through it for painkillers, my shaking hand just makes a mess of things.

"God damnit!" I shout. This feeling of helplessness is intolerable. My muscles tense, exacerbating the pain and shaking.

This is the kind of moment where the Colonel's advice is all but useless. When your own body is fighting against your will, you can't just grit your teeth and push through. Sometimes you have to take the time to let your body heal. Unfortunately for me, and my body, I'm not a patient person. But I'm willing to give it a few minutes.

I decide not to fight. It's against my nature, but I manage it. Sitting still, I wrap the cloak and electric blanket fully around my naked body. Then I lie back on the bed, legs out straight, arms over my chest like I'm the lost wife of King Tut. A deep breath and slow exhale help me relax. I close my eyes, focusing on loosening my muscles and absorbing the warmth of the electric blanket, which miraculously is still plugged in, thanks to the ridiculously long extension cord.

The pain instantly subsides. Pins and needles dance over my skin, prickling as the warmth eats away the cold that seeped to my core. Several shivers rise from my feet and stop at my head. Another deep breath relaxes my thoughts. In the back of my mind, I'm still aware that there are six giant whales en route to kill us, but I keep myself from thinking about them. Instead, I think about Willem. Our first night together.

I didn't feel like doing the downtown thing again—the local "everyone knows everyone" bar scene gets obnoxious when no one knows *you*. So we retreated to his house. Despite the cold outside, the place felt warm. It's a small house, heated by a woodstove and a fireplace. Decorations are sparse, but almost all items in the house have some historical value or story attached. For the first hour, he regaled me with tales of wood-carvers, stonemasons, and blacksmiths of old. Not much has survived from the days of Norse Vikings, especially on Greenland, where only a few foundations and potsherds remain to be found, but he had authentic-looking replicas.

I became bored with the past, but not with the man telling me stories. He was gentle the entire time, and kind in a way that should be impossible for a man who'd fought Draugar and escaped. He never spoke about the incident that night. It would have been easy to slip in some information about Torstein's giant ax, or how the settlement had been destroyed by Draugar, or any number of things. But he didn't. He seemed far more interested in me, which pretty much sealed the deal, though he didn't know it. I sent him to the kitchen for a drink, and when he returned I was as nude as I am right now under this blanket.

The rest of the night was a blur, and when I woke up—

Wake up!

I sit bolt upright with a gasp.

Was I asleep? Was I thinking about that night? Or dreaming about it?

I slip out of bed and step to the portal. I can see nothing but blue sky and blue ocean. No whales. But that doesn't mean anything.

I unbutton the cloak and let it drop to the floor. I pull out fresh clothes—Jakob will be thrilled that they are once again all black—and halfway through hiking up my pants, I realize that I'm not shaking and the pain is nearly gone. Seems I just needed to warm up, though I suspect I'm going to hurt sorely in the morning. More so the following day.

Fully dressed, I snatch the cloak from the floor, yank the plug out of the electric blanket so I don't set the ship on fire, and head for the door. I'm wearing sneakers now in place of my boots, but find myself moving faster because of it. In fact, I'm running by the time I reach the end of the hall and take the stairs to the main deck two at a time.

When I emerge into the light of day once more, all of the warmth regained through the electric blanket and fond memories is sapped away by the chilly ocean breeze and sight of three massive bull sperm whales breaching in unison just a few hundred feet off the stern. Willem is there, manning the rear gun. Talbot is on the starboard gun and Helena on the port. Klein squats at the center of the deck with a wooden crate of explosive harpoon tips, ready to help reload the first person to fire a shot. But the whales are still too far out to fire with any kind of accuracy, and they're gaining slowly because we're still moving away at full speed. It probably goes against Jakob's nature to run from a fight, especially with a whale, but it will give us the most time.

A puff of misty air catches my attention. It's followed by five more. The orcas are on an intercept course, moving in tight formation. *Why are they helping us?* I wonder. *Can they sense something wrong? Are they intelligent enough to identify Draugar as enemies? Is this vengeance?* I suspect we'll never know why the killers are helping us. Hell, they might not even be helping us. Their arrival at this moment might be coincidence. If so, hallelujah to the god of coincidence because he saved my life. Of course, I *did* pray for help... but I'm not quite ready to believe a higher power sent an orca pod to save me, though I have no doubt that's what Helena believes.

When I step up next to Klein, he flinches and falls back, catching himself on his hands. "Geezum crow," he whispers, then says to me, "That was fast."

"Fast?"

"You've been gone just ten minutes," he says.

Guess I didn't fall asleep. "What can I do?"

"Not much, I suppose." He rubs his nose. "Figure we can run to whoever fires off a shot, pull in the line, help reload, and get off another shot. Nice and efficient. There are three whales, so it's not inconceivable we'll have more than one gun to reload at a time."

I've heard everything he says, but a single detail jumps out. "Just three whales? What happened to the blues?"

"They were farther back," he says. "But they haven't surfaced in five minutes."

"Blues can stay under for thirty minutes," I say and then mentally kick myself. "But these aren't blue whales. They don't need to surface at all."

Klein looks down like he can see through the hull to the water below.

"Yeah, sucks," I say. "Each one can weigh up to two hundred tons."

"Just two of them weigh as much as the *Raven*!" he says.

"Yeah, but if just one of them decides to swan-dive on the back deck like that humpback did, we're done." I sigh. "You sure there isn't something else I could be doing?"

His brow furrows. "Not unless you know how to fire a grenade launcher."

I stand up straighter as a fiendish grin slips onto my face. "We have a grenade launcher?"

"You know how to use one?" Klein asks.

"Did you forget who my father was?"

He scratches his head, upsetting his comb-over. "Right. The Colonel. But that doesn't mean you can—"

"Ain't a gun I don't know how to shoot," I say.

Klein stands, takes note of the whales' location, and starts back toward the supply closet. "You sound like Talbot."

"I guarantee you, I've fired some guns the UFO Ranger has never even heard of."

I watch him work the combination on the supply closet lock. It's my birthday. "Did Jakob set the combination?"

"Yeah," he replies. "Why?" Then I see his eyes dart back and forth for a moment, and before I can respond, he says, "Oh. Your birthday. Interesting." He pulls the lock and swings open the doors.

I gasp. Not only is there a grenade launcher, but there are several assault rifles, handguns, swords, axes, and boxes of ammo. "Hot damn, where the hell did Jakob get all this?"

"Uh," Klein says, adjusting his glasses. "I sort of pilfered a few weapons contacts from the office before I left."

"Jakob bought weapons from an arms dealer?"

Klein waves his hands in front of him. "No one will ever know, of course, but I—"

"I'm not worried about that," I say. "It's just awesome." I take the grenade launcher—a Mark 14 six-shot revolver-style weapon that can pop off six 40mm rounds in three seconds, open it up, and give it a quick look-see. It's in nice condition, and the storage closet, which I can now see is heavy duty and designed to hold weapons, has protected it from the elements nicely. The Mark 14 isn't large and weighs just eighteen pounds fully loaded, so I can manage it just fine. Even better, it has a five-hundred-foot range, which means I can take the fight to the sperm whales a little bit sooner.

"Why weren't you using this?" I ask as I open a case of fragmentation rounds and load the weapon.

"I—I don't know how," he says. He takes out his girlie-size handgun. "I can barely operate this peashooter."

I slap the launcher closed and stand. "Well, you're about to get a lesson in modern warfare, Colonel-style."

As I turn to the rear of the boat, I hear Helena shout a Greenlandic curse. Two hundred feet behind the *Raven*, the orcas have engaged the bull whales. I see blood in the water already, from the center bull, I think, but the monster still has some fight left, a fact displayed when it dives and catches an orca off guard with its fluke. The massively powerful tail snaps up and catches the much smaller killer in the side, flinging it out of the water.

As the orca arcs back toward the ocean, a second bull rises from the deep and snatches it from the air like a Frisbee-fetching dog. Definitely not typical sperm whale behavior. The whale slaps back down into the water, taking the killer with it. Our would-be defender belongs to them now. And if we don't do something soon, the other four will be turned against us, too.

25

I walk toward the rear of the ship, looking through the grenade launcher's sight. I center the red crosshair on the spot where I think the whale farthest to the right will breach again. When I reach the stern rail to the right of Willem, I plant one foot on the lower bar and lean forward, bracing myself against recoil. The Mark 14 has very little kick and its low-pressure chamber fires nearly silently, but I'm not planning on squeezing off a single round. When you've got thirty tons of mean to kill and have a weapon that can spurt six grenades in three seconds, that's exactly what you do.

That's the plan anyway. But the whale, who hasn't surfaced yet, isn't playing along.

"I thought you'd like that," Willem says.

Without looking away, I say, "Should have told me about it sooner."

"Try not to shoot anything on deck," he teases.

I lower the weapon and look over at him. He turns to me with a grin that's one part mocking me and one part some kind of genetic Viking battlegasm. I'm about to tell him as much when the whale chooses that exact moment to breach.

We both turn and aim, but it's too late. The breach was quick, timed perfectly to get a look but avoid getting peppered with a

40mm hail à la Jane Harper. "That seem a little too well timed?" I ask, not taking my eyes off the ocean. I won't do that again.

"How could it know we were distracted?" he asks.

The center whale surfaces and I nearly shoot, but the ocean around it is swirling pink with blood. Lots of blood. The sperm whale pounds its tail at the water but can't move. Its fluke is missing. Score one for the killer whales.

The victory wasn't without cost, though. The bodies of two orcas float to the surface. One is unmoving, probably dead, and slides back beneath the waves. The second is having some kind of spasm, its fluke slapping the water, while it swims on its side with its mouth locked open. When it completes a revolution, I see that its dorsal fin is missing and its back is bent at an unnatural angle. Its spine is broken. That tail is on autopilot. The killer slips beneath the water, its fluke pushing it down to the depths, where it will drown.

Twin puffs of steam pull my aim to the right. Two tall dorsal fins cut through the water, moving away at high speed. The two remaining orcas are retreating. Seems even porpoises abide by the "live to fight another day" mentality.

"Here they come!" Willem shouts, pulling my attention back to the stern.

Twin mounds of water surge toward the *Raven* as the two remaining sperm whales kick into high gear and charge. They're just a few feet below the surface, easy targets for Willem and me.

"Wait," Willem says. "We can't miss."

Technically, I can miss five times, but I don't say anything. I'd rather put all six rounds into the Draugr's head and make sure the job is done. The whales continue on their path, closing to within fifty feet. What are they doing? Ramming the back of the ship won't do much. If they were going to breach and try to crush us, they'd have to go deep first.

When they close to within thirty feet and hold their distance, I'm even more confused, but I know not to look a gift horse in the mouth. Whatever it is they're up to, I don't think they've equated a Mark 14 into the plan.

Then I see it. A band of white spread out between them.

"What is that?" I ask. "Between them."

"Not sure," Willem says. "But they're close enough."

The whales close in, breaking the surface as though offering themselves to us. As they rise, the line stretched between them comes into view. It's a rope. A thick rope. The ramifications of what they're attempting makes me hold my breath. It's the oldest trick in the antiwhaling handbook. The large rope won't be hacked to bits by the prop, it will be sucked in and wrapped tight until the blades can no longer spin. If the engine keeps running at that point, it could burn out. The only defense against it is cutting power to the engines and sending in a diver to cut the line free. "They're going to prop-foul us."

That they're employing the technique chills me, not because it's intelligent—I already knew the Draugar are smart—but because I have no doubt they learned how to prop-foul from the *Sentinel*'s crew. They could have absorbed the knowledge from McAfee, Peach, or even Jenny. *Poor Jenny.* That they might be using my friend's mind against me now makes my jaw clench tight with rage. *These fuckers are going too far.*

"Fire!" Willem shouts.

Don't need to tell me twice.

The boom of Willem's harpoon firing drowns out the four coughs from the grenade launcher. But the sound is nothing compared to the simultaneous explosions that tear through the air when our projectiles find their marks. Willem's harpoon strikes the starboard side whale dead center in the head, tearing through several inches of skin and flesh before sinking into the spermaceti-filled case and detonating. A geyser of red and yellow bursts from the wound.

The four grenades launched from the Mark 14 find their target as well, each one striking the crater created by the previous shell. In two seconds, the four fragmentation grenades punch a hole all the way through the whale's head, partly severing it from the whale's body. While the water fills with a slick of fleshy gore and slick chunks of yellowish wax, the whale's forward momentum is arrested. It falls behind and sinks.

"Jane!" Willem shouts.

I turn and find that while his whale sports a crater the size of a kiddie pool, it still has some fight left in it and the rope clutched in its jaws.

I zero in on the wound, which makes a convenient target, and squeeze the trigger twice, firing my last two grenades. The second shot must reach its brain because as the insides of its head burst into the outside world, the body seizes and goes still. The rope slides free from its mouth and bobs in the water behind us.

My small measure of relief is erased by the memory of three missing colossal blue whales. I turn around and shout, "Has anyone seen the blues?"

Talbot shakes his head. "Not a dang thing."

"Nothing over here," Helena says.

Klein is approaching with a fresh spearhead for Willem. I already know he couldn't see anything more from his position at the center of the deck. I see Nate standing on deck three, which is the roof of the bridge. He's got the best view on the ship. "Nate!"

He doesn't acknowledge me. I shout louder and wave my arms. "Nate!"

His head turns subtly, but I can see he's looking at me now.

"Can you see the blue whales? There are three of them!"

Nothing. No reply. He just stares at me.

I squeeze the grenade launcher's grip. "Nate, I swear to God if you are having some kind of whale love pout fest up there, I'm going to beat the living shit out of you until you beg me to feed you to them."

Still nothing. *Is he in some kind of shock?* Whatever the reason, he's useless.

"Oh shit," Klein says. "Oh shit. Go faster!"

Willem and Klein are doing their best to quickly reel in the spent harpoon while piling the cable in neat loops so it can be fired again. Beyond them, out to sea, is a single killer whale. As its back arcs up and out of the water, I see a series of bloody puncture wounds. This is the orca that was bitten.

Draugr, I think.

My fear is confirmed when the beast rises again, clutching the rope in its jaws. We've been outsmarted *again*. The sperm whales weren't attacking, they were *distracting*. More than that, we used up our ammo on them, leaving us no way to stop the freshly turned orca.

How did they know? How did they know!

I run for the supply closet as the orca closes the distance.

The closet doors shake as I whip them open and descend on the box of grenades like a rabid Tasmanian devil. I take out two rounds, probably far more roughly than is recommended, and put them on the deck. I pop open the six-shot revolver, dump out the spent cartridges, twist the chamber back into position, and slap in two fresh rounds. Not a lot of a margin for error, but I'm not going to have time to fire six rounds. If I miss with these two shots, I won't have a chance to fire more anyway. With the launcher reloaded, I sprint to the rear rail.

Halfway there, Willem and Klein give up on reloading the harpoon, draw their handguns, and send a volley of lead over the rail. They're aiming nearly straight down. Not a good sign and a wasted effort. The 9mm rounds couldn't stop a non-Draugr orca, never mind one that's technically already dead.

I nearly fall over the rail when I arrive and point the grenade launcher's barrel over the side. I see the sleek black shape of the killer slide beneath the dive deck. My finger finds the trigger and squeezes, but the weapon is yanked from my hand before I can fire.

"Jane, no!" Willem shouts as he takes the weapon.

The ship shakes a moment later. The orca has struck the prop. Blood and gore plume out behind the ship as the nine-ton killer is diced by the giant propeller blades. But did the rope catch?

A grinding sound and sudden deceleration confirm the suicide attack's success. The prop has been fouled.

Being an experienced whaler who has dealt with antiwhaling organizations in the past, Jakob reacts quickly, shutting down the engine. The silence that follows is eerie until I break it.

"Willem, what the hell!" I shout. "Why didn't you let me shoot it!"

"We can fix a fouled prop," he says. "But we can't fix it if you blow it up."

I just grind my teeth. It's the closest thing he'll get to a concession and he knows it, so he doesn't say anything else about it.

The ship slows. We're dead in the water. And to get moving again, someone will have to go in the water and cut away the cable. Being the only one on board with diving experience, I can guess who that someone is going to be.

Three gentle thumps from below furrow my brow, but I relax when I feel our speed pick up. "Did Jakob restart the engine?"

Willem's frown is deep. "No." He walks to the port rail and looks over the side of the ship.

"But we're moving," I say.

"It's not us," he says, then points. "It's them."

I look over the rail and see nothing but ocean. But the deep blue waves are suddenly disturbed by a swirl of water that flattens the surface and lets me catch a glimpse of a massive fluke. The three giants have wedged their bodies up against the hull and are now directing the ship's motion. The Draugar never intended to kill or sink us. The whole thing was an elaborately choreographed kidnapping. With our engine disabled and the whales largely shielded by the *Raven*'s hull, there is nothing we can do now except go along for the ride.

Jakob arrives at the rail. He leans over and takes a look. I expect to see him respond with righteous anger, or perhaps even defeat, but when he leans back up, he's smiling. "Our search is over, Raven. They're taking us, just like they did the others. We'll find the other ships."

"Jakob," I say, disbelieving the man's optimism. "Even if we find the other ships, there isn't much we can do. We're dead in the water. Our prop is fouled."

The old captain gives me his best crafty Viking grin, raises an eyebrow, and says, "Is it?"

26

With no way to fight against the giant Draugar ferrying us through the ocean, the crew stands down and gathers on the main deck. Only Nate isn't present, which is probably in his best interest since I'm still pissed about his silence. I know now that he couldn't have helped, but if he wants to be on this ship, he needs to help out, even if all that means is replying, "I don't see anything."

"You're really okay with this?" I ask Jakob.

He nods. "They're taking us where we want to go."

"I thought we wanted a sample?" I ask.

Jakob's eyes flick to the deck for just a second, but it's his tell. He's about to lie to me.

I cross my arms. "As much as I like you, Jakob, the next words out of your mouth better be the truth."

He meets my eyes with a challenge. I might be his Raven, but he's not used to being spoken to like that on his ship.

"I'm your first mate," I remind him. "Secrets are *not* part of the deal."

"You're right," he says, wandering away from the group. He looks out at the endless ocean. His shoulders sag a touch before he turns around. "I'm afraid I haven't been totally forthcoming—"

No duh.

"—with any of you."

That's actually a surprise.

Willem steps closer. "Father?"

When Jakob's forehead crisscrosses with angst, Willem adds, "What have you done?"

Jakob steels himself with a deep breath and asks, "Do you remember the man bit by an orca several months ago?"

"When we were still in the hospital?" I ask.

"I tracked him down," Jakob says.

"Why didn't you say something?" Willem asks. "Where is he?"

Jakob's lips twitch. "He's dead. By my hand. I killed him."

"He was infected." It's not a question. I have no doubt about it. Not only because the man was bit by an orca, which was no doubt infected by Draugar, but because Jakob would never kill a human being, despite his ancestors' penchant for violence.

"Part of him remained," Jakob says. "The pain brought him out."

"You didn't torture him?" Helena asks, her voice cut with concern.

I turn on her, annoyed, but before I can question her knowledge of Jakob's character, he says, "It was not my intention."

I turn back to Jakob, silently demanding an explanation.

"I caught up with him in the mountains. He was heading north, for what purpose, I'm not sure. When I confronted him, he attacked. When my blade in his chest didn't stop him…I took off his feet."

"Father…" Helena says, raising her hand to her mouth. For a big Viking warrior, she's kind of a softy. Then again, she's religious, and killing whales is quite a bit different than hacking off a man's feet.

"He was already dead, my dear," Jakob says. "If you are here with us, you must believe it."

Helena just lowers her head.

Willem tries to put a comforting hand on her shoulder, but she shrugs away.

"His mind only partially returned," Jakob says. "And only when the pain was greatest. But he knew everything."

"He'd been part of the hive mind," I say.

With a nod, Jakob continues. "Every word he uttered was a struggle. Against the pain. Against the parasites. But he knew. So he fought."

"What did you learn?" Klein asks, more interested in raw information than details of pain and blood, which quite frankly is how I feel, too.

"That they remembered me," Jakob says. "They knew my name." He looks at Willem. "And yours." He looks at me. "And yours."

This news is disconcerting, to say the least, but it's not exactly helpful. When no one speaks, Jakob continues. "He spoke of the ships. It's how I knew to look for them. He told me they intended to return again to the mainland. That they were searching for something."

"What?" I ask.

"He could not say. When he spoke of their intentions, there was resistance. Between his words, the Draugar shouted threats. I learned about the boats, but not the purpose for them. I learned there is something in the mountains they desire, but not what."

There's more. I can see it in his eyes. "*Jakob,*" I say, slathering the word with impatience.

"Before I set him free, he was able to reveal one detail." Jakob looks at me. For some reason, he thinks this revelation will affect me the most. "There are three Queens."

Well, he was right. This is unexpected and horrible news. I killed the first Queen. Crushed it with my bare hands. But before that happened, I very nearly *became* the Queen. I offered myself to the thing so that Willem and Jakob could be spared. That's not how it played out, but if the Draugar remember me, it's likely they also remember the promise I made. "Do you think—"

"They remember?" Jakob finishes. His head bobs up and down. "They do."

"You knew this when you brought me out here?" I say. It's a rhetorical question. I already know the answer. He did. "What am I, Jakob, bait?" I don't give him a chance to answer. "You came out here, convinced all these people to join you. Your son. Your daughter. Your friends—Malik is *dead*. And you had no intention of collecting a sample, did you?"

"Jane, you don't know that," Willem says. He understands my temperament, that I'm getting close to knocking Jakob's block off, and is trying to make peace, but I'm not finished.

"He could have taken a sample from the Draugr after he lopped off his feet," I say to Willem before turning back to Jakob. "But that's not what you did, is it?"

"I burned his body," Jakob says, a little anger of his own sneaking into his voice. *Thataboy. Let's have this out, Old Norse style. Show me what the old dog has left in him.*

"Why, Jakob? Why did you maim, torture, and kill a man? Why did you set him on fire? What did his screams sound like as he burned? Human? Something else? Why?"

"Because it was the right thing to do!" Jakob shouts, his face turning red. "Because he wasn't a human being anymore! Because if I let him live, the others would know we survived, that *you* survived!"

His last statement sucks away some of my anger.

"The parasites were fleeing his body," Jakob says. "They had to be destroyed. They all need to be destroyed."

I agree with this. With everything. Even setting the poor bastard on fire, but something still feels wrong. "Why me? I don't understand. Why me?"

"Because the only time I saw fear in his white eyes was when he spoke *your* name. You killed their Queen, Raven. They remember that. They fear you. You are not bait. You are the spear tip."

"She's nothing," an unfamiliar voice says. When the group turns around, the only person there is Nate. "'Sup, peeps," he says.

We're all so confused by the strange voice that we keep looking around. When it's clear there is no one else there, I ask, "Nate, was that you just now?"

He doesn't reply. He's placed one hand over his right eye.

"You feeling okay, son?" Talbot asks.

"Huh?" Nate says, looking confused. "Sorry, I have a killer headache."

Speaking of killing someone. "That why you didn't respond when I was yelling at you?"

"You were yelling at me?" he asks. The question sounds earnest, but I'm not buying it.

"When you were standing on the upper deck? When we were busy fighting the zombie-whales? Ringing any bells?"

Nate's face screws up with a mix of emotions. I don't think he's feeling any of them. It's more like he's not in control.

Not in control…

"Mind moving your hand away from your eye, Nate?" I ask.

He looks at me. "What for? My head is raging, man. Frikken eye feels ready to burst."

I take aim with the grenade launcher. "Open your eye."

Everyone takes a few steps away from Nate, but no one says a word. If anyone is afraid I've gone off the deep end, the fear is erased when Nate says, *"You belong to us,"* in a voice that is not his, and then adds, "Dub-TF, Jane, chill," in his own voice.

"She doesn't belong to you," Jakob says.

Nate cringes away from Jakob. "The hell, man! I don't want— *she will join us soon*—anybody!"

"He can't hear it," Willem says. "He doesn't know."

"Know what?" Nate shouts.

I look down the sight of the grenade launcher. Everyone takes a few more steps back.

"Jane!" Nate pleads. "What—"

"Show. Me. Your. Eye." I don't need to follow the statement with a threat. He sees my finger go to the trigger.

He pulls his hand away but still has the eye clenched shut. I aim the Mark 14 toward the closed eye. The sight slightly magnifies the target, giving me a closer look without actually stepping forward.

The eye flicks open a few times, and then snaps open wide.

"Nate..." I whisper.

The kid's eye is gone. All that remains is the clear membrane that used to house it. A clear fluid now fills the orb, and within that fluid wriggles a single, white parasite.

The kid's face reflects abject fear. "What is it? Why are you looking at me like that? *I see you, Jane Harper.*"

I stride forward, filled with rage, not because I'm face-to-face with a parasite that knows my name but because of what it did to Nate, and what I know his fate is going to be. I should probably shoot him here and now, but I can't bring myself to do it.

Nate backs away from me, but he doesn't seem to have full control over his limbs now. "Jane. What's happening? What are you doing? Wait. Wait!"

When I reach the kid, I turn the grenade launcher around and slam the butt of the weapon into his forehead. He crumples to the floor, unconscious.

The crew gathers around.

"Why didn't you kill him?" Helena asks. I don't get the sense that she wanted me to kill him, just that she's confused why I didn't.

I frown. She's not going to like the answer. "For the same reason Jakob didn't immediately kill the Draugr he found in the mountains." I look her in the eyes. "We need answers."

27

"You're not really going to go through with this," Helena says. She's put herself between the mess hall door and me, Jakob, and Klein. Willem and Talbot are on the bridge, keeping watch. Helena was supposed to be with them, but it seems her conscience has gotten the best of her.

I glance past her wide shoulders and see Nate strapped down to a table. It's a horrible sight; I'll admit it. He's still unconscious, and his face is coated with dry blood from where I struck him. His arms are pulled up and tied to the table legs, as are his feet. Two thick ropes at his waist and chest bind his body to the table.

"It's necessary," Jakob says.

"I don't believe that," she replies. "If we start torturing people, are we any better?"

My patience evaporates. "Helena, I like you, but you need to open your eyes. We're not thugs or terrorists or even 'the man,'" I say with some air quotes.

"I work for the man," Klein says.

I thrust an index finger at him without looking. "Shut up, Klein. We're not doing this for kicks. What happens in this room will probably join my fresh collection of nightmares for the next few years. Maybe forever. I really don't want to go into this room. I don't want to talk to Nate or see that thing in his eye. I don't want any of this to be real. But it is. It's fucked up, but this is the world now, even if the world doesn't yet know about it. But they will. If these parasitic assholes take the fight to mainland Greenland, we're going to have fifty-eight thousand Draugar to deal with. And when the bloodbath ends—if it ends—everyone you know and love will be dead or worse.

"I'm going into this room. Right now. And I'm going to do what needs to be done so we can avoid that happening." I step up close to her and crane my head up to stare her in the eyes. I'm dwarfed by her size. It's a real-life Hulk Hogan–versus–Andre the Giant moment. But there are no body slams or chest slaps. She just frowns and steps to the side. I'm not sure if it's because she's taken my explanation to heart or if she just doesn't feel like crushing me. Either way works for me, though a small part of me wishes she'd beaten me to a pulp so I wouldn't have to take part in this interrogation.

Jakob and Klein follow me into the room. Klein turns and closes the door, blocking out Helena's scowl. Nate hasn't regained consciousness yet, so we gather by his feet, where Jakob is rubbing his thumb across the edge of a knife.

My imagination gets the best of me, and I picture the blade being used against Nate, who has really done nothing to harm us. "Jakob," I say, "if I'm understanding this right, the parasite doesn't give answers in response to pain, the pain simply helps center, or bring back, the mind of the host."

"That is how it seemed to work, yes," he says.

"So as long as we're talking to Nate, we don't need that."

He nods.

"Then put it away until we do," I say. "Our job isn't to terrify Nate."

Jakob closes the folding knife and slips it into his pocket.

Klein walks to Nate's head. "I'd like to make a few points before we start. I may not be running around the globe shooting people, but I am a spy. And a good one. From what you said"—he points at me—"Nate might just have one parasite inside him, currently located in his eye. But it's shown it has at least partial control over his body and speech, though the kid doesn't seem aware of it. The really worrisome part is that while Nate has just one parasite inside him, it seems clear that it is still part of the collective."

Sonofabitch, he's right. Nate might be unconscious, but I have no doubt the parasite is still wriggling around beneath his closed eye. The kid might not be aware of what's going on, but the parasite is likely still monitoring his senses. Which means it's hearing us now, which means—"They're listening to us."

Klein nods. "Unless we kill the kid, toss him overboard, or lock him in a soundproof room, everything he hears, sees, smells, feels, or tastes is going straight to *them*. He's the ultimate bug. And I'm fairly certain he was *meant* to be a bug. Maybe not specifically for us, but for whoever came along and picked up his distress signal."

"You're sure?" Jakob asks.

"I wouldn't be if it weren't for the coordinated attack," Klein says. "The only way the Draugar whales could have known Jane and Willem were out of ammunition is if Nate saw this, understood it with his human mind, and then the parasite communicated the information with the collective, allowing them to seamlessly, precisely, and effectively assault the ship in a way we could not defend against."

"He's right," I say. "Nate was watching us from the wheelhouse roof. He could see everything."

"*They* could see everything," Klein says. "Just as easily as they can hear us, even now. So if it speaks through him, we're not talking to a single parasite. We're talking to the hive mind."

"To the Queen," I say. "Or one of the remaining two."

"I'm not sure how they're connected," Klein says. "Nate is physically close to the three whales below us, so that's the initial connection, and they surely contain thousands, if not millions of parasites each, which makes them sizable amplifiers. But there's no way to know their range. Maybe the three whales are enough. Maybe there are other creatures between us and the Queen."

"Or maybe the Queen is in one of the whales," I say. It's a horrible thought, but quite possible.

"Or that," Klein agrees. "The point is, we're interrogating them, not the other way around."

In other words, don't reveal anything of strategic importance, like the fact that the prop foul didn't get too tight and that to free ourselves all we need to do is reverse the engine. "Got it," I say. "Now let's wake him up and get this over with."

"*I am awake,*" Nate says, but it's not his voice. His clear eye pops open. I still expect there to be a human eye there, glancing around at each of us, but the clear orb doesn't shift. The worm inside it does.

"What do you want?" I ask it.

The tiny parasite wriggles in my direction. I can see its two tiny black eyes.

"To live," it says. "Same as you."

This time, the voice is more like Nate's. It's learning his speech pattern, mimicking his inflections and accent.

"Bullshit," I say. "Why are you here?"

"We have the right," it says. "BT-dubs, we were here first."

Could it be true? Did these parasites evolve before the human race? Doesn't matter, I decide. I can't trust anything the parasite says. *Don't get distracted, Jane.* "Nate. Can you hear me, Nate?"

"Aww, Jane, don't you effing like me anymore?"

The voice of my friend Jenny hits me like a punch to the nuts, if I had them. I step back, the hairs on my arms standing upright.

"Not your most Van Helsing moment," the thing says, still duplicating Jenny's voice and speech pattern. "Cool that you kept the cloak, though."

I unbutton the cloak and toss it into a chair, suddenly repulsed by it. My repulsion gets filtered through a lifetime of hard-knock lessons combined with a genetic disposition for fight rather than flight, both supplied by the Colonel, and comes out as violence. I step forward, saying, "I want to speak to Nathaniel!" Then I slug him in the shoulder.

Nate's other eye pops open, and his body bends against the rope holding him down as a shout of surprise and pain erupts from his lips. Now that the shock's worn off and he realizes he can't move, his breathing quickens. If we had a heart monitor, I'm sure we'd see his pulse skyrocketing.

"It's okay, kid," I say, despite things being decidedly *not* okay.

His good eye rotates toward me. "Jane! What's happening? Why can't I move?"

"It's for your own good, Nate," I say. "You're going to have to trust me."

"You...you hit me," he says, remembering. "Why did you—*you're wasting your time, Jane*—hit me? Who said that?"

He looks around the room, seeing Klein and Jakob, but somehow knows it wasn't either of them who spoke. "Is there someone else in—*it will be easier if you don't fight*—room?" Nate freezes, going still. "Dubs...that was me, wasn't it?"

I place a hand on his arm. "You have one of them in you."

His eye locks on me. "Am I...dead?"

That's actually a really good question, because it doesn't seem like it. His mind is compromised, without a doubt, but he seems to be sharing control, and I seriously doubt the parasite has made any changes to his body. Despite being infected, he might still be fully human and alive. Which creates a sort of moral dilemma.

"Jakob, the man you...spoke to before. He was..."

"Draugr," he confirms. "Not like this."

He understands the conundrum. What are we willing to do to somebody who isn't yet against us? Maybe it will be easier, I think, now that Nate knows.

"Nate, you're infected, but it's just one parasite," I tell him. "You're still alive. Still human. And in control."

"Can you get it out?" he asks.

"Not yet," I say, though I have no idea if such a thing is possible. "But I need you to listen. With your thoughts. Hear them, Nate."

"Hear who?"

"The hive mind," I say. "The collective consciousness. Whatever you want to call it."

"Like Locutus," he says.

I remember the *Star Trek* episode where Picard became one with the Borg collective mind. Truth really is stranger than fiction. "Yes. Like Locutus."

The kid closes his eye and relaxes. The clear eye remains open. I can feel the worm looking at me, and it takes all my strength to not reach out and rip the orb from his skull.

"I hear them," he says. "I think I...what?" Then he starts laughing. The cackle rolls through several different voices, and I feel like I'm performing an exorcism. It's really not all that different. I'm speaking to a nonhuman entity that has taken over the body of a man. Maybe exorcism stories are really parasitic infections?

The laugh stops abruptly with a gasp. Nate's eye opens wide. His face twists with an expression of pain. What the hell happened?

"My leg," Nate says. "It hurts!"

I look down and find that Jakob has stabbed Nate's calf. It's not a deep or mortal wound, but it must hurt like hell.

I lean in close to Nate's head. "Ignore the pain," I tell him. "Listen to the voices. Tell me what they want!"

He grinds his teeth. "You, Jane Harper! We want you."

It's trying to throw me. Distract me. "Nate! Tell me what they want!"

Jakob twists the knife, eliciting a scream that can probably be heard on the bridge.

Nate returns for a moment. I can see it when his forehead screws up. "Host!" he screams. "Host! They want the host!"

The door bursts open. Helena storms in, looking ready to bust skulls. But the interview is over. Nate's body goes limp. He's unconscious again. But I don't think it's from the pain. I think we were getting close to something. The parasite switched him off. I suspect we could start again, bring Nate back with another dose of pain, but I don't think that's going to happen with Helena in the room.

Her eyes glance at Nate's placid face, then down to the wound on his leg and the knife in Jakob's hand. I'm sure we're about to get a lecture, but instead she says, "Willem sent me. Something is on the radar. Something large."

"Another whale?" Jakob asks.

"Bigger," she says. "Much bigger."

28

After a quick double check of Nate's bonds to make sure escape is impossible, we shut off the lights and close the door to limit what he can sense. I don't feel comfortable leaving him down here alone, but Helena insists that Willem wants everyone on the bridge.

Part of me suspects that Willem just asked for Jakob, and that Helena is using the request as a way to pull us away from the dirty business of extracting information from Nate. But when my leg starts hurting and my walk becomes a limp, the giantess wraps an arm around me and says, "Lean on me," so I decide to cut her some slack. Having a moral compass on board is probably a good thing anyway. History is full of good causes that become distorted into atrocities.

I half expect to see an army of whales filling the ocean when we arrive on the bridge, but there's nothing but blue skies and calm waters all the way to the horizon. If it weren't for the fact that we were being carried to our collective doom by three zombie blue whales, it'd be a nice day to get sun on the deck. Of course, the chilly air kind of kills that, too.

Willem's face, however, reveals that not everything is hunky-dory on the USS *Raven*. I look for Talbot but don't see him.

"What is it?" Jakob asks.

"Better if you come and see," he says, stepping aside so we can see the radar screen. As the radar starts a new three-hundred-sixty-degree sweep of the surrounding eleven miles, a large portion of the top of the screen turns green.

"What the hell is that?" I ask.

Jakob says nothing. Nor do Willem or Helena.

I try to work out the size. "It's nearly two thousand feet wide! It has to be an island."

"There are no islands out here," Helena says.

She knows the waters off Greenland as well as anyone, so I have no reason to doubt her knowledge, aside from the giant green blob filling the radar screen as if the Jolly Green Giant dropped a load in the North Atlantic.

"Then what is it?" Willem says.

Willem's smart. Possibly the smartest person on the ship aside from Klein. He knows the history of this place, the culture, the ocean, and our enemy. If he's been thinking on this for several minutes already and not come up with an explanation, I doubt we're going to have an epiphany.

But then Jakob does. "It's the ships. All of them. Together."

My eyes return to the radar screen. The shape of the target is roughly oval—shaped something like an aircraft carrier, though I know that's not what it is because it's twice the size.

"Makes sense," Klein says. "Based on the individual sizes of the ships we know have disappeared, a grouping this size is plausible. The question is why."

"Question of the day, Klein," I say. "What we do know is that that's where we're headed." I look up at the horizon, expecting to see the floating island, but nothing is there. "How long will it take to get there?"

"We're moving at roughly seven knots," Willem says. "Give or take a knot."

Klein whispers to himself for a moment, then says, "Somewhere around forty minutes, though we'll be able to see it in a half hour."

"How many people were on board the *Poseidon Adventure*?" I ask. But then I remember the news report and say, "Twenty-five hundred. What about the other ships?"

"Most were working ships," Klein says. "Maybe five hundred more, tops."

"Some three thousand people," I say. "In military terms, that's a brigade."

"Is…that bad?" Helena asks.

"My father led a brigade once," I say. "They could take and hold a city like Nuuk overnight. Hell, they could kill everyone overnight. But that's not what these things do. They'll kill some people, sure, to eat them. The rest join the party. If three thousand Draugar make landfall, they'll double their numbers overnight. They'll spread through the country about as fast as they can run. Anyone who didn't leave right away—by plane—would be overrun within a few weeks. It's pretty much a doomsday scenario."

"Which is why we're going to sink them," Jakob says. "All of them."

I turn to him. "With what? A grenade launcher? We'll be lucky to ding the cruise liner."

"We'll figure it out when we get there," he says.

The rear door to the bridge opens, drawing our attention. Talbot walks in, fixing his belt. The cowboy had to take a leak. He nods at us, "What'd I miss?" Then he stops cold and looks at me. "How'd you get here before me?"

"I've been here for a few minutes," I say. "I came with Jakob and—where did you see me?"

"Leaving the mess," he says. "When you didn't reply, I figured things weren't going well with the interrogation, so I didn't push it. You were wearing that cloak."

Leaving the mess. The cloak. I can feel the muscles in my back constricting. "I left my cloak with Nate. In the mess."

Klein draws his weapon and heads for the door. "It wasn't you."

I'm right behind him. The entire crew files through the ship like a mob chasing down Frankenstein's monster. We're missing the pitchforks, but each and every one of us is armed with a handgun of some type. Even Helena.

Willem heads down to the second deck with Talbot and Helena. I take the main deck hallway, aiming for the mess, just to confirm my doppelgänger is Nate.

I find the mess hall door wide open. The table is covered in loose rope and blood, but no body. "How did he break the ropes?"

"He's Draugr," Jakob says.

The Draugar are stronger than the average man, in part because they can push past the pain that might give a normal person pause, but I suspect the parasites also enhance the muscles. Maybe reinforce the bones. Could just be that slime they coat everything with. Could be something else. But there's a problem with Jakob's theory.

"Nate had a single parasite in his eye," I say. "Otherwise he was himself. And still human."

"He's not human anymore," Jakob says. He glances down at my gun. "Be ready."

What Jakob is really saying is, the gloves are off. If there is a Draugr on board, we're all in danger. One bite. That's all it takes, and the parasites can spread. It's a death sentence, not just because the parasites would claim mind and body, but because Jakob, or I, would shoot the victim dead. Just like we will Nate when we find him. Poor kid.

Willem charges up the staircase a little farther down the hall. "He's not down there." Klein is with him, but not Helena.

"Where's Helena?" I ask.

"Back deck," Willem says.

Back deck. It's really the only place we haven't checked. But why would Nate—shit. "The weapons locker!"

We swarm down the hall and through the door at the end. A wall of cold air greets us, along with a sight none of us are expecting: Draugr-Nate, who is currently wearing my cloak, engaged in hand-to-hand combat with Helena.

And she's a sight to behold. Nate is clearly stronger and faster than he has any right to be, and he's fighting with a skill that doesn't belong to him. But Helena, it's like watching a blond Wonder Woman mixed with, well, just Wonder Woman. Nate swings a series of blows that, had he been a larger man like Willem or Torstein, would have had a devastating effect, but Nate's shorter arms fail to connect. Helena ducks the last swing and delivers an uppercut to his lower jaw that sends him stumbling back.

All four of my male counterparts raise their weapons and take aim, but Helena is between them and Nate. "Put down your weapons, idiots!" I shout, before charging forward. It's time for some women's lib.

"Helena!" I shout.

She glances back. Sees that I'm coming.

"Stay away from his mouth!" I say. "No more head shots!"

Nate recovers and moves toward her. I can't see him, though—just hear him—but he can't see me, either, which is perfect.

I hit sprint speed, coming up fast behind Helena. "Duck!"

When she bows down fast, putting her trust in me, I think, *Good girl*, and then leap into the air. I sail over her back, extend both legs, and drive my heels into Nate's chest. I'm not a big person, but I'm fast, have strong legs, and can pack a punch when I use my entire body like a wrecking ball. I feel his rib cage bend under my feet for a fraction of a second before I hear them crack, one by one. Sounds like my father cracking his knuckles.

With my forward momentum arrested, I fall to the deck like Wile E. Coyote after running over a cliff ledge. The hard deck greets me mercilessly, but the rough landing pales in comparison to what I've just done to the Draugr. Unfortunately, my attack has barely fazed it. It's hard to stop something that can't feel, or doesn't mind, pain. Even harder to stop something that doesn't need to breathe. Or pump blood through a heart.

Before I can get back to my feet, the Draugr charges forward, mouth agape. I've got a clear view of Nate's now-white tongue. One bite. Just one bite. And I'm done.

He dives.

I kick out, aiming to implode his face with my heel.

And miss.

When he lands a foot short of me, I nearly laugh because of how poorly we both judged the distance, but then I feel Helena's hands beneath my arms. She pulls me out of range and deposits me on my feet.

Nate recovers once more, undaunted, and heads toward us.

She looks at me. There's fire in her eyes. "Together."

I grin. "Hell yes."

We meet Nate halfway, just ten feet from the starboard rail. He lunges at Helena, but her long arms strike first, knocking him off balance. When he stumbles back, I follow her punch with a kick to his gut. His body pitches forward but snaps back a moment later when Helena lifts her leg and drives it into his chest.

Nate's body is lifted off the deck. He stumbles backward and slams into the rail with a *clang*. The backward momentum pulls the cloak up over his head. He tears it away, dropping it to the deck. He's far from done. Nate springs off the metal rails like they were wrestling ring ropes. But the skill he displayed earlier is now gone. Instead of punching, he shoves. The effect is freakish.

Helena sails across the deck, sliding to a stop by the feet of the men, who are still aiming their weapons, waiting for the chance to shoot without also hitting Helena or me. I can see them shouting at me, probably to duck, but I'm not hearing them. Not really. I'm in that place where common sense takes a backseat to instinct.

Nate makes a gurgling sort of roar as he charges me, mouth open, teeth bared and ready to bite. But if Helena is Wonder Woman, I'm Batman—Frank Miller's Batman—which is to say, I fight dirty. I kick out hard, this time judging the distance perfectly, connecting with his kneecap and inverting it with a loud crack.

Nate screams in pain as he falls to the ground. And I do mean Nate. The pain brought him back.

"Jane!" he shouts. "Do something! Save me!"

The kid is breaking my heart. But there's nothing I can do for him, except take advantage of this break in the Draugr's control. I lift him to his feet and shove him against the starboard rail. He turns and sees the water below.

His eyes go wide with fear, but he doesn't fight. Instead, he turns to me and says, "The host. Jane, don't let them find the ho—" His voice morphs into a shriek, and he lunges for my throat.

A single shot rips through the air. Nate's head snaps back as a dot appears on his forehead and his parasite-ridden brains exit through the back of his skull. His body lolls back over the rail and then, tugged by gravity, slips over the top and falls into the North Atlantic.

29

When the reality of what has just happened hits me, I drop to my knees. Nate was a good kid and, unlike most people, willing to fight for something he believed in. His cyberspeak rubbed me the wrong way, but his passion was admirable. *Was* admirable. Him and the parasites trapped in his lifeless body are fish food now.

"We killed him," I say when I feel a hand on my shoulder.

"Ain't no way that's the truth," Talbot says.

I'm surprised that it's Talbot and turn toward the man.

"That boy was dead long before we plucked him from the water, and you know that, sure as I do."

He's right, of course. And my logical side can argue the point until I'm old and wrinkly, but I'm not sure it will ever feel true. The moment he went from human being to Draugr, something in my mind snapped and I didn't just attack to defend myself; I took pleasure in the fight. Hell, if Nate hadn't come back right at the end, I might not have a guilty conscience at all. But he *did* come back. Some part of the infected still remains, and while they're beyond hope of retrieval, and I have no doubts that killing them is a mercy, erasing that last part of them should be done solemnly.

"If it makes you feel better," Talbot says. "I put the bullet in him."

I knew that the moment the expert shot whizzed past me and poked a hole dead center in Nate's head.

"Had to be done." He grows serious. "But next time, git out of the damn way. Y'all coulda been killed."

Right again. I'm going to have to find a way to swallow my anger at the Draugar and start thinking before I act. I got lucky this time. The sharpshooting cowboy might not always be around to save me.

He offers his hand to me. "C'mon. Being all weepy and sad ain't becoming for the Mighty Raven."

His says the last part with a dramatic flourish that makes me smile. I take his hand and get back to my feet.

"He mentioned 'the host' again," I say, wiping the moisture from my eyes. "I think it might be more than we thought. Heard anything about that from the conspiracy nuts?"

Talbot thinks on it and takes so long I think he might have taken offense to me saying "conspiracy nuts," but then he shakes his head. "Can't say that I have. Nothing of the sort."

Feeling discouraged, I look at the deck and see that it's covered in loose weapons and ammo. We didn't lose everything, but a quick glance at the cabinet reveals that Nate managed to throw a good portion of our arsenal overboard before Helena confronted him.

I catch a glimpse of Jakob and Klein leading Helena inside the ship. She's holding her side but looks okay otherwise. Before ducking through the door, she looks my way and gives a nod. In Greenlandic body language, it's the kind of nod that says, "Well done," "I respect you," or "We're friends," but in this case, I think it's all three.

Talbot crouches next to me and picks up my cloak. "This belongs to you."

I take it from him but don't put it on despite the chilly ocean air. I give it a once-over, looking for any parasitical stowaways. Finding none, I fold the cloak over my arm and turn to greet Willem. He's got his "tsk, tsk, Jane" face on, so I raise an eyebrow that says, "Don't say a damn word."

When he offers an apologetic smile, I realize we've just had an entire conversation without saying a word.

Talbot notices, too, and voices what I'm thinking. "You two are like an old married couple." He spares us from the awkward moment by adding, "Help me collect the guns. See what kind of damage the kid did."

Twenty minutes later, we've got what remains of our weapons laid out on the chart room table.

Jakob enters the room. "We'll see it in five minutes," he says, referring to what he believes is a conglomeration of ships. "What do we have?"

Talbot verbally inventories our weapons. "One pump-action shotgun. Twenty shells. Two AK-47s. Five magazines between the two. One hundred fifty rounds total. Three 9mm handguns. Six magazines. Plus the handguns y'all are carrying." He draws his revolver, which now has one less live round in its chambers. "I kept my ammo in my quarters, so I've still got sixty rounds for the ol' peacemaker here."

"And I still have my peacemaker," I say, hefting up the Mark 14 grenade launcher. "Just three rounds left, though."

Jakob doesn't look happy. "That's it?"

We've got enough guns and ammo to form a small militia, but it's not enough. Not even close. We could be facing three thousand killers, and even if our aim is perfect, we only have enough to take out a few hundred. Not that guns are the only way to handle

Draugar. "Any swords on board? A machete for hacking up whales? Maybe a fire ax?"

Jakob looks up at Willem and gives a nod.

Willem exits without a word. *Vikings and their nods*, I think. These guys are the embodiment of the strong, silent type. I sometimes wonder why the duo has taken such a shine to me, given my tendency to run off at the mouth. Must be my charming personality.

Willem returns holding a wrapped-up wool blanket. He lays it down on the clear portion of table, and I hear the clang of metal from within. The sound triggers an almost Pavlovian response. I lean forward in anticipation.

When Willem pulls the blanket away, he reveals a collection of assorted bladed weapons. Three swords, one double-headed ax, and two hatchets. Helena steps into the room, her eyes like those of a dog that's just been called to dinner. *Hello, fellow Pavlovian*, I think. She looks over the weapons for just a moment before reaching down and taking both hatchets. She leaves with the weapons as fast as she arrived.

I guess the Greenlandic method for calling dibs is to just take what you want before anyone else, a theory that's confirmed when Willem snags the double-bladed ax—which makes him look more what he is: the much less decayed, still living, descendant of Torstein. Talbot and Jakob are quick to grab the larger of the three swords, leaving a pitiful-looking weapon lying on the table.

The two-foot blade is old and rusted, more likely to cause tetanus than a mortal wound. No doubt drawn by the sound of clanging weapons, Klein enters the room. He looks down at the last sword.

"I'd offer to arm wrestle you for it, but I'm fairly certain you would win," he says.

"Thanks, but you can have it," I say. "I think I'd rather use my knife."

A sheathed sword slides into view, clutched in Jakob's hand. The curved shape of the black lacquered hardwood scabbard, ornate guard, and finely wrapped hilt identify the weapon as a *katana*—a Japanese samurai sword. Jakob's free hand takes the hilt and pulls, revealing a gleaming, brand-new, razor-sharp blade. But the fierce-looking metal isn't what captures my attention, it's the engraved raven at the bottom of the blade. I recognize the symbol immediately as the Olavson family crest, which is tattooed on Jakob's and Willem's arms. Torstein's, too. Jakob didn't just buy this sword for me, he had it *made* for me.

Before I can thank him or ask why he had a Japanese sword, rather than something in a Norse design, made for me, he places the weapon in my hand and I understand. The blade is light. Really light. I might have a hard time swinging the bulky blades that Jakob and Talbot scooped up, but this...this is going to sing through the air.

My grin is impossible to hide. "Jakob..."

"You like it?"

"It's beautiful," I say, but then feel silly for gushing. "Let me guess, you named it Raven? Seems to be about the limit of your ability to name things."

He scoffs and waves a hand at me. "Vikings do *not* name swords."

With a smile, I untie the cord and slip it over my head and shoulder. After I've cinched it tight, the weapon hangs comfortably from my back. I reach back and take hold of the hilt. Easy to reach. I don't bother drawing it out. I've held swords before. My father even taught me the basics of using one. But I'm far from a samurai. Getting the weapon back into the scabbard won't be easy, and I don't feel like embarrassing myself. Odds are, if I have to take it out, I'll need it out for a while.

"Hey," Helena says from the bridge. "Hey! I think I can see it."

The crew filters into the bridge, heading for the front windows. The speck in the distance isn't hard to make out—it's the only thing that isn't blue. The object appears small, but three miles of perspective can do that. That we can see it at all from this distance tells me the thing is huge. Jakob looks through a pair of binoculars. I can see him frown even through the cloak of his gray beard. He passes the binoculars to me.

It's still too far to make out details like people, or serial numbers, but there is no doubt that Jakob hit the nail on the head. The cruise ship sits at the core of a large flotilla. They appear to be bound together somehow, forming some kind of megaship, with the largest vessels framing the cruise liner and the smaller ones lining the outside edge.

I scan the boats, looking for the green-hulled *Arctic Rainbow*. I find it near the front outer edge. It's a fairly large ship, added to the front of the pack. Something about the ship catches my attention. It's bobbing up and down. I focus on the *Arctic Rainbow*'s green hull and see a splash of white at the bow. Then another.

"Holy shit…"

I look at the other ships and find the same telltale flare of white surf.

"What is it?" Willem asks.

I lower the binoculars. "It's moving." I look at the sky, note the position of the sun, and then take the island-ship's direction. "Toward Greenland."

30

For fifteen minutes we watch the distant shape resolve into a megalithic merger of ships. It's a mix of private and commercial vessels, new and old, wooden, metal, and fiberglass, all connected by a web of cables, thick ropes, and anchor chains. The Draugar seem to have no preference for color, size, or style of ship. Even crew size appears to be a nonissue; some of the smaller fishing boats couldn't have had more than four crew. The end result is nothing short of monstrous. It's a floating city, and it absolutely dwarfs us. We're still five minutes from reaching the outer fringe, but the ships fill our view and even blot out the lowering sun.

We're going to be here overnight, I realize. The idea of facing Draugar is bad enough. Facing them in the dark is absolutely horrifying. Still, there's at least an hour of light left in the day. Maybe that will be enough.

Right. We're going to sink two thousand feet of ships in a single hour. We'd have an easier time getting the old gals at Saint Mary's Convent to have a wet T-shirt contest.

I pick up a pair of binoculars and take a fresh look. But everything's the same as it was fifteen minutes ago—a collection of ships, moving in unison, with not a soul in sight.

"Nobody's home," Klein says, lowering his own pair of binoculars. "Maybe they set it on a collision course and let it go?"

"Don't call her a cowgirl till you've seen her ride," Talbot says, twirling his mustache.

"What?" Klein asks.

"I think he's trying to say that looks can be deceiving," I say, pointing to the cruise ship. "Main deck. Starboard beam."

The figure—a woman I think, given the height and bulk around the hips—hasn't moved since I saw her. She might have been there the whole time or just arrived. But she's new to me.

"I see her," Klein says. "What's she doing?"

"Watching us," Jakob says.

"Like Nate," I add. "Evaluating us. They must know Nate is dead, but they might not know how many weapons we have. So the question is, do we take them by surprise or try to intimidate?"

"Intimidation worked for our ancestors," Willem says.

I remember Jakob's story about how the Norse raiders approached from the sea in ships made to look like dragons, banging drums and shouting war cries. Their enemies could hear and see them coming from a mile off. And often by the time they arrived at the village or monastery they were raiding, no one remained to put up a fight. Muninn and Torstein had used the same tactic on the island, and it had nearly worked. If Jakob, a fellow Norsemen, hadn't revealed the purpose behind their intimidation, I might have lacked the resolve to see things through.

"But these aren't monks," I say. "They're Draugar. I'm not sure we can intimidate them."

"Their hosts may not know fear," Jakob says, "but the parasites, as a collection, do. Remember how they shied away from the caves where they'd been entombed? And they fear you, the Raven who killed their Queen."

"One of three," I say.

"And if another resides on this ship?" he asks.

I don't answer, mostly because he might be right. I don't like the idea of the Draugar seeing me as a specific threat. I'd rather be a nobody—a nameless grunt—than the person who squished the Queen. If these things hold a grudge the way people do, then bringing us out here might be all about taking vengeance on me. And if that's true, every life lost is on my shoulders.

"If we hide our defenses, we might lure them in," Klein says. "Draw out the Queen."

"They're too smart," Talbot says. "They've been one step ahead of us, and quite frankly, I'm sick of taking a lickin'. I'm 'bout ready to dish one out."

"Captain?" I say to Jakob. "It's your call."

He looks me in the eyes. "You already know, Jane."

"Right. Viking assault it is." It's the right call, not because we'll intimidate the Draugar, but because it's so bold they'll never see it coming. Maybe. "What's our goal?"

"Sink the cruise ship," Willem says.

"Kill the Queen," Jakob adds.

"Hopefully both at the same time," I say. "And if we can, find out what the host is. That's not asking too much, right?"

"We could simplify it for you if it would help," Willem says, then grins. "Something like, fuck their shit up."

Willem manages to get a chuckle out of everyone, even Helena, who has remained silent.

"Humor in the face of certain death," I say. "What could be more Viking than that?" I glance out the window and see that we're just a minute or two out from the front edge of the ship-island. Time to get serious. "Klein, how fast are they moving?"

"Couple knots, tops," he replies.

"Can we move sideways safely at that speed?" I ask.

"Of course," Jakob says. "What are you thinking?"

I quickly detail my plan, which involves some skill, a fair amount of luck, and a shit-yourself big explosion, to the group, and despite the high level of risk involved, everyone is on board. After loading up on weapons and ammo, we conceal most of it under winter gear and head for the forward deck—everyone except Jakob, that is. He's at the wheel.

As we near the moving island, the whales transporting the *Raven* start turning the ship to port so that the starboard side of the ship will rest against the outer edge of the bound ships. I have no doubt they will then try to add the *Raven* to their collection. But the real problem is that if a wave of Draugar try to board the ship, we'll have a hard time defending the entire port side.

I stand at the front of the ship, watching our approach and slow turn. I'm wearing my cloak again, which sort of disgusts me after Nate wore it, but it helps obscure the sword—only the hilt can be seen, poking out of the cloak by my head. I have two handguns tucked into my belt behind my back and three spare magazines in my pockets, along with my Taser and knife.

Despite all being armed, we brandish no weapons, and have most hidden. The goal is to show no fear but keep our actual capabilities, or lack thereof, a secret. I'm sure more than a few of us would like to fly to Africa, find a nice patch of sand, dig a hole, and put our heads in it, but we manage to put on a respectable tough guy act. 'Course, it's not too hard when Willem, Helena, and Talbot are the real deal. Klein looks a little unsure of himself, which is understandable given that his toughest sparring partner is the occasional paper jam. And me? I'm not exactly a wuss, but I'm pretty frikken terrified right now. This is a fight I had hoped to never repeat.

I look out over the rail, judging our distance, speed, and rate of turn. *Close enough*, I think. I push a button on the radio I'm carrying. "Okay, Jakob, hard to starboard. Do it now!"

The ship begins to shift immediately as Jakob spins the wheel like a madman. The whales fouled the prop, but not the rudder. There's a thud as the heavy ship bumps into one of the whales below, but we're suddenly straight again.

"Hold on!" Willem shouts.

I grip the forward harpoon gun as we T-bone the ship-island. The first of the vessels we strike, a medium-size fishing boat, is split in two by the *Raven*'s ice-breaking double hull. But it manages to slow us down before we hit the two larger vessels beyond the first. With a shriek of metal, the *Raven* wedges between two slightly smaller industrial fishing ships.

When we come to a stop, I peek over the rail. *Perfect.* The decks of the fishing ships are six feet below the front deck of the *Raven*. Not only have we created an easily defensible bottleneck, but any Draugar attempting to board will have to overcome the six-foot climb first.

I've chosen Helena and Klein to stay behind. Helena is staying because she's still holding her ribs, which I suspect are broken. I might have a chunk missing from my leg, but it just hurts. Broken ribs can make moving in general tough but can also make it hard to breathe. Klein is staying because, well, he's a desk jockey, and we're going to be doing a lot of moving. Even old man Jakob is in better shape. But they may yet have the hardest job. If the Draugar take the ship, we're screwed. So they're probably going to have their hands full.

Jakob runs onto the main deck. He's got a shotgun in his hands, a spare gun in his pocket, and a sword hanging from his belt. The ship's keys jangle in his hand before he shoves them in his pocket. If we don't make it back, the *Raven* will become a permanent part of the flotilla.

"No horned helmet?" I ask with a mock frown.

Before he can reply, a booming voice echoes over the ocean. "*Hello* and *welcome* to the *Poseidon Adventure!*"

The hell? The woman is speaking through a megaphone with the exaggerated excitement of a grown-up Dora the Explorer.

"We hope you'll enjoy your stay with us and take part—"

I take a look through my binoculars. For the most part, she looks like any other poorly paid wannabe actress trying to make a living, except that her eyes are solid white. "She's Draugr," I say. "And not the Queen."

"—*three* pools, *fifteen* restaurants—"

"What are they doing?" Helena asks.

"Fucking with us," I reply. "Let's return the favor." I turn to Jakob. "Can you make the shot?"

He doesn't reply. Instead, he gets behind the harpoon gun and takes aim. The explosive head on this harpoon has been removed, but it will still be like shooting a mouse with a howitzer.

"—enjoy shuffleboard or any one of our five dance clubs—"

Choom! The harpoon exits the cannon as a blur trailing a long trail of white. Just when I think the line will go taut too soon, there is a loud, wet crack from up on the main deck of the cruise liner. Jakob has fired the harpoon with incredible accuracy, piercing the Draugr's chest and pinning it to the wall behind it. The line strung between the two ships will help prevent the whales from moving the *Raven* while we're gone.

With a shout, Jakob climbs over the rail and leaps down onto one of the fishing vessels. Willem follows with an impressive war whoop of his own. For a moment it feels silly. I'm not sure anyone is even watching. But then I hear them. Grunting, shrieking, and shuffling. The Draugar are coming, rising from the bowels of the surrounding ships.

Letting out a war cry of my own, I leap onto the fishing vessel behind Talbot and charge toward the cruise ship. The battle for the *Poseidon Adventure* is about to begin.

31

By the time we reach the hull of the *Poseidon Adventure*, there is nothing to climb and a seven-foot height difference between us and the third deck. Working together like we're part of some summer-camp team challenge, Jakob and Talbot hoist Willem and me up onto the ship's deck. I flop over the rail and fall to the deck, which is strangely cushy. Suspecting the truth about what I've landed on, I roll away fast, get to my feet, and look down into the eyes of a corpse.

It's a man. I can tell from the name patch on his coveralls—Rob—but there is little else I can glean. His limbs have been torn to shreds. Gnawed on. Eaten. His head is cracked open, and his brain extracted. He was probably consumed by his friends after they became Draugar.

Willem sees the body when he hops over the rail, but he only gives it a moment's glance. Then he's reaching back over the rail for his father. I move to help Talbot up but hear footsteps behind me. "Here it comes!" I shout, turning around to face the Draugr.

Correction: *Draugar*. Plural. They pour out of the main deck's doorway like clowns from a car. The only reason we're not immediately overrun is that most of them are severely injured in some form or another. Some have flesh wounds, but others are missing limbs, walking on broken legs, or have holes in them.

The crews of these ships didn't go down without a fight. *Good for them*, I think. But ultimately, they didn't stand a chance. Just like the four of us.

I draw one of the two handguns from behind my back and fire three quick shots. When three of the zombies drop to the deck with holes in their heads, I think, *At least my aim is still good.*

Six shots later, five more Draugar lie on the deck in a heap. I eject the magazine and let it fall to my feet before snatching a fresh one from my pocket and slapping it home. I rack the slide, chambering the first round. "Hurry up!" There are already more zombies than I can shoot. If not for their injuries and the pile of bodies now hindering their progress, I'd be overrun.

I squeeze off three more rounds, dropping two more Draugar. When the next two trip over their fallen brethren and fall to the deck, I chance a look back and see Talbot coming over the rail. The ship between us and the cruise liner is a medium-size freighter, its deck covered with a patchwork of red, yellow, and blue metal shipping containers. It's the second-largest ship in the floating island, its hull ten feet higher than our current position. It's going to take all of our summer-camp teamwork to scale the wall.

"Go ahead!" I shout.

"We're not going without you," Willem replies.

Jakob fires his shotgun four times. The *schuck-chuk-boom* of each pump-action shot is a satisfying sound, as is the resulting effect. Six more zombies drop, pinning the two that fell. But all he's done is bought Willem more time to argue with me.

"Go, Willem. Now!" I move away from him, around the bodies, firing off six more shots. Only three of the undead go down with this volley, but my goal is to distract more than kill. The emerging horde focuses on me as I reload my handgun again.

Just two more magazines and the second gun, I remind myself. At this rate, my ammo will be spent long before I reach the cruise ship. *If* I reach the cruise ship.

Willem moves to the starboard bow with Jakob and Talbot. None of them say a word. I've made my gamble, and like it or not, they need to see it through. As I head down the port side, I see Willem shoving Jakob up the side of the container ship. Jakob grabs the rail and is helped up by Willem shoving his feet from below.

They're going to make it, I think. A groan turns me around. Three zombies emerge from a side door, cutting me off. *They're not zombies*, I remind myself. *They're Draugar. They're smart.*

I fire at them, nearly point-blank. Their parasite-laden brains spray against the beige wall. "Not so smart now."

More shuffling feet and groaning voices emerge from the side hall. I'm not exactly Einstein right now, either. As though to confirm my assessment of my own mental capacity, Draugar round the corner on the deck ahead. The deck behind me is already thick with shambling men—a collection of men with blood-soaked beards, cold-weather gear, and vacant white eyeballs. And still more are approaching the exit just ahead.

I look over the rail and find the vessel below overrun with living dead, reaching up for me. A staccato burst of assault rifle fire pulls my eyes up. Klein has just mowed down a group of zombies trying to board the *Raven*. Even more are headed their way. The collective has targeted them as well. But that's not my concern. The horde about to tear me limb from limb is a much more pressing issue. One I can't possibly defend against.

So I don't. I tuck the gun into my waistband behind my back. With Draugar just feet away in every direction, I decide to follow the only path left available to me.

Up.

The deck above is just seven feet higher, less if I can get to the top of the rail. The port rail wobbles slightly as I climb it, and I nearly spill into the mosh pit of undead waiting below, but the rusty metal holds and I regain my balance. Channeling my inner Michael Jordan, I bend at the knees and spring up, reaching for the deck above. My hands clasp the freezing-cold lower rail of the upper deck, but now I'm dangling in front of the Draugar like meat in a butcher's shop.

I pull hard, loosening the cracking, bubbled yellow paint on the rail. A shower of sharp flakes falls onto my face, stinging my eyes. I clench my eyes shut and grunt as I swing a leg up onto the upper deck.

I'm going to make it, I think, pulling myself up more quickly. But then my lower leg is snagged. Something is pulling at it. I nearly lose my grip, but knowing I'll be torn to pieces if I fall inspires me to hold on tight. I kick out with my stuck foot and connect with something hard. But I'm not kicking a person who can be stunned, I'm kicking a Draugr that couldn't care less.

With one arm wrapped around the rail, I reach back for my gun and pull it out. When I turn to take aim, I see the Draugr that has me. He's a long-haired, thick-bearded fellow who looks like he should be hugging trees somewhere. Instead, he's hugging my foot. His mouth opens wide as he lunges forward. His jaws squeeze tight and his teeth grind, clamping down hard on my foot. Pain lances through my body, along with the knowledge that I might be a dead woman walking.

This is it. My worst fear made reality.

A Draugr. I'm going to be a Draugr.

And if that's true—if I'm infected with one of those parasitic bastards—the next shot I take will be through my own skull.

32

A lifetime spent with a limp is better than having to shoot myself in the head, so I lower the barrel of my handgun dangerously close to my foot and pull the trigger. The Draugr whose teeth are locked on to my foot goes limp, but his mouth doesn't open. Instead of trying to pull me down, his deadweight is hanging from me. But this time when I kick my foot, there isn't any resistance. My foot slides from his mouth, and I yank it up out of reach as the other zombies swarm together like two converging armies on the battlefield.

Out of reach, I cling to the rail above the throng and catch my breath. I search the top of my sneaker for punctures but find none. Draugar may be stronger than normal people, and immune to pain, but human teeth are human teeth, and they're not designed to cut through sneakers. I've escaped what I thought was certain death with some bruised toes.

I hear Willem's voice in the distance, barely audible over the moaning zombie din. "Jane!" He's on the deck of the container ship. He waves his arms at me. "We made it! Get moving!" He points toward the aft of my vessel. "Go! They're coming!"

A head floats into view at the back end of the second deck. The Draugar are using the exterior stairs to give chase. Fighting the urge to punt the first one down the staircase, I climb over the rail and run aft, as Willem wanted. At one of the two exterior entrances to the bridge, I open the door, intent on taking a shortcut to the ship's starboard side. What I find inside slows me down, not because it's trying to eat or infect me, but because the man inside is fully human.

The man—dressed in some kind of frilly pink and yellow cabaret outfit—cowers away from me. Then he must realize that I'm not here to kill him and shouts, "Go away! Leave me alone!"

"Who are you?" I ask, glancing back to make sure I'm not yet being followed. "What's your name?"

"Steven," he says.

I figure the guy is part of some kind of song-and-dance routine performed on the *Poseidon Adventure*. Either that or the crew of this ship was into some kinky shit. "You're from the cruise ship?" I ask.

He gives a furtive nod. "I'm a dancer."

"No shit," I say, looking at the flowery pom-poms billowing from his lower arms and legs. I reach a hand out to him and say, "Come with me if you want to live."

I nearly lay on a Schwarzenegger accent but hold back, which is good because the guy is already looking at me cockeyed.

"Seriously," I say, staring pointedly at the detritus surrounding Steven—wrappers, old water bottles, something gross I can't identify. I also catch a whiff of human waste. "I can tell you've been hiding here for a while, but you can't anymore. They're right behind me."

Steven looks terrified. "They—killed them. Killed them all. I—I can't."

Then I say the last thing this joker is expecting. "Suit yourself." I head for the door, yank it open, and leave without looking back. I've got bigger problems to deal with, and dragging around a guy dressed like a fly-fishing lure will attract all sorts of attention anyway.

Once outside the bridge, I look to the right and see what Willem was pointing at. A large anchor lies on the deck. The metal cable attached to it is strung from the top of the rail of this deck to the bottom of the container ship's main deck. I run to the anchor line and take a look back. With a gasp, I raise my handgun and nearly put a bullet in Steven's head.

"I can't believe you just left me!" he says with a whine that makes his outfit seem fitting.

Of all the people in the world I could have found hiding on this ship, it had to be a cabaret dancer! When I was a kid, the Colonel was roped into going to a Broadway show. Dragged me along for the ride. We both hated it—he was missing a football game and I was missing WrestleMania—and the whole way home he grumbled, "Fucking nancy dancers." The mantra confused me at the time, but Steven is helping me understand my father's severe annoyance. My father judged most people he met on how he perceived they would do on the battlefield. Dancers were near the bottom of his draft list, right along with beat poets, landscape painters, and just about everyone in Portland, Oregon, many of whom were my friends.

"Move," I say, shoving the guy to the side and pulling the trigger twice. The first round strikes the zombie that's farther away. It falls to the side, folds over the rail, and topples out of view. The second stumbles forward and falls facedown on the deck just a foot from Steven.

He shrieks and jumps back, but that reaction is nothing compared to what he does when he looks down and sees the softball-size exit hole blown in the back of the man's skull. Inside the hollow is a mash of brains and bone, but the flesh is moving—crawling with parasites. The white worms wriggle out of the dead body, searching for a new host.

Steven waves his hands in front of his chest, making a squeal like the sound I imagine a hyena makes while giving birth. He bounces on his feet like he's running in place and then leans over the rail and pukes his guts. But even that doesn't help, because he pukes right into the shredded face of a Draugr reaching up for him.

When he comes back up, Steven is still shrieking. How this guy survived surrounded by all these Draugar is beyond me. *Maybe he didn't*, I realize. *Maybe he's like Nate?*

"Let me see your eyes," I say, but he's in another world. There are more Draugar coming now. Time is short. So I do the only thing I can think of; I haul off and clock the guy in the face. Not hard enough to break anything, but I put enough pepper into the blow to knock the silly out of him. At least for a moment.

He holds his cheek and looks at me, tears in his eyes.

For God's sake.

I get a good look at his tear-filled blue eyes. No signs of a parasite, but that's how Nate started, too. "Have you been bit?"

His eyes widen. "Zombies! I knew it!"

I don't correct him, but I do point my gun at his head.

"No!" he shouts. "I haven't been bit!"

"Do you remember everything?" I ask, lowering the gun. "Have you had any blackouts? Any missing time?"

"No, nothing like that, I swear." He points at the turquoise design painted on the hull of the *Poseidon Adventure*. "I hid in the laundry room for two days. When things quieted down, I came here. Thought they wouldn't think to look for me here."

The first thing I realize is that Steven somehow thinks this is about him. Might be some kind of twisted survivor's guilt. But that's not what stands out the most. "You hid in a laundry room, and you're wearing this." I look over his outfit. "Why?"

With a huff, he tears off his frilly sleeves. "Happy?"

"Not in the slightest," I say. The sound of approaching Draugar grows louder. I hear the pop of gunfire in the distance. Assault rifles. Handguns. A shotgun. Chat time is over. "You know your way around the *Poseidon*?"

"Yeah," he says with a nod. "Been with the dance crew for three years."

I point my gun at him again and then waggle it at the chain stretched out between the ships. "Get moving."

He looks at the chain and then at the Draugar waiting below with fear-filled eyes. "I—I can't."

I sigh. "Go. Now. Or I'll shoot you in the knee and leave you here."

I think he's about to argue the point, but he proves himself to not be a complete idiot by moving to the anchor chain. Whether I shoot him or not, if he stays here for another minute, he's zombie food. While Steven works his way out onto the chain, dangling just a foot above the outstretched arms below, I target several Draugar coming at us.

Steven lets out a yelp every time I pull the trigger, but he keeps moving. By the time I slap in my last remaining magazine, he's halfway across. Despite his frail personality, he's lithe, muscular, and agile. With his legs wrapped around the chain, he pulls with his arms, sliding quickly across as deftly as any marine. If he wasn't gussied up like a peacock, the Colonel might even approve.

The chain is thick and will no doubt hold us both, so I tuck my gun into my pants, wrap my cloak over my waist so it doesn't hang down too low, and slide out onto the chain. Unlike Steven, I *have* done this before, and despite his head start, I make such quick time that I've nearly caught him by the time he reaches the container ship. Climbing aboard from the anchor chain is awkward but made easier when Steven helps pull me up.

"Thanks," I say, and then, "Shit!" I put my hand atop Steven's shaved head and push him down before jumping back. The lunging woman topples over Steven's back and face-plants on the steel deck with a crunch that I think must be her teeth.

Steven is quick to his feet, kicking away from the zombie-woman. His eyes look like they're about to explode out of his head, but his tightly pursed lips contain his scream—that is, until I take the woman's hair, lift her head up, and slam it into the deck over and over until I feel her skull give in.

With the nasty business finished, I turn back to Steven and find him gazing at me like I'm frikken Genghis Khan reborn. "Zombies, remember? No reason to hold back on the already dead."

"Yeah, but, couldn't you have just tossed her overboard or something?"

I glare at him. "I have anger issues. Plus, they've killed a lot of my friends."

This seems to strike a chord. His fear slips away, replaced by a scowl. "Mine, too."

Movement behind Steven catches my attention. A mob of Draugar lopes toward us. The way Steven's mouth drops a little when he looks over my shoulder tells me the situation behind me is similar. *The container ship is overrun*, I think, and then I notice that while I still hear the occasional rattle of automatic gunfire, I haven't heard a handgun or shotgun in a few minutes. *Did they make it off the ship, or were they overcome?*

"This way!" Steven says, proving useful. He's halfway up a ladder attached to the side of a six-foot-tall container. When he nears the top, he has to leap across to the ladder attached to the end of the container above, but he manages the jump with ease. I follow him up and slide on top long before the horde reaches us.

A field of containers stretches out before us. It's a vast flat space the size of a football field cut down the middle by a six-foot divide. Relief floods me as I see Willem, Jakob, and Talbot standing on the far side of the divide, but my elation is short-lived. They're not just standing there, they're waving at us. Frantically. And shouting something.

Run.

I look back and see at least fifty zombies barreling toward us, white eyes, white tongues, and all. And there are more coming, pouring out of the broken bridge windows above the containers. The worst part is that their formerly incoherent moaning has become a long, drawn-out word, spoken lustfully. "Jaaaane. Jaaane!"

33

Why do they have to make this personal? Fine. I killed one of the Queens. I get it. But why bother with the personal taunts? *They're afraid*, I remember. Of me. They're trying to freak me out. Make me screw up. If there is a Queen on board, it's probably aware of my progress. The question is, will the Queen find a hole to hide in, or will it fight to the end?

There's only one way to find out, of course, locate the Queen and kill it. Again.

To do that, I need to survive the next thirty seconds.

The horde closing in on us is moving quickly, but the living dead aren't exactly spring chickens. They're strong, sure, but a little less limber than they might have been in life. Of course, these Draugar are primarily seafaring blokes—sailors, fisherman, whalers, though I now see the occasional tourist mixed in—and many of them are seriously injured. In fact, it seems like most of them are injured. And I mean hacked, cut, or broken. Not just bites.

Where are all the people who just got bit and turned?

A question for another time. I'm about to tell Steven to run, but the flamboyantly clad man is already dashing across the field of containers, trailing a rainbow blur like a human Nyan Cat.

I give chase. The containers beneath our feet boom like war drums with each footfall but do little to drown out the incessant calling of my name.

Like a gazelle born to jump—or a dancer born to dance—Steven leaps out over the six-foot divide and manages to make it look good. Willem helps slow him on the other side.

"Jane!" The voice is right behind me. I don't look. Can't. A single misstep could cost me my life, and the gap is just ten feet away. I see Talbot raise his pistol—the peacemaker—so I expect the report. The high-pitched buzz of the bullet narrowly missing my head, not so much, but I hear a splat that sounds like a watermelon meeting its end at a Gallagher show and know that the nearest zombie has been dispatched.

And just in time. My injured leg protests as I leap over the divide, pulling a shout from my mouth. But then I'm airborne, soaring over a twenty-foot drop. I glance down and see a mob of Draugar. Their white eyes track my progress across the space, mouths open, tongues squirming, arms outstretched.

My foot falls short and catches on the container's side. Lunging with my arms, I pitch forward. Jakob is there. His big arms catch me, scoop me up, and deposit me back on the container in time to see the rushing horde fall into the gap like a waterfall of undead lemmings. Not one of them attempts to jump the divide.

Most fall straight over the edge, dropping atop the throng below. My ears fill with the sound of snapping bones and a wet splatter of skulls striking the deck below. Some of the Draugar are moving fast enough that they smash their faces against the metal container below my feet. One is even high enough that he attempts to clamp down on the container's edge, but his teeth shatter and he falls with the rest.

"They're intelligent," I observe. "But they're not quick."

"Must take them time to transmit thoughts," Talbot adds. "Makes 'em slow."

"But they're good at the long game," I say. "Maybe better than us."

"Then we stay unpredictable," Jakob says.

I think about the *Raven*. How we drove the ship into the side of the floating island and stormed aboard. We've got unpredictable down to a science.

With the immediate threat writhing on the deck twenty feet below, I turn to find Willem holding Steven at arm's length, holding the man by his throat.

"Who is this?" he asks.

"My *name* is Steven!" He squirms to get away but can't move. Steven might be cut and fit, but he's fairly small when compared to the big Viking historian.

"Wasn't talking to you," Willem says, tightening his grip. Steven winces and stops fighting.

"He's okay," I say. "A little too"—I wave my hands at the man like he smells foul—"you know. But he's not infected. No missing time."

"Why's he gussied up like my favorite lure?" Talbot asks.

"I'm a dancer," Steven says when Willem lets him go. He rubs his throat. "I worked on the *Poseidon*."

"Good," Jakob says. "He can show us around."

"What if I don't want to?" Steven asks. He's clearly not thrilled about my choice in raiding party companions.

Jakob levels his shotgun at Steven's stomach. "You don't have a choice."

"That's enough, macho men," I say, placing a hand on the shotgun and pushing it down. "He already doesn't have a choice."

Steven is about to complain, but I cut him off. "Look around, Tinker Bell, you're on a floating island populated by zombies in the middle of the North Atlantic. We're the only people for a hundred miles who have weapons and a boat that can get us the hell out of here."

His eyes light up at this news. I point toward the *Raven* as distant gunfire erupts. The black hull of the large whaling ship is easy to spot, as are the two people at its bow, cutting down a still-growing gathering of zombies. The bodies piling up below the raised hull will soon make a convenient ramp. We need to hurry.

But movement beyond the *Raven* catches my attention. The ocean is alive with whales, walruses, and porpoises. Untold numbers of them. Even if we do make it back to the *Raven*, I'm not sure we'll be able to escape.

"Look," I say, "whether or not Jakob here puts a round in your head, if you don't come with us, you're a dead man. Personally, I'd prefer the bullet to being eaten. Or becoming one of them. I'm not going to lie to you. Your odds of surviving the day"—I note the darkening sky—"or night are slim. But on your own, you're basically just a bedazzled snack."

I don't wait for him to show he's convinced. He really does have no choice. I head for the starboard side of the freight vessel.

"Can I at least have a weapon?" Steven asks.

I stop and look at the others. There's no way in hell any of them are going to give up their guns or blades. As a matter of fact, I won't, either. I dig into my pocket and pull out my Taser. "Just press the two metal prongs against the target and push the button." I depress the trigger and let him see the small arc of electricity.

"That's it?" he says with exaggerated abhorrence.

"Maybe you'd like a demonstration?" I ask, taking a threatening step toward him.

He raises his hands. "No, no. It's fine."

I hand him the weapon. "If you can, zap them in the head."

He forces a shit-eating grin.

34

Three minutes of climbing and zombie killing later, we reach the main deck of the *Poseidon Adventure* and climb over the rail. A vertical conga line of zombies is still ascending the ladder behind us.

"Where is everyone?" Willem asks.

The main deck is covered with a chaotic mass of deck chairs and the occasional bloodstain, but there isn't a Draugr in sight. Not even a body.

"They could be belowdecks," Steven says. "The *Poseidon* is easily big enough to hold everyone. They could just be sitting in their rooms, waiting for someone to come along."

"How do we get to the fuel tanks?" Jakob asks.

"Fuel tanks?" Steven repeats. A flicker of concern lights his eyes, but he answers. "Second deck. Amidships. But we have to pass through the passenger decks to get there. If I was right about the zombies being—"

Jakob nods. "Take us there—wait, take us to maintenance first. We need to pick up a few things first."

"You guys are crazy," Steven says. "You know that, right?"

"We're the only people here," I say, raising my eyebrows and offering an exaggerated nod that says something close to *No shit*.

He sighs and heads for a nearby hatch. "This way."

"Wait," Jakob says and points toward the ship's bow. "That way."

For a moment, I think Jakob is accusing Steven of leading us astray, but then I understand. He's thinking about the long game. If the Draugar can't figure out what we're up to, then they can't block us. Won't make much of a difference if Steven is right about the majority of zombies being belowdecks, which makes sense since we've only seen a few hundred tops.

Steven leads us to the bridge and opens the door, treating us to some raw evidence of the carnage wrought on the ship's passengers.

Intestines hang around the high-tech bridge like garlands. Dark brown splotches of old blood coat the computer systems, floor, and bridge windows, blocking the view. The smell is something like a sewer full of old pennies, which is actually a nicer way of saying shit and blood. Despite the gore, there isn't a single body. They've either been removed or just got up and walked away after the parasites tended to their ruined bodies.

Still, with zombies after us, who cares about the stench? Steven lets out a whimper but doesn't say a word. Jakob is the first to step inside, followed by me and Willem. Talbot gives Steven a little nudge. He's staying behind our guide, probably to make sure he doesn't bolt.

I turn back to Willem. "Lock the doors."

Willem quickly spins the locks on the thick metal door through which we entered. The six locking pins slide into place. Nothing short of modern explosives can get through the door now. Not even water. He tiptoes through the fleshy muck, slowly heading for the second door.

"The systems look like they're active," Steven says, and he's right, the bridge is lit up with blinking lights, glowing screens, and flashing sensors. With a splash of green, the bridge would look like Christmas in hell. "C-couldn't we just purge the gas tanks from here or something? There has to be a way we can strand the ships."

"We don't want to strand the ships," I say. "We want to sink them and kill everything on them." I pause. "Except for us."

Steven shrinks in defeat. There are probably a number of things we could do from the bridge that might hinder the Draugars' plans, but by how much? We don't even know what those plans are, and it's likely that the propulsion provided by all the other ships tethered together would be enough to carry the island on its merry way. No, the only direction we want these ships going is down.

Willem reaches the second door and quickly locks it. Just as he finishes, there's a loud *thump* on the first door. The small, thick glass window reveals a peeling, bloody face with white eyes. It can't get in, but it can see what we're up to.

"Move away from the rear door!" I whisper.

The group quickly moves.

"Act like we're interested in the ship's systems."

As the charade gets under way, I pick up a discarded shirt, tear it in two, and toss half to Willem. "Cover the door window." There's no way we can cover the forward-facing windows. They're huge. But they're also largely coated in dried blood, and unless the Draugar know how to rappel, I don't think it's a concern.

The banging on the door grows frantic. The man outside is missing more skin on his face than he has, and one eye looks partially deflated. He's hard to see thanks to the setting sun, but his face is caught in the glow of the bridge lights.

I'm not sure why, but I return the man's stare. *I see you*, I try to say with my eyes, *and I'm not afraid*. When a stiff breeze catches the man's comb-over, it pulls the flap of hair vertical. But it doesn't stop there; the skin of his skull lifts like a second comb-over. The image is ghastly but so ridiculous that I crack a smile.

The zombie reacts first by curling its lips in a snarl. Then it flings itself at the door, kicking and thrashing like a kid in a toy aisle who didn't get a Nerf Vortex Nitron Blaster. I flip the tantrum thrower the bird and tuck the shredded shirt behind a steel bar above the door. The shirt dangles down, covering the window.

The banging instantly stops.

Out of sight out of mind? I doubt it.

Probably working their way around to the other doors. Time to go.

Willem must be thinking the same thing. "This way?" he asks, pointing toward the open door at the back of the room.

Steven scrunches up his lips like he doesn't want to answer, but then he nods quickly.

Talbot takes the lead, sidestepping slowly toward the door. Standing next to the door frame, he takes a quick peek around it and then pivots in front of the door, raising his gun and scanning for targets. The maneuver is so rehearsed and natural that I remember the man was an honest-to-goodness Texas Ranger before he joined the UFO-loving Dark Side. He's done this before. Well, he hasn't stormed a ship full of zombies, but he's probably raided a home or two. Maybe a bank full of hostages. Or a drug factory.

"Talbot, take the lead," I say, then motion to Steven. "You next."

"M-me?"

I roll my eyes and step up behind Talbot. "Just tell us where to go."

"Take the stairs down three decks," he says. "That will put us just behind the theater." He gets a wistful look in his eyes. Then Jakob pokes him in the back with the barrel of his gun. "Okay, okay."

As we descend the red-carpeted staircase, the feel of the ship immediately changes. The exterior is all white and turquoise, like some kind of polished dinner plate. And the bridge is like the bridge of USS *Enterprise*—the starship, not the aircraft carrier, though the aircraft carrier probably looks similar, too. But the beige-and-red-striped wallpaper lining the walls, brass railings, and corny modern art lining the walls smack of Las Vegas.

At least the rug is plush, I think. It will muffle our movement through the ship.

At the bottom of the first flight, Talbot pauses and points to a gaudy-looking brass sconce. "Why're the lights still on? If they didn't want us in here, they shoulda shut off the lights."

My first thought is that he's right and we must be walking into a trap, but then I remember the cave. We were freezing and afraid, Jakob, Willem, Chase, and me. That night, in the pitch-black of the cave, a man named Jackson—a Draugr—came in after us. But he couldn't see us. He nearly drooled a parasite into my mouth, but in the dark, he was as blind as the rest of us. "They can't see in the dark," I say. "Even if they take a mammal that can see in low light, they inhabit the eyeballs. They can't improve their vision, which is as limited as ours."

Talbot accepts the answer and starts down the stairs once more.

When the staircase ends two flights down, Steven says, "We're on the fourth deck, just behind the showroom. We can go around or through the showroom, cut through the duty-free shops, and take the main stairway down to the second deck. One of the maintenance shops is toward the bow end of that deck, so we'll have to backtrack a little, but I'm pretty sure we can access the maintenance tunnels there, too, which will get us to the gas tanks."

I hear the "but" coming before he says it. "But?"

"You can't just walk in there. Unless the door was left open, which I suppose is possible, 'cause, you know, we'll need a maintenance crew or senior crew keycard to unlock the door."

"Any idea on where to find one?" I ask.

"Well I'm sure there are more than a few zombies carrying them around," he says.

At first I think he's joking, which pisses me off, but then I realize he's not. "Fuck."

"What about the captain's quarters?" Willem asks. "He must keep a spare."

Jakob nods at this. "He'd be a fool not to."

Steven shakes his head. "Captain's quarters are on deck three."

Jakob's eyebrows rise. "The captain spoils himself."

Steven smiles and gets that wistful look again. "He spoils everyone he likes."

I clear my throat. "We'll try to find a card on the way. If that doesn't pan out and the door isn't already open, we'll worry about getting up to Captain Happy Tappy's quarters." I'm about to give the go-ahead when I see Talbot cock his head to the side. "What is it?"

"Music," he says. "I think."

We all listen. I hear something, but it's indistinct. Muffled through walls. Steven, on the other hand, lights up. He's about to speak when a loud squeak drowns out the distant music.

Talbot points up the stairwell, then shushes us with a finger to his lips. He leans out over the rail and turns his head up.

The door above squeaks loudly again, and then slams shut. Talbot holds out his index finger and mouths the words, "One person."

An electric whirring sound comes from above as something rumbles over the rug. I can actually feel the floor shaking beneath me. Whoever it is, they've eaten one too many Twinkies, or maybe people. I join Talbot at the rail, looking up, hoping to see something that indicates whether we're dealing with a Draugr or human. The latter seems unlikely, but if Steven can survive, it's possible that there are other survivors on board.

A hand grips the rail two floors up. The fingers, which sport chipped ruby red nails, are grotesquely fat and bloated. They look ready to split, like overcooked sausages. The head slides into view, peering over the rail with white eyes. The woman's pushed-in nose and flaccid jowls remind me of a bulldog. She's wearing layers of old makeup, but is strangely blood-free. Her blond hair dangles from twin ponytails—what a past boyfriend referred to as handlebars, because men can't resist riding a girl with ponytails. But I'm pretty sure he'd change his mind if he ever had a look-see at Chubby Cheeks here.

Shit.

But the Draugr reacts to our presence with a wet-sounding rasp. *Why isn't she attacking?* I wonder. Because she doesn't have to. Every Draugr on board, on the surrounding vessels, or swimming around the island inside hijacked marine mammals has just seen what this one has seen. We won't be alone for long.

I'm about to bolt when Handlebar Helga starts twitching her head up and down.

The hell?

With each upward motion, the undead woman makes a sound that's one part belch, one part frog croak. Thinking of frogs, I notice her triple chin growing larger. It's expanding like a balloon.

"That gal's been rode hard and put away wet," Talbot says.

I barely hear him. "Look out!" I shout, jumping away.

But Talbot doesn't move. He just stares straight up, captivated by the horrible sight. There's a retching sound, followed by a pop. Talbot only has time to widen his eyes before a blob of fat, bloody, and maggoty parasites drops onto his face.

35

My mind recoils from what's just happened. It ranks near the top of Jane Harper's nastiness chart. The fat zombie actually launched a parasite-laden projectile formed from its insides. The softball-size glob splattered when it struck Talbot, sending dollops of wriggling fat to the rugged floor at my feet, but most of the viscous stuff burst all over the cowboy's face. It's in his eyes. His nose. His mouth. His mustache is thick with the stuff.

At first, his reaction is similar to someone who's just gotten a pie in the face. He scrapes the goo from his eyes with his fingers and spits out a wad.

He's already dead, I know, but he hasn't quite realized it yet. Whatever parasites reached his face would have wasted no time wriggling inside him.

"Talbot..." I say.

I don't know if it's the despair in my voice or the feel of parasites beneath his fingers as he rubs the gunk from his face, but his movements become frantic. "Shit! Shit!" He removes his jacket and uses it to roughly scour the remnants of the fat-bomb from his face. When he stops, he looks like himself again, though his skin now has an oily sheen.

He looks sick when he looks at us again. "Knew my curiosity would git me killed someday." He winces. "I can feel 'em in there. Diggin'."

He raises the peacemaker, and I think he's going to shoot himself.

"I can do that for you," Jakob says. And I know he can. He shot his oldest friend, Alvin, to prevent him from becoming a Draugr.

Talbot gives a nod. "I reckon you could, but that's not how I'm gonna leave this world."

A spasm racks his body. The parasites work quickly. It won't be long before he's just another mindless zombie. Well, not quite mindless. Some tortured part of him will remain, but he'll also be part of the collective. He stands and looks up the stairwell.

There's a whir of an electric motor. The door above squeaks. The lard-spewer is leaving.

Talbot starts up the stairs.

"What are you doing?" I ask, wondering why he doesn't want to be killed. It's a strange way to think, but the alternative is far worse.

Talbot stops at the top of the first staircase. "I'm gonna kill the sombitch. Next time you see me, Raven, you put a bullet in my brain. No hesitation. You put me down."

I give a nod, and he's charging up the next flight of stairs, off to exact his vengeance before he becomes one of the enemy.

"Let's go," I say, turning to Steven.

"That's it?" He looks aghast. "Your friend is about to become *one of them*, and you're all, 'Let's go?' How can you be so—"

I slap him. Hard. I don't know if it knocks some sense into him, or out of him, but it shuts him up. "When you've seen your friends come back from the dead, talked to their severed head after it's been transplanted onto a thousand-year-old body, or watched someone you know sacrifice themselves—then you can bitch about my response to it. Until then, you can shut the fuck up."

A glimmer of blue light catches my attention. The little bastard is thinking about Tasing me. "Let me make this clear for you. If you're not with us, you're against us. And if you're against us, you're with *them*. And if you're with them…"

Jakob brings the point home by pumping his shotgun.

"You people are insane," Steven says.

I've got a thousand quips lined up, most of which insult his masculinity or make me look crazier, but I keep them to myself. Silence is the best kind of intimidation.

Steven sighs. His shoulders slouch. "Fine."

Willem opens the door slowly and peeks into the plush hallway on the other side. Wall-to-wall blue Oriental rug stretches down the hall, which is lit by recessed lighting in the ceiling. A few blood-streaked handprints mar the yellowish walls and the railings that stretch down the hall, but the space is empty, which begs the question, Where is everyone? This place should be swarming.

No one has an answer, so we push forward into the hall. When the door closes behind us, the pressure changes and the music we heard earlier comes through more clearly. It's a mix of horns and an up-tempo beat, like a combination of big band music and salsa.

Steven stops, straightening. He recognized the music before but forgot about it when fatty-bo-batty showed up.

"The cabaret!" he says with a gasp. "They must be okay!"

He rushes past Willem and sprints down the hall.

"Steven!" I hiss at him, afraid to yell and draw attention. But there's no stopping the man. He passes ten open doors and two hallways without incident before turning right.

Willem, Jakob, and I stand still. We share glances at each other.

"Should we leave him?" I ask.

"He's not giving us much of a choice," Willem says.

"We might need him," Jakob says.

I can't fathom a reason why we'd need Steven beyond his being our guide, but even that might not be necessary. "I remember his instructions for reaching the second deck, and those are everywhere." I point to a black plastic diagram of the ship mounted at the intersection ahead of us with a big You Are Here posted toward the front of the ship.

Jakob gives a slow nod. "We might need to find a keycard."

Right. Damn keycards. "Fine. Let's get him. But if he runs again, I'm letting him go."

Jakob just continues his nod.

A closer look at the large map reveals that the hall we're in abuts the showroom. I point at it. "That's where the music is coming from. So who's putting on a show?"

As is often the case, no one has an answer to the question. The answer lies fifty feet ahead, down a hall to the right, and then what? The map isn't that detailed.

"Let's go," Willem says, taking the lead. As he walks ahead of me, my eyes are drawn to the big ax slung over his shoulder. None of us have had to use our melee weapons yet, but we've got to be getting close. No time to count rounds, though. It'll be pretty obvious when I run out of ammo.

Jakob must have been thinking along the same lines because I hear him reloading the shotgun behind me. Five shells go in. "That's all of them," he announces.

We round the corner and face a nearly identical-looking hallway. No wonder there are maps everywhere. The only difference between this hall and the last is a set of double doors at the end and a small glassed-in ticket booth embedded in the wall. A velvet rope that had hung between two brass poles now lies on the floor, possibly unclipped by Steven. One of the double doors is slowly closing. A loud salsa beat booms from the opening.

I rush forward, ignoring Jakob's and Willem's hushed complaints. Just as the air cylinder slowing the door's progress gives up the fight, my hand stops it from slamming shut. I open it slowly as the Latin beat washes over me. I'm not sure the slamming door would have been heard over the din coming from the showroom, but I didn't want to risk it. I kick down the doorstop and let go slowly. The door remains open.

Doors line the opposite side of the wide hall beyond, one every fifteen feet. The door farthest from us on the left is wide open. Beyond the open door, the hallway angles to the right, destination unknown.

I point to the open door and then head for it, gun leading the way. The soft rug and blasting salsa music make my approach silent. Mimicking Talbot's breech technique, I take a quick peek through the door. The room isn't a room. It's a box seat. The chairs are gilded with gold paint and upholstered with maroon velvet. This is where the rich and introverts sit. Steven's standing just a few feet in front of me.

I move forward slowly and tap Steven's shoulder with the barrel of my gun. He turns with a start but manages to not squeal or wave his hands about.

He's got a big manicured smile on his face. "Isn't it wonderful?"

Wonderful? I step up next to him and take in the showroom. I can barely see the heads of the audience below, but the bright light blooming from the stage reveals the tops of their heads. It's a full house. Well, except for the box seats. We seem to be the only ones with a privileged view of the show.

There are dancers onstage, all dressed in outfits matching Steven's, kicking their legs and strutting their stuff. The music—a recording synced with the frantic light show—blares. I can feel the bass kicking my chest. If I liked this sort of thing, I'd say they're doing a pretty good job. But I don't, so I focus on answering the nagging question repeating in my head in time with the beat. *What. The. Fuck?*

Steven grips my arm. "Isn't it marvelous?" The only thing that keeps me from slapping him again is the fear of being found out, and even taking that into consideration, it's a close call. Someone really needs to beat the perpetual optimism out of him before he gets himself killed.

Steven gasps and his grip tightens as he whispers, "Shamaya!"

Too late.

The woman in question twirls onto the stage, where she's surrounded by the female dancers. While she spins in one direction, kicking out her leg with each twirl, the ring of women twirl around her in the other direction. The choreography and timing are all perfect.

Steven gazes at the woman. He's clearly smitten with her, which is surprising because I'd pegged him as batting for the other team.

"The show must go on," he whispers.

No, actually, it doesn't. And it shouldn't be.

The music reaches a crescendo. The lights focus on the dancers, who suddenly stop, frozen in place with near-impossible precision. And then, as one, they bow. The show has ended, and some part of my brain knows the audience is about to erupt into uproarious cheers and clapping, but only one person does—the idiot standing right next to me.

36

Steven's clapping slowly fades along with this smile as he realizes his error. A loud shuffling sound rises from below as the audience of three hundred collectively shifts to get a look at Steven and me. I quickly motion for Willem and Jakob to step back, hoping they won't be seen. But it's too late for me. I can feel six hundred eyes staring at me.

No, more than six hundred. There is no doubt in my mind that everyone in the audience is already Draugar. That means there are actually tens of thousands of eyes looking at me, but they might as well be one giant eye. The collective sees me. The Queen sees me.

The women onstage stand up straight, arms slack by their sides.

"Shamaya," Steven says, and I sense he's about to take action.

"Look at her eyes," I say. "It's not her."

With the dance complete and the well-lit dancers looking straight at me, it's now easy to see their white eyes.

"She's dead," I say.

With a quivering lip, he relents. "Okay…" He looks at me. "Okay."

I'm about to drag Steven out of the box and bolt, when a voice stops me. "Jane? Jane, is that you?"

It's a woman's voice. I recognize it but can't place it without a face. A woman steps up from the front row and climbs the steps onto the stage. She turns my way and puts a hand over her eyes. The shadow cast by her hand hides her face, but mine is still clearly visible. "It is you! How have you been?"

How have I been?

The woman places her hands on her hips, revealing her face—Diane Simmons. The captain of Greenpeace's *Arctic Rainbow*.

"Diane?" I say. I really had no intention in engaging in conversation, but I'm caught off guard by her appearance and natural demeanor.

"She's got white eyes, too," Steven points out.

"I can see that," I whisper back.

"I'm impressed you made it this far," she says. "But I'm glad you did."

Unlike Steven, Diane really does bat for the other team. She's smart, funny, and most guys find her attractive, but she's got more love for whales than she does for the less fair sex. Me, on the other hand…She had more than eyes for me. She had hands, too. I could have slapped her with a sexual harassment suit, but I couldn't bring myself to damage Greenpeace's reputation. Not because of the whales, but because it would have affected a lot of friends. So I took care of things Jane Harper style. Just a single broken finger, and we came to an understanding. Even managed to work together afterward. And when she spoke to me, all of her poorly concealed attraction was absent.

Now, that tinge of longing has returned to her voice, along with some not so subtle words. "I missed you, babe. Why don't you come down here?"

"Thanks," I say. "I'll pass."

She shrugs. "Heard about that mess in the Arctic. Did you really do all those awful things I've heard about?"

I squint at her. "What did you hear?"

"Jane," Willem whispers from behind. "We should go."

I casually extend my index finger, indicating that I want a minute. The wise thing would be to run and not stop, but I've got a feeling about something.

"All those poor people, dead. Murdered." She frowns. "You killed them, didn't you? Thousands of them."

And there's the switch. We're no longer talking about people. We're talking about the parasites. If they value each and every parasite with the same worth that humans place on each other, I'm probably viewed with the same level of abhorrence as Adolf Hitler. I not only killed thousands of them, but I also killed the Queen.

"You don't need to reply," she says. "We remember." I sense a shift in her gaze. "We don't remember him, though."

The cabaret dancers onstage reach out to Steven in unison. "Why don't you come join us onstage? Lead the next act."

Steven follows my lead and stays silent. It's a good thing, too, because he's only got one more strike—and then I'll shove a parasite down his throat so I don't feel guilty when I put a bullet in his head.

"No? Too bad," Diane says. The dancers lower their arms, frown, and cock their heads to the side. "I've been trying to understand your culture. The memory is there, experienced by thousands, but seeing things for myself provides a true experience. I must admit, I find your species confusing."

She raises a hand, indicating the stage. "This...spectacle is—what would Jenny say? Effing horrible."

She's at least 150 feet away. It's a hard shot, but there's no wind and she's out in the open. When the time comes, I'm going to take off her head. Not because she's taunting me, but because I know now that she's the Queen.

There's no hesitation in the way she speaks. She says, "I," not "we." The hive mind might think as one, but the Queen is the core, the force that binds a million different tiny minds into one entity. The problem is that once the host is dead, the Queen can leave and take up residence in any of the hundreds of people in the showroom.

"Have you come to fulfill your promise, Queen Harper?" Diane asks. "The offer still stands." But she doesn't wait for an answer. "No, of course not. You're here to kill me. That's what Malik tells me, anyway," she says.

I hear motion behind me, and Willem whispering, "Father, no."

Truth is, hearing Malik's name has me on edge, too. The only silver lining is that Malik was taken before I came up with our suicide mission. Doesn't seem likely that we'll get to see it through, but we'll still be hard to predict.

Diane turns toward the audience. "Malik, why don't you come out here where Jane can see you?"

Dear God, no.

When Malik appears onstage, his loping walk has been replaced with a prance. He's walking on his toes, like a ballerina. He's still dressed in his coveralls and cold-weather jacket. His steel-toed work boots thump across the stage. His hair is as shaggy as ever, and his beard looks like a fuzzy pom-pom below his chin. But the personality of the big fisherman is nowhere to be seen.

Which makes my next act a hell of a lot easier.

I raise my handgun, look down the sight, and squeeze the trigger until all the rounds are spent. Four bullets zing across the open space of the showroom. The first catches a dancer in the knee and sends her to the stage floor without even an expression of pain. The second shot finds only wood. But the third shot catches Malik in the chest, and the fourth shot finds my intended target—his head.

The big man drops to the stage in a heap, falling at Queen Diane's feet. Without a word, she crouches down by Malik's body. She reaches out to his mouth, props it open, and then inserts her hand. A writhing column of white rises from his mouth, covering her arm and rising to her shoulder. When it reaches her mouth, she opens it and allows the mass of homeless parasites to enter the refuge of her body. When the parasitical rescue mission is complete, she stands and says, "Still have that fiery temper, I see."

"Fuck you," I say, no longer able to stay silent. "I am going to kill you. Every last one of you wriggling little bastards."

She grins like she knows better, and I nearly draw my second pistol. But it would be a waste of bullets. I shot Malik to set him free. I owed him that much. Shooting Diane won't kill the Queen, and Diane can wait a little longer for her freedom. Doesn't stop me from returning a verbal volley of my own, though. "You're insignificant. Lower life-forms. Incapable of surviving without hosts. You're weak. Pitiful. And I'm going to stomp each one of you little shits to paste beneath my foot."

Diane opens her mouth to speak, but I cut her off. "And when I find you—and I swear to God in heaven that I will find you—I'm going to wrap my hands around your wriggling limp body and squeeze until your brains spray from your beady black eyes and your guts burst from your tiny little mouth. You remember that, too, don't you? When I killed your sister."

Her face contorts like she's about to retch her rescued brethren all over the stage. The noise that emanates from below is something resembling a scream, but it sounds a little more like a roar.

I shout over it. "And when I'm done with you, I'm going to find sister number three and make it a triple play. You're never going to find the host."

When those last two words leave my mouth, the screaming stops. The showroom goes silent, aside from Steven's rapid-paced breathing. The lights come on, burning my eyes. The first thing I see is the resplendent decor. It's a facade, but all of the red and gold makes the place look like an authentic Victorian-era opera house.

The audience, however, is the stuff of nightmares.

Not only are they white-eyed Draugr. Not only are they staring directly at me. Not only are their voices rising as one into an ear-splitting screech. But they're also children. Each and every one of them. The youngest is maybe three. The oldest perhaps a tweenager.

"They're kids," Steven says. "They're all kids." He slowly backs away from the edge of the box, shaking his head. Not one pair of white eyes tracks his movements.

I stay rooted in place, looking at all the little faces staring up at me. In the war of offenses between species, the Draugar have just crossed the line. Not just because they turned the children, but because I'm not sure if I can kill a kid, even if it's not really a kid anymore. Not up close and personal, anyway. I don't think my psyche could recover from that. That said, I still have no trouble sinking the ship. The kids deserve to be set free, and billions more are at risk if we don't stop them here and now.

As one, the children scream, launch themselves from their seats, and charge toward the exits at the rear of the showroom. Their feet echo like thunder, rolling through the showroom. I take one last look at Diane and find her staring at me, blank-faced and white-eyed like one of the aliens in *They Live*.

Where's Rowdy Roddy Piper when you need him? I think, and then run from the box.

Back in the hall, Willem stands at the far end by the door, holding it open. "C'mon," he shouts. His eyes go wide. "Hurry!"

I can hear them before I see them. The rumble of three hundred small feet grows loud behind me. I glance back when I reach the door and see a writhing wall of child-size Draugar closing the distance. Willem slams the door closed behind us, and Jakob is already waiting with one of the brass poles used to hold the velvet cord. He slides it through the door handles, just as the horde pushes on the other side. The doors flex and creak, but hold. Had the mob been adult Draugar, the result might have been different.

We've turned to flee down the hall when a new sound pricks my ears. It's barely discernible above the pounding on the door—the electric whir of a motorized cart.

Talbot's mission of revenge ended in failure.

Chunka Love is back.

37

The motorized cart slides into view at the end of the hall. It's black and expensive looking, though the front is marred by blood and chunks of dried flesh—probably from plowing through corpses littering the floor. Not that we've seen any bodies, but they're here somewhere. The whirring engine sounds strained, like it's been worked too hard, too long.

Please let the battery die, I think, but then I realize she's blocking our path.

The doors behind us shake violently, but the improvised lock holds.

When the woman comes fully into view, my stomach knots. Her heavily made-up face and blond handlebars were bad enough. But she's completed the look by wearing a tight pair of hot pink short shorts that show off her cottage-cheesy, spider-veined legs. But the shorts are almost completely hidden by her unbridled belly, which hangs down from the bottom of a too-tight T-shirt like a loose curtain of skin. In fact, the skin is so loose that I suspect she's been using her belly fat to hock up parasite bombs like the one that got Talbot.

For a moment, I wonder why the parasites would alter a human being in such a way, but then realize that not one of us has moved an inch since she blocked our path. Shock is the secret to her success.

Beep, beep, beep. The electric cart chimes as the Draugr-woman completes a three-point turn so that she's facing us.

When I see her neck bulging, I snap out of my trance. "Look out!" I shout, shoving my three compatriots through the open door to our right.

I hear a hocking pop and then a wet thud. I jump at the sound and spin around. A large blob of what looks like Crisco mixed with ketchup and maggots slowly slides down the glass of the ticket booth. I can barely see the fat lady beyond, but she's growing larger.

Not larger. Closer.

The whir of her electric cart is like fingernails on a chalkboard.

"Stand back," Jakob says. He steps out into the hall and fires off four shotgun rounds. Sparks spray as many of the pellets ricochet off the cart. Gore splatters against the hallway walls as the body is shredded.

I peek out into the hall as the smoke from Jakob's barrage clears. For a moment, I think he's managed to actually take the Draugr's head clean off. A wet hacking says otherwise. The head isn't missing, it's tilted back, protected by the thing's girth.

Jakob pumps the shotgun, preparing to fire his last two rounds, but I grab his arm and yank him back inside the ticket booth. The Draugr's head springs up and fires a fatty wad, which sails just past Jakob's head and strikes the locked double doors. The wet splat against the doors seems to enrage the horde of tiny Draugar on the other side.

She's not trying to kill us, I realize. *She's just slowing us down.*

The doors shake loudly, and I chance a look. The wad struck the pole, tilting it slightly and coating it with slick fat. As the door shakes, I see the pole shift.

Jakob was never her target.

The throaty gurgle repeats as the Draugr prepares to catapult a fresh wad of raw nastiness.

"We need to stop it," I say. "Before it opens the door."

"How?" Steven asks. "He just shot the shit out of it and only managed to spring a few leaks."

A wet pop signifies the firing of a projectile. It slams against the door with a rattle of metal. I expect the doors to swing open and the ticket booth to swarm with pint-size Draugar, but the woman starts hocking up fat.

I look at her through the glass. Her stomach convulses in waves as the loose material is gathered from her prodigious reserve and moved into her sack-like under-chin.

"We'll do it the old-fashioned way," I say. I step up to the door, tense as I prepare to spring into action.

"Jane..." Willem says with growing concern.

Jakob mimics his son's tone, saying, "Raven..."

I ignore them and glance through the window one more time. She's just ten feet from the booth but still focused on the door. If she hits it just one more time, we might all be screwed. I'm determined to not let that happen. It's going to take a sacrifice, though.

The pouch of flesh beneath her chin goes suddenly taut like a bullfrog's vocal sac as it fills with liquid fat. *Any second now.* I pull the hood of my cloak up over my head.

The Draugr cocks its head back slightly. Its jaw drops open. The neck flexes.

Here it comes!

I leap into the hallway, turn my back to the Draugr, and flare open my cloak, filling the hallway with a black shroud. I catch a glimpse of the double doors, which are still shaking.

The pole holding them shut is about to slide free. "The doors!" I shout.

I cringe as a fleshy *pop* fills the hall. The impact nearly knocks me over, but Jakob catches me. Willem runs out behind him and heads for the door. He pushes the post back in place with his foot. The fat- and parasite-covered metal is too dangerous to touch with a bare hand.

After freeing the button on my cloak, I let it fall to the floor. It drops fast, pulled down by the weight of the fat now clinging to it.

When the hocking sound begins anew, I turn to face the Draugr. The waves of flesh undulate over her body even faster than before. She knows what's coming. The collective knows what's coming. It's not the first time we've done this dance.

I reach back and take hold of the samurai sword's handle. The metallic *zing* of the blade sliding free of the scabbard drowns out the banging on the doors and the hocking Draugr. The sound focuses me.

Gripping the handle with two hands, I raise the blade to the right of my head. I cover the distance between me and the obese Draugr in three strides. With a quick horizontal swipe of the *katana*, I slit the expanding sac lengthwise. Chunky lard, full of clam-like globs, slides out of the sliced flesh and fills the air with a scent something like dead fish and skunk ass. It looks like someone cut open a really big, spoiled crab rangoon and squeezed out the filling.

With its only weapon disabled, the Draugr's chubby digits work the cart's tiny joystick. *Beep, beep, beep.* I have no trouble keeping pace. She stops when I lower the sword tip in front of her face.

Knowing the Queen can see and hear me through this woman, I meet her parasite-filled eyes and say, "Every last one of you."

A quick jab puts the woman out of her misery and seals the fate of the several thousand parasites occupying her body.

The banging on the door stops just long enough for me to hear Diane screaming in anger, her voice echoing in the showroom beyond the double doors.

While I wipe my blade off on the clean side of my discarded cloak, Willem hops away from the doors. The pole is back in place. "I'm not sure how long that will hold," he says. "It's pretty slick." He gets a look at the now-dead Draugr and scowls.

We faced an oversize Draugr once before. There was no fat left on his formerly obese body, but after a long soak in the ocean, his folds of loose skin became supple once more...just before peeling free of his body and covering me like a blanket. "Remind you of Captain Loose Skin, too?"

He nods. "I wonder if he used the same technique on our ancestors."

"A mystery to be solved hopefully never," I say before working my way around the portly corpse. When we're all in the clear, I turn to Steven. "Which way?"

He looks shaken. I'm sure he's about to marvel at our blasé response to dispatching this hideous woman, so I take his arm with my left hand and squeeze. "None of this would have happened if you hadn't clapped."

"I thought they were—"

"I don't give a damn what you thought," I say. "From now on, if you want to live through this, you don't think. You just do what we tell you. Agreed?"

"Yeah. S-sure."

"Now," I say, "Which way?"

For a second I'm afraid I'm going to have to remind him where we're going, but then he points to the right and says, "We can reach the duty-free shops this way. Go through the employee entrance.

But if they know the ship as good as the people they've…possessed, then they could already be there."

I'd really rather not face down a Draugar horde, but I say, "That's a chance we're going to have to take. Just try not to break into a dance routine or flag down any friends."

He looks down at his feet for a moment. If he's crying, I swear I'm going to nut-shot him and find my own way. But then he catches me off guard by saying, "Thanks. For everything. I'd be dead several times over by now if it wasn't for you."

I appreciate the gesture, but this isn't the time for a Dr. Phil breakthrough. "Glad you've had an epiphany, but I'd like to not be here when the man-eating children break through those doors, so get a move on, Strawberry Shortcake."

With a sheepish smile, Steven leads us to the duty-free shops.

38

"We're here," Steven says, stopping by a door that's labeled "Employees Only," which seems like a no-brainer because the entrance to this hallway had a similar label. "This is one of four duty-free shops. It's connected to one of the others, which is close to the main atrium. That's the way we want to go."

When we respond with silence, he grows nervous and says, "You're going first, right?"

I step up to the door with a sigh. "We need to have a chat about chivalry."

"We are being chivalrous," Willem says with a slight grin. "Ladies first."

After giving him a well-deserved middle finger, I lean into the door's push handle and open it slowly. The door is well oiled and doesn't make a sound. With just enough room to fit my head through, I take a look. The duty-free shop is a well-designed space with lots of curved walls and oval compartments, each of which displays a different type of product. There are necklaces, sunglasses, perfumes, soaps, and hats—all brand-name, all costing a small fortune. The ceiling is a series of square mirrors that reflect the gleaming hardwood floor and splotches of light provided by ample recessed bulbs. But the most wonderful sight inside the duty-free shop? It's completely devoid of Draugar.

I step inside and motion for the others to follow. I haven't seen the entire shop, so I place a finger to my lips, indicating the need for stealth, which really goes without saying at this point. But you never know when fancy-pants Steven will decide to announce our presence. If there's a surprise in the next room, I want to see it first.

While tiptoeing to the break between sections, I catch the scent of something foul. It's nothing compared to the stench wafting off the obese Draugr woman, but it smells worse than the unwashed hippies I worked alongside on the *Sentinel*, and that's no small feat. I hold out my hand to the others. The effect is like a Gorgon's stare. Willem, Jakob, and Steven freeze in place, spread out in a single-file line.

I slide up to the entryway and slowly poke my head around the door frame. The next room is full of designer clothing hanging on racks. Looking out over the space, I can't see a thing, but the eau de death persists. Motion catches my attention, but not from ahead.

It's above.

I look up and see it. A lone Draugr. It stands on the far side of a clothing rack, shifting back and forth. Its small stature makes me think it's one of the children, but then I see the gray, wispy hair and age spots pocking the scalp beneath. It's an old man.

Beyond him I can see the wide-open hallway that leads to the atrium. Despite there being a Draugr waiting in the other room, his appearance doesn't bother me nearly as much as the otherwise complete lack of undead. *Where the hell is everyone?* I find it hard to believe that with three thousand people available, this entire ship wouldn't be swarming with savages seeking us out.

But all is quiet, and the only Draugr standing watch over the area leading to the showroom is Grandpa Munster. Sure, he's got a shield of children to protect him, but—

A pattern emerges.

The young and weak.
The old and frail.
The obese and incapable.
The severely wounded.

These are the Draugar we've encountered thus far. Why? Are they protecting the more healthy and uninjured people for some reason?

And because our path isn't blocked by a horde of children or undead geriatrics, I think it's safe to assume that their endgame is still a mystery. They might even be reining in their defenses to protect the Queen in the showroom. Most of what I said about killing the Queen and crushing her wormy body was misdirection. As much as I'd like it dead, I have no desire to see another Queen, nor touch it with my bare hands, let alone squeeze out its guts.

The problem is that if this old codger, or any other Draugr, sees us heading in the opposite direction, the jig will be up. And that leads to two questions. First, can I kill him without being seen? Second, does killing the human host sever the link to the hive mind, or will the parasites still be able to see us and transmit that information to the others?

I suspect that mammalian minds work like some kind of signal booster. If I'm right, severing the connection should leave the Draugar blind to what we're doing. But I also think the sudden silence of the hundreds of parasites populating the man's body won't go unnoticed. If they're as smart as I think they are, others will come to inspect. Maybe even send in the cavalry.

I step back to the others, pull them in close, and whisper, "There's just one. I can take care of him, quick and quiet. They won't know which way we're headed, but I think others will come running to find out what happened."

"We'll need to move fast," Willem says. He turns to Steven. "You can lead the way?"

Steven looks petrified but nods without delay. Feeling a twinge of sympathy for our guide, I take out my knife, unfold it, and hand it to him. "You don't need to kill them all. Just incapacitate. Back of the knees. Back of the neck. Achilles tendon. Don't bother with body shots. They won't even feel it. The odds of you punching the knife through a human skull is slim, so don't attempt it unless you're out of options."

He takes the blade in his shaking hand.

"Remember," Jakob says. "Maintenance first."

"Then a keycard if we need it," Willem adds.

"Don't stop moving," Jakob says. "If someone falls behind. Or is caught. None of you are to stop."

None of *us*. Jakob knows he's older and slower than the rest of us. He's talking about himself. I don't say anything, mostly because I agree with him, and I don't want Willem to hate me for it.

"Even if none of us makes it off of this ship alive," Jakob continues, "this ship and everyone on board needs to sink to the bottom of the Atlantic. Agreed?"

"Yes," says Willem without hesitation.

"You know how I feel," I say.

All eyes shift to Steven. "For Shamaya," he says. "Yes."

Attaboy, I think.

"Stay by the door," I say. "When you hear the Draugr drop, treat it like the start of a race."

When I get all nods, I move back to my position by the open door frame and look up at the mirrored ceiling. The Draugr hasn't moved. Without a glance back, I tiptoe into the duty-free clothing department, staying low behind the racks of clothes.

Halfway across the room, I pause. The stench of old man death has increased. I can hear a slight squeak from his flip-flops as he shifts back and forth. But nothing else, from the man or from the hallway beyond the shop exit. I take a peek to confirm that the space outside holds no immediate surprises. Finding none, I tighten my grip on the *katana* and round the right side of the clothing rack.

As the old Draugr comes into view, I stop. He's wearing a gaudy Hawaiian shirt and turquoise shorts. The top of a paperback novel titled *Pulse* pokes out of the top of his shorts pocket. Something about the dog-eared novel makes me remember that this was a human being not so long ago. He has to be at least eighty, and looks like many of the old-timers I saw at the VA hospitals when my father would take me to visit one of his injured men.

Sorry, Pops, I think and then bring the sword up at a forty-five-degree angle. I feel a tug on the blade as it passes through the tough esophagus and then the spinal column, but I've managed to sever his head and drop the Draugr in a single strike.

Parasitic worms flow from the headless body rather than blood. The head falls at my feet and starts to roll toward me. I tear a shirt off the rack and toss it over the severed neck and head, just in case the parasites within can still communicate with the others.

Footsteps approach from behind. Steven dashes past me. His face is grim as he leads the charge from the duty-free. I follow close behind with Willem and Jakob. The hallway outside is a spectacle of its own, with fluorescent lights, a fountain, and lines of benches. But it's also deserted.

Thirty feet of hallway passes in a blur. As we approach the end, Steven breaks the rules.

He stops.

When I reach his side, I see why.

39

The atrium is nine stories tall and lit up like a pinball machine. The decor is old-world—columns, statues, and ornately carved wooden railings—mixed with the modern. An LED chandelier casting rainbows on the floor and walls hangs from the center of the ceiling. Two long, curved, tapering staircases lead to the third floor, and four glass elevators in each corner rise to the others.

A bar cuts through the center of the space, blocking a direct path to the descending stairs on the opposite side of the massive space. Flashing lights rise from the depths of our target staircase, and I can see the tops of lit letters spelling out CASINO. But that's not our destination. We need to reach the floor *below* the casino, which at the moment seems unlikely. It's all very impressive, but it's not what stopped Steven.

The mangled horde from outside has found its way inside the *Poseidon Adventure*, and congregated in the atrium. They turn to us as one and cock their heads to the side as if they're as surprised by our appearance as we are by theirs. Gnarled zombies—scores of them—occupy each floor. They stare at us from staircases, through the elevator glass, and over the rails of every floor.

My gaze flicks from face to face. They're torn, decayed, and beaten. Not a one of them is uninjured. When my shock over the horde's sudden appearance fades, I remember our urgency. Just fifteen Draugar occupy the lowest floor, spread out around the enclosed bar.

Sword in hand, I charge down the steps. "Move!"

The first Draugr I reach—a man dressed for a night of fine dining—recovers from the horde's mass surprise a moment too late. I see the tiny black speck eyes of the parasite worms filling his eyes shift toward my sword's blade. I played softball in college, and I put all those years of practice to good use. Step in. Swing hard. Keep your eye on the…head. The blade connects with the undead man's temple. I feel the impact, but it's far less than I expected. The strong, sharp blade severs skin, bone, and brain with equal efficiency. I follow through, completing the arc, and watch the top of his skull and brain flip to the floor, where it lands alongside his collapsed body.

With a shout, Willem brings his ax down on a Draugr who has just started moving. The sound of the strike reminds me of a coconut being split. The heavy metal chops through the man's head and stops in his neck. Willem kicks out hard, striking the man's solar plexus, and sends him flying, freeing the ax, which he quickly brings to bear on a woman who's charging him.

The horde is in motion now. Those on the bottom floor move in to attack. The group on the third floor charges down the dual staircases, though *charge* is a generous word. It's really more of a hobble. One of the bunch, whose foot is twisted to the side at a sick angle, topples forward and plows through the Draugar in front of him. It's like watching a Looney Tunes snowball grow larger as it rolls down a hill, enveloping people on the way.

A fast-moving zombie lumbers toward me, arms outstretched and fingers hooked. Ducking low, I swing hard and remove his legs. He falls hard to the side but barely breaks stride as he starts pulling himself forward with his hands. He sticks out his parasite-laden tongue. I can see each one of the maggoty monsters wriggling, eager to find my flesh and take my mind. A quick sword thrust to the top of his head takes the fight out of him.

Jakob appears by my side. I haven't seen him take on a zombie yet, but the gore dripping from his sword says otherwise. "Keep moving," he says, stepping over the man I've just dropped and hacking at the first Draugr to reach the bottom of the stairs.

I look for Willem and find him already on the other side of the atrium, clearing the Draugar blocking our path to the stairs with wide, powerful swings of the double-bladed ax. His attacks aren't exactly precision, but the flying gore and limbs leave no doubt as to his effectiveness. Dead or incapacitated, it doesn't matter. We just want to get through.

A flash of color pulls my attention to the bar. Steven leaps over the side. The zombie pursuing him slams into the bar, stymied by the polished hardwood wall. Steven stands up and looks at the thing, and his eyes widen. As do mine when I see what he's looking at.

The zombie trying to reach him is wearing a white uniform. His cap is missing, but the blue shoulder board with three gold bands and a fourth looped band identify the man as the *Poseidon Adventure*'s captain.

A chain dangles from his neck and disappears beneath his heavily bloodstained reefer jacket.

The keycard.

I change course, heading for the bar, but only make it two steps. A blur passes in front of me, falling from above. A wet thud forces me back. When I look down, I see a stream of parasites crawling from the ruined head of a twisted Draugr. I take another step back.

Whack!

I spin around and find a second Draugr in a similar state. What the—*whack!*

This time I see it. The Draugr came from above. I look up in time to see a fourth man leap from the eighth floor like a BASE jumper.

"Look out!" I shout to Jakob. In the three seconds it takes the dive-bombing zombie to reach the floor, Jakob ducks to the side. He narrowly avoids being crushed but has no time to think about the close call.

The glass elevators are descending. The wave of zombies reaching the bottom floor will soon be joined by their more resourceful counterparts.

"Keep toward the center," I shout to anyone who's listening. Then I take my own advice, leaping over the suicidal zombies and heading for the bar.

Steven looks unsure of how to handle the captain.

I doubt he has the gumption to stab his commanding officer in the head, so I offer him an alternative as I hop over the bar. "Taser him!"

Steven looks at the Taser in his hand like he'd forgotten it was there. He pushes the trigger, activating the blue arc of electricity, and shoves the two metal electrodes against the captain's outstretched arms.

The zombie twitches, frozen in place. The parasites are unable to control the host body while fifty thousand volts course through it.

"Hold it there!" I shout, running up beside him. Without thinking, I reach out and snatch the chain. The resulting shock flings me backward. I fall to the floor, stunned but conscious. And when I look down, I see the chain gripped in my hand, along with a keycard.

To my great surprise, Steven jabs the captain in the side of the head before turning to help me up.

"You okay?" he asks.

"Look out!" I say, pulling him down.

A zombie crashes down on the bar with a crack, his back folding over. *Sonofabitch must have got a running start.*

When I stand back up, the situation has gone from shitty to fucked. The elevators are opening. The stairs leading to the bottom floor are thick with undead, many of whom have spilled out into the atrium. And the Draugr projectiles continue to rain down from above as they sacrifice themselves for the protection of the hive.

"Jane!" Willem shouts from the descending staircase. "Hurry up!"

Even if we make it to the stairs, we're going to have an angry horde hot on our heels. We might be faster, but we're also still human, and eventually our bodies will betray us. The Draugar have no such concerns. I'm about to tell Jakob and Willem to carry on without us when I remember the keycard. They might make it all the way to maintenance only to find the door locked.

Glass shatters. "Help me!" Steven shouts.

He's tossing bottles of liquor at the floor around the bar, saturating rug and zombies alike. Doesn't take a genius to figure out what he's up to, so I grab as many bottles as I can, whipping them at the floor and distant stairs. When I'm satisfied with the job, I dump two bottles on the bar and down its outside edge.

I take the Taser from Steven and hand him the keycard. "Go!" I shout. "Get them to the fuel tanks."

"But—"

"Now, damnit!"

Steve springs into action, leaping over the far side of the bar, where Willem and Jakob await.

Jakob separates a Draugr's head from its shoulders and turns to face Steven. He nearly cuts the man down, but the brightly colored outfit makes him easy to identify. The blade stops short of Steven's neck.

Jakob looks from the keycard to me. I hold up the Taser, indicating what I'm about to do. "Make him go," I say.

Giving me a look that's part regret, part respect, and one of his patented Viking nods, he turns for the stairs, grabbing Willem's arm to pull him along, not giving him a chance to look back. The trio disappears down the stairs.

A few Draugar give chase, but the rest are stopped when I trigger the Taser and place the electrodes down on the alcohol-soaked bar. Flames erupt, nearly singeing my hand. The blaze rockets across the bar, down the side, and across the rug. The lowest floor of the atrium is quickly transformed into the lowest level of hell.

And I'm caught in the middle of it.

40

The burst of heat from the conflagration makes me duck back behind the bar. There's a steady, rising *whoosh* as the fire spreads across the atrium floor. The flames quickly move beyond the alcohol, eating through the rug and carried farther beyond by burning Draugar. They don't normally react to physical pain, but the parasites inside the flaming hosts must know they can't escape, because they're flailing around, rolling on the floor and slapping their bodies. The revolting scent of melting flesh and popping hot body fat mixes with the strong odor of alcohol, twisting my stomach. As screams rise, I wonder if that small part of humanity that resides in each undead is brought forward by the intense pain.

God, I hope not.

The thought is too much to bear, so I push it from my mind and focus on not becoming another human torch.

The flames rise up the staircases, burning through rug and Draugar, but the fire isn't everywhere. There are still some clear paths, especially by the elevator nearest the casino—the area we didn't douse with booze.

The elevator doors open and belch out a dozen ragged-looking tourists. Two of them, a man and woman, wear bathrobes. A matching set. Another woman is wearing just her underwear, a cute matching set of black lace accented by bits of whoever it was that she devoured. A few are well dressed, ready for a day of gambling or lounge hopping. And the rest are wearing the jackets needed for spending time in the Arctic Ocean air.

What a shitty way to end a vacation.

The group heads for the stairwell, shielding their faces and the parasites behind their eyes from the flames. But they're not fleeing the fire; they're chasing the others. As Nate probably would have said, this is unacceptabru.

I pick up a bottle and whip it at the group before jumping over the side of the bar not engulfed in flames. I land on the opposite side about the same time the bottle clocks the underwear model in the back of the head.

She turns and sees me, which means they've all seen me.

The group, which is halfway down the stairs, pauses and turns toward me.

Whack!

A kamakazombie lands right next to me, its ample belly splitting open and loosing its contents as a red-and-white marbleized smear.

If I don't get out of here soon, I'm dead. But I can't let this group follow the others. Not because Willem and Jakob couldn't handle them, but because they might figure out what we're up to.

When the tall brunette turns, I see the injury that has her thrown in with this gnarly lot. Her stomach is torn open. While a lot of her guts are missing and likely eaten, what remains crawls with parasites, each working to coat her insides with their gooey preservative.

She'd be easy to cut down. The long *katana* ensures that the Draugar won't be able to get too close—that is, when I face them one at a time. But I don't want to kill her yet. Facing off against these twelve is not only dangerous but too slow. Sooner or later, more of these bastards will find a way past the wall of fire. If I'm still here when that happens, I'm screwed. Story of my recent life. Move or die.

The woman is a good foot taller than me, and that hole in her stomach kind of puts a monkey wrench in my plan. So instead of kicking her hard in the stomach, I leap up and jam my foot against her chest. The blow stumbles her back. She collides with the others, but the group catches her and props her up again.

So much for the bowling-ball plan.

Time for plan B.

I draw my spare pistol and fire it seven times before the ammo runs out.

Five zombies, including hottie-bo-bottie and four of the winter-clad gang, drop to the floor. There are still seven undead closing in, but I've blazed a trail of bodies straight down the middle of the pack. I waste no time dashing forward, stepping on the dead as I run through the group. I swing out with my sword. It's a random swing, but it manages to eviscerate the bathrobed man. He trips on his insides and pitches forward.

With the stairs just ahead, I think I'm home free when something snags my ankle. My forward momentum snaps to a stop, and I flop to the floor like I've been lassoed. I look back and see the bathrobed man. He managed to grab hold of my ankle when he fell forward.

His grip tightens with inhuman strength. I feel my scabbed-over leg wound reopen as the skin below it is compressed. A scream of pain bursts from my mouth, but it's coupled with action. I bring the sword down, severing the arm and the tendons pulling the fingers tight.

The hand falls away, but the pain remains. I channel my inner Jesse the Body Ventura, tell myself, *I ain't got time to bleed*, and roll backward. The roll takes me away from the six remaining Draugr but over the side of the top step.

As I fall back, I have the presence of mind to fling the sword down ahead of me. It's not that I don't need the weapon anymore—I do—but falling down stairs with a razor-sharp sword is akin to walking into a doctor's office with a paper cut and shouting, "Take the arm!"

Without the sword hacking off my limbs or taking my attention, I manage to partially control my descent and keep myself from being knocked silly. I'll probably be covered in purple polka-dot bruises if I live to see another day, but I make it down the steps in record time, recover the sword, and still have time to taunt the nearest Draugr.

"Hurry up, Suzy-Q!" I shout as I separate the bathrobed woman's legs at the shin. She topples to the side, catching herself on the next step down. But the well-dressed man beside her steps on her head, twists his already shredded ankle, and falls. He rolls down the stairs far less gracefully than I did. When he reaches my feet, I put him out of his misery.

I consider taking care of the others and following after Willem and Jakob, but that idea is quickly squelched by the sound of an alarm, which is followed quickly by the sound of spraying water. The ship's computer system is smart enough to trigger the sprinklers where the fire is without saturating the entire ship, but not smart enough to realize those flames were the only thing keeping the Draugar at bay.

Running feet and loud moans drown out the hissing spray. They're coming for me. And since I've managed to kill another few thousand of their kind, I have a feeling my end will be slow and painful.

I turn and run but don't follow the next flight of stairs down. Instead, I enter the casino. Flashing lights, dinging bells, and mechanical voices surround me. "Howdy, partner," says a slot machine as I pass. "Give me a whirl!"

Rows of slots stretch down the center of the casino. Pews for the Church of the Almighty Dollar. Toward the end of the slots, I see a gray-haired woman sitting at one of the machines. Her head is dipped forward, but her hand is raised and clutching a quarter that's halfway in the slot. I prepare to strike her down with the sword, but there's something different about her. She looks…dead. Like *dead* dead, rather than living dead. When I step up next to her, I see her eyes. The color is faded, but I can still see the brown of her eyes. Not a Draugr. Never a Draugr. She died playing slots while the ship around her went to hell. Old bag went out the way she wanted to, I guess.

I duck behind the old woman's machine as the horde reaches the bottom of the stairs. I'm not sure if out of sight, out of mind will stumble them up, but I need to catch my breath.

The motion-sensitive slot machines near the entrance start jabbering. The electronic solicitations are greeted with angry grunts. The sound of smashing machinery follows. Are they angry at the machines or my disappearance?

Whatever the cause, it seems to have slowed them down long enough for me to suck in a few breaths. But there are more voices joining the chorus. The sound of awkward footfalls grows louder. They're congregating at the entrance.

I look to my left. The wall of slots will hide me from them if I stay low. If I can make it to the side of the room, I might be able to reach the far side before they spot me heading for the exit.

Committing to the plan, I carefully slip the sword into the scabbard still slung over my back. I'm going to need both hands free to crawl. I push off the slot machine and onto my knees.

A metallic *cling* freezes me in place. The sound of a coin making its way through the inside of the slot machine feels like gunshot. I cringe, knowing it was my motion that knocked the woman's hand loose.

The din at the entrance quiets in response to the sound. But nothing moves.

Well, nothing except the old woman. I can almost see her ghost hovering above her corpse, saying, "One more game!" and then shoving her old body forward. I hear a bang, which can only be the woman's face striking the glass. Then her hand falls and strikes the lever just hard enough to trigger the digital slot machine.

The thing ticks loudly. I can't see the images scrolling by, but I know they are. Then one by one, they stop.

An alarm blares.

A spinning red light flashes.

Coins rattle into the metal tray.

Granny Smith is a winner. Which makes me the world's biggest loser.

The horde and I burst into motion at the same time. A quick look back as I leap out of my hiding place reveals at least fifty of the mangled monsters.

The space beyond the slots is more spaced out, with roulette, card, and craps tables. While the tables aren't a problem, the chairs that surrounded them are now strewn about the room, forming a chaotic maze. I leap, twist, and hop my way through rather than clearing a path. The Draugar will have a harder time with the obstacles than I do.

I'm close to the far side exit when a single zombie stumbles into view, blocking my path. He's an average-size man in a casual jacket. Part of his leg is missing, as are several of his teeth.

They're moving to cut me off, I think. A second man stumbles into the entrance, this one dressed as a waiter except the arm that might normally hold a tray of food is missing at the shoulder.

There must be a staircase beyond the doors. Knowing that more could arrive at any moment, I rush toward the open arms and maws of my nightmares made real.

41

With just twenty feet between me and the two Draugar blocking my path, I reach for my sword but then decide against it. Using the blade will mean stopping to swing, parry, and swing again. It's a delay that could allow the horde at my heels time to close the gap.

I see a chair, intending to use it as a shield and ram my way past the two men, but find a better option. A roulette table has been tipped on its side. It looks like it was attacked by an ax; blood smears hint at the demise of whoever tried to use the table as a shield. It's the roulette wheel that grabs my attention. The thick wooden disk is separated from the table, leaning against it.

Without stopping, I take hold of the top of the wheel and lift. "Ugh." I grunt at the effort. It's a lot heavier than I thought. At least fifty pounds. But the adrenaline pulsing through my body enables me to lift it. I take two more steps forward, spinning as I move. Centrifugal force makes the wheel nearly impossible to hold on to, but that's also the idea.

I let go of the wheel and send a spinning blur of red and black toward the pair blocking my path. The solid disk strikes the first man in the face, knocking out his few remaining teeth, imploding his jaw, and knocking him back. He and the wheel smash into the waiter, and they fall together like a pair of dominoes.

The waiter is pinned, but that doesn't stop him from reaching up for me as I leap over him. He probably would have caught me, too, if he hadn't tried to use his missing arm. Instead of catching me, he just looks silly. I've heard that people who lose limbs can sometimes still feel the arm or leg like it's still there, sometimes even having an itch that's impossible to scratch. Seems the parasite's sense of the world is dependent on how the host brain processes external information—except for sight, they've hijacked that sense directly. But they can only smell, feel, and hear the world as well as their host can. I doubt they can taste a thing, though, not with the way they turn the tongue into a parasite delivery system.

I clear the two fallen undead unscathed and dash through the open end of the casino. Had there been doors, I might stop and try to lock them, but the entrance to the casino is open wide, ready to pilfer money from passengers 24/7. So I don't slow as I enter the large hall beyond.

The hallway is short but wide, really just a junction. The staircases descend on either side of the casino entrance. I can hear shuffling feet from above as more Draugar move to cut me off. A hallway branches off to the left, labeled "Promenade Bar, Library, Starboard Deck." A hallway on the opposite side reads "Internet Café, Salon, Port Deck." Straight ahead are two sets of glass double doors—shattered—beneath a sign that reads "Yan's Sushi Bar." No offense to Yan, but rotting raw fish is not a scent that will improve what is already the world's most nauseous experience. A second sign on the wall of the port hall catches my attention. It's a crude drawing of a small boat with the text "In case of emergency—Lifeboats this way."

If I can't lose the Draugar in the maze of hallways, rooms, and bars, then maybe I can hide from them in a lifeboat. With no time to debate, I head left.

The mash of intersecting hallways, though clearly labeled, really is a maze, and while there may not be a minotaur waiting at the ship's core, I think I'd prefer the half-bull, half-human myth to the swarm of zombies. I follow the lifeboat signs, turning left, then right, then left again. The sound of pursuing footsteps fades with every turn. Without a single direction to head or clear target, the hive is going to have to think in several directions at once. They'll follow me for sure, but not all of them.

I push through a door and am shocked as cold air hits me. I'm outside. The cruise ship, along with every other ship bound to the moving island, has its lights on, illuminating the ocean with a brightness equivalent to the noonday sun. Shivering, I close the door and latch it shut. It's not locked, but the metal latch offers some warning if anything opens the door.

I step up to the rail and take in the view. The stars of the night sky are obscured by the artificial light.

They can't see in the dark, either, I remind myself. My relief at being able to see is quickly consumed by the realization that I can also *be seen*.

Jangling chains draw my attention up to the ceiling. Several chains with carabiners at the end hang there. There are three groups of four. What the—*damn*.

"They're gone," I whisper. A quick glance to the right reveals more of the same. Three long lifeboats had once hung here. The winches on the overhang above confirm it, but now the cables are stretched out and attached to the neighboring ship's rail.

Some of them escaped, I think. Word of the zombie infection must have spread faster than the infection itself, and some of the people made it off the ship. *And now they're out there.* I look at the dark ocean beyond the conglomeration of ships. *Probably freezing. Lost. Desperate. In short, a hell of a lot better than being here.*

But they've also taken my hiding place.

The deck to my right stretches two hundred feet before ending at an entrance. But about half that distance is another entrance. I have no idea where it goes, but the sign with the little stick figure descending a staircase that hangs above the door means it heads down. And since Willem, Jakob, and Steven are on the floor below me, down is good.

I sprint for the door. The sound of my feet on the open deck sounds like thunder in the quiet night. If there are any Draugar on the ships below, or within earshot, the collective will have a pretty good idea of where I've gone.

Metal squeaks behind me. I've got company.

That was fast.

As I pull open the staircase door, I look back and see the metal deck door swing open. Dead feet step onto the deck, but I'm hidden from the zombie's line of sight. If I can get this door closed before they—

A groaning croak comes from the staircase.

I shout in surprise as a woman dressed like some Disney princess rushes up the stairs and clutches my sweater. We spill backward, out onto the deck. My back strikes the rail, and I start to tip over it. If not for the woman's hooked fingers holding my sweater, I would have toppled over the rail and fallen fifty feet to the deck of the neighboring ship.

The woman's strong arms yank me forward. Her teeth and parasite-filled tongue go for my neck. I use the woman's strength against her, turning her pull into my push and slamming my forehead into her face. The blow crushes the woman's delicate nose. It doesn't cause any pain to the parasites, but the force of it knocks her back and untangles one of her hands from my clothes. Unfortunately, the same attack that has saved my life has also knocked me senseless.

I blink away the lights dancing in my vision in time to see her coming at me again. Thick blood oozes from her ruined nose. Her mouth opens wide. Her wriggling tongue emerges with a length that would impress Gene Simmons. But this time, I don't need to use my head to fend off the attack. I've got a free arm. And I use it.

The punch's force doesn't come from any kind of learned fighting technique or any advice doled out by the Colonel. It comes from instinct and is powered by a mixture of abject fear and righteous anger, which in this case is a winning combination. The uppercut punch strikes the woman's chin, driving her jaw up. Teeth meet and sever flesh weakened by burrowing parasites, and the tongue flies free, dropping over the rail.

The sudden removal of her tongue seems to confuse the Draugr. Before she can recover, I take the collar of her frilly yellow dress, pull her forward, and sidestep. Her waist folds over the rail. Her feet come up, and she flips out into space. Two seconds later, there's a wet thud as the woman completes the world's worst dismount.

Thumping feet put a damper on my victory. Five Draugar pound down the deck toward me. Their loping run looks like something out of *Planet of the Apes*.

After escaping through two doors and closing the second one behind me, I find myself at a T-junction. To the left is an endless hallway with doors lining either side. Some have trays of food set outside them. Some have Do Not Disturb placards hanging from the knobs. To the right is more of the same. Doors. *More fucking doors!* I swear the designer of this ship must have had a door fetish. I suppose it's possible. Some people get their rocks off by dressing like stuffed animals, so why not doorknobs? Or maybe it's the wood grain? Or hinges? Whatever the reason, this seems excessive. The hall must run the length of the ship.

The door behind me shakes as the pursuing zombies careen into it. *They must have fallen down the stairs*, I think. In another second they're going to open that door, and on my busted ankle there's no way I can run away fast enough.

Fuck it, I think for the third time since Willem and Jakob picked me up at the bar. I don't really want to fight these zombies. Not only am I exhausted and wounded, but the sword will be hard to use in the tight hall. There's no room to swing sideways with any strength, and if I swing over my head, I'm likely to lodge the blade in the seven-foot-high ceiling. But it's not like I've got a choice.

I turn around, backing up a bit, draw my sword, and wait for the Draugar.

42

While the door handle jiggles, a blotch of bright red on the blue and gold rug right by my foot catches my attention. It looks like a credit card, but where the number should be, there's a *Poseidon Adventure* logo.

It's a room key.

I glance at the doors running down both sides of the hall. Specifically the doors near me. *Could it be?*

The door handle turns all the way. I have just seconds before the latch pops and they spill into the hall and see me.

My ankle protests when I squat down and snatch the card from the floor, and it screams when I stand quickly and lunge to the door. I shove the card into the lock of the nearest door and pull it out. The little lights on the lock stay red.

Damnit!

I hobble to the next door, fifteen feet down the hall. Without looking back to see if I'm about to become a meal, I put the card into the lock and pull it out. The lights glow green. There's a mechanical whir and click. I shove the door handle down, push into the room, and quickly close the door behind me. I slow the door just before it slams shut, then carefully bring the handle back up so the lock engages silently.

In a few more seconds, I hear footfalls and grunting voices. Soon, I hear hands running along the wall, the door. They're looking for me.

I stand at the door, trying not to breathe, though my body craves air. Each breath is shaky with panic. *Slow down*, I tell myself. *Breathe.* I pull in a long, slow breath and hold it for several seconds before letting it out again. My panic ebbs. My breathing slows. I'm quiet and in control.

Bang! The door rattles.

I hop away from it but manage not to make any sound.

The door handle shifts up and down, but without a keycard, the Draugar won't be able to get in.

Which is good.

Not so good: I might be stuck here.

The water probably works, so I can last awhile, though not too long without food. But none of that matters, since Jakob and Willem are planning to turn this ship into the world's biggest bonfire. They might wait for me, but when I don't show, they're going to assume I'm dead. Staying in this room means dying for sure.

A body shifts across the door, bangs on it one more time, and then moves on. More bangs resonate from farther down the hall. They're testing all the doors.

They have no idea where I went, I think with some relief. If they keep moving, I can leave and be on my way. Not that it'll be easy. The ship is now crawling with packs of zombies who have a hard-on for Jane Harper, the Queen slayer.

When the shifting, banging, and footfalls of the Draugar fade, I lock the brass swing-bar door guard and retreat farther into the room.

I don't have much time to dawdle, but the relaxing space draws me in like a saucy siren luring mythological sailors to their doom.

The space looks like your average hotel suite, but it is a good number of square feet smaller. The queen-size bed, still nicely made by whichever cleanup crew scoured the floor last, takes up at least a fourth of the space. The rest of the room is taken up by a couch, a wall-mounted desk, and its chair. A dinner-platter-size round window is at the far side of the room. I make a mental note to stay away from it. The room is lit by a single bedside lamp, which was left on. If I move too close to the window, any watchful eyes outside might see me.

A red pillow sits at the front of a four-pillow wall leaning against the bed's faux maple headboard. At the center of the embroidered *Poseidon Adventure* logo is a chocolate.

I sit on the bed and place the sword next to me. With the practiced hand of a woman who used to be a teenage girl with boy trouble, I strip the wrapping off the chocolate and pop it in my mouth. The creamy pleasure feels almost wrong—decadence on a death cruise. It melts away my tension, and I feel myself leaning back.

I stare at the plain white ceiling while I suck on the candy. In the emptiness of my view, guilt washes over me. I should be working on a plan. Or at the very least, fighting for my life. Not eating chocolate and lying on a bed!

The bed becomes uncomfortable. I sit up and consider spitting out the chocolate, but I'm not that much of a sadomasochist. I chew the chocolate quickly and swallow.

When I push myself, my hand strikes something solid. A TV remote.

The large flat-screen is mounted to the wall. I look at the remote, then the TV again. There could be news about the ships. Or about the survivors who got away on the lifeboats. Hell, it would be nice just to see some people whose faces aren't peeling off. My finger rubs the remote's power button. *I could mute it*, I think. *I could—quit pussyfooting around.* My inner monologue puts the kibosh on my emotional craving for distraction.

And without the distraction, I remember that my ankle is throbbing. *Going to have to take care of that.* I scour the room for luggage and find none. The only thing of note is an awful framed print of multicolored ships and anchors, like some kind of cruise-themed Warhol painting.

I head for the double closet door embedded in the wall next to the front door. Inside, I find four drawers full of men's clothing, a rack of more clothes, shoes, and a variety of other typical vacation sundries. I take the bottle of ibuprofen and toss it on the bed, too. Then I turn my attention to the minifridge next to the drawers. The door opens with a tug, revealing two bottles of water. I take one out, twist off the top, and chug. I toss the second on the bed. I'm about to close the door when I see a small ice unit. I open the secondary door and pull out the miniature ice tray inside. After recovering a sock from a drawer, I sit back on the bed, fill the sock with ice, and remove the shoe from my injured foot.

There's some bruising and swelling, but it's not nearly as bad as I thought. I place the ice against the injury and hold it for as long as I can bear, which actually isn't that long. Not because the ice is too cold, but because the ship could go up in a ball of fire any moment now.

When I remove the ice, the swelling has gone down. It's still going to hurt, but I should be able to function. Remembering the ibuprofen, I pop the cap, shake four pills into my hand, and chase them down with a swig from the second water bottle.

Putting my shoe back on hurts. A lot. So much so that I nearly repeat my "fuck it" catchphrase and go barefoot. But I push past the pain and tie the laces. Once the shoe is tight, the pressure actually feels good.

I stand and test my weight. Not great, but better.

I'm as ready as I'm ever going to be, I think. *Well, almost.*

After a quick pit stop in the bathroom, which is barely big enough to bend over in, I head to the door. There's a map of the floor on the back of the door. At least eighty rooms stretch from the front of the ship to the back, then wrap around and continue on the other side. Four well-marked exits lead up and out to the exterior deck above, but there are also three larger stairwells at the center of the ship leading to the bars, shops, and casino—one at the stern and two at the forward end. The stairs nearest the center show an entrance to a long section of the ship's core labeled "Maintenance."

That's where Steven said they would be able to access the ship's fuel tanks.

With a destination in mind, I unlock and quietly open the door, and then just stand there, listening.

Not a sound. If there are any zombies waiting for me, they're not moving or breathing.

I poke my head out like a wide-eyed panicky gopher popping out of its hole, chance a quick peek left, then right. Nothing. The hall is empty.

Actually, that might not be true. Many of the lights have been broken, and everything after the first fifty feet is plunged into darkness on the right. I need to go left, which is good, but anything could be hiding in the murk on the right. Of course, I've already exposed myself, so there's no real reason to stick around.

I head left and move as fast as I can. I get only ten steps before a voice from behind stops me. "Well, howdy there, Raven."

It's not so much the phrase that turns me around as it is the voice and accent. "Talbot?"

I hold my *katana* out in front of me, ready for anything.

Except for what I get.

"Your engine's running, but ain't nobody driving," he says.

"What?" I say, confused by the statement. I'm pretty sure he just called me stupid, but I'm not sure why. "Come out where I can see you."

"This ain't my first rodeo," he says. "Why don't you come here?"

This isn't Talbot, I remind myself. I saw him get infected. Saw the worms. It's his body, but it's not him.

"Come out," I say, growing angry at the fact that the Draugar are using my friend against me. "Now."

"Well, don't you think the sun comes up just to hear you crow."

"Stop it," I growl. The way they're picking Texas Talbotisms from his brain is really starting to piss me off.

"Big hat, no cattle."

"I'll kill you."

"You're as full of wind as a corn-eatin' horse."

That's it. I raise the sword and step toward the darkness.

"It's so dry the trees are bribin' the dogs."

That doesn't even make sense! I speed up, aiming for the shifting shadow I can see just a few feet beyond the darkness. If I swing at an angle, I can put a lot of power into the blow and hopefully connect with his head.

The shifting figure steps forward into the light.

All of my plans unravel.

I stop moving.

My jaw drops.

The sword lowers.

Some part of my mind snaps.

It's Talbot.

But not.

43

Talbot's body is whole and hale. His gun is holstered on his hip. His mustache twitches in the same way. And his voice seems unchanged. His eyes, like all Draugars', are white, but that's not the source of my horror. It's that his feet aren't touching the floor.

Talbot is floating.

He moves a step closer.

Not floating, I realize. *He's being held. But by what?*

I back up a step, and Talbot keeps pace.

That's when the rest of…*it* comes into view.

Arms and legs jut out in every direction. Some push against the floor. Some against the walls. Some against the ceiling. Talbot has been made the figurehead of a conglomeration of human body parts. And his isn't the only full body in the group. I see several more still partially concealed by shadow. I grind my teeth. Some of them are child-size. The bodies seem to be bound together by rubbery mucus. It's like a human caterpillar, but instead of spiky hair, it has human limbs—still-functional limbs.

When the thing moves forward, it's propelled through the hallway by all of its limbs working together. The people are no longer individuals under the control of parasites, they're one organism joined together.

It's the Queen, I realize. The last time I saw something like this was when the island-locked Queen merged a man's legs and Jenny's head with the decayed body of Áshildr, the Queen's vessel.

The parasite watching me through Talbot's eyes must see the understanding in my expression because Diane's face rises up behind Talbot's head. She laughs. "It's the closest thing to beautiful I could do with these horrible bodies."

The Queen-thing moves closer, revealing even more bodies. The part of the abomination now in the light stretches ten feet back. For all I know the shadows might hide another ten or fifty. She might have merged the horde and all those poor children. And the worst part is that the Queen could be *anywhere* inside the mass. Killing the portion that is Talbot, or Diane, won't make a difference. They're all interconnected and have more brains than I can possibly hope to destroy with a sword. Or a bazooka, for that matter.

"Why are you doing this?" I ask.

"Come closer, Raven," Talbot says. "Gimme a hug, and you'll know everything."

I step back as he/it/them floats closer still. The distance between us is shrinking. I'm starting to feel like a rat facing a king cobra. It's just biding its time, putting the fear of God in me. When it decides to strike, it's going to be a blur. My only hope is to keep it talking long enough for me to reach the maintenance area at least a hundred feet behind me.

"I get why you want to kill me," I say. "But what about the rest of the world? The people from this ship. From the other ships. Why kill them?"

Diane shakes her head. "We're an endangered species, Jane. Why wouldn't you want to protect us? Isn't that what you do?"

I keep my backward pace slow and steady. "Killing one species to save another isn't—"

"Killing?" Diane says. "Why, Jane, they're not dead."

Talbot's head goes slack for a moment. When it lifts again, his expression has changed. Instead of anger and loathing, there is fear and horror. Looking through the eyes of the parasites, he sees me. "Jane?"

He looks down at his hands. At his mucus-covered body and the arms protruding from his sides like a spider's limbs. His lips quiver. "I can feel them. I can feel all of them." His eyes widen. "I was right. I was right about everything—yeargh!" He quakes with pain.

"Tell her, Ed," Diane says. "Tell her you're not dead."

He shakes his head. "We're not dead." His voice is shaky. Weak. Defeated. "We're not dead." His voice is more firm. "But we're in hell."

He grits his teeth. His body arcs. The parasites are causing him pain. "Kill us, Raven," he manages to say, and I'm pretty sure he's actually speaking for the lot of them. "Kill us!"

He screams as the pain becomes intense. Then he's a rag doll again. His arms and legs have gone limp. His head hangs. But his mind is still there. I know because he's weeping. Draugar don't cry.

"You see," Diane says. "The relationship is symbiotic. Both species live."

I'm not sure if she's taunting me or if she honestly believes what she's saying.

"Evolved parasitic species don't interfere with the health of the host," she says. "But the most successful are those that actually benefit the host, as we do. Our hosts live indefinitely."

I let a snicker slip out and quickly feel worried about it. This is decidedly *not* funny. So I'm either mocking her or close to hysteria, neither of which strikes me as a good thing, and I suspect the truth is a little of both.

"Talbot," I say. His head comes up a little. "What do you think? Is this beneficial to you?"

He groans again, not wanting anything to do with anything that reminds him of what he's become. But my real intention is to confuse the Queen. "It's like a weight on your hip," I add.

Step back.

"Weight on your hip," Diane says, testing out the phrase. She has no idea what I'm saying. But will Talbot? And if so, will that understanding transmit to the Queen?

Talbot takes a sharp breath.

His head comes up.

His white eyes go wide.

Diane's head looks at him in confusion. And then understanding.

Whatever time it takes for the Queen to transmit her thoughts to the parasites controlling Talbot, it isn't as fast as his quick draw. Talbot's pistol slides from the holster in a blink. The weapon rises. The barrel is leveled.

Talbot's eyes scrunch in pain as he fights the creatures reasserting their control over his mind. With the last of his free will, Talbot pulls the trigger.

I shout in pain at the loud pounding sound of the gunshot's blast, reverberating in the small hall. Talbot's head bursts and splatters against the wall.

He did it, I think. *He set himself free.*

A pain-filled scream rises from Diane's lips, soon joined by the next head. And the next. A wave of high-pitched wails rolls back through the hall as each of them experience Talbot's suicide.

They felt the pain, I think. *They all felt it!* But I don't think it was Talbot's death that set them off. It was the parasites inside his hollowed-out brain. When Talbot put a bullet through his own head, he took a good number of parasites with him.

The monster quakes. Diane lets out a gurgled shout. Her eyes are wide and staring at the ceiling. Talbot's body moves, but he's flopping around due to the movements of the others, not under his own power. His dead body is being shed from the whole. He slips toward the floor as tendrils of mucus stretch and snap.

This is the only chance I'm going to get.

I turn and run.

Diane and a hundred other voices shriek angrily. The sound is nearly loud enough to make me stumble. But I push past the pain stabbing my ankle with each step.

When the shriek repeats, I look back.

Oh shit!

Talbot's body has been discarded.

Hundreds of limbs work as one, pushing the monster forward like a subway car though a tunnel.

The entrance to the stairwell that leads to maintenance is just thirty feet ahead on the right. I ignore the thunder of countless feet and hands pounding the hall's four surfaces and run faster.

But I'm not nearly fast enough.

The living train closes the distance and strikes me from behind. I fall to the floor, just ten feet from my goal.

The pounding run of merged bodies slows, but the sound is replaced by another, far more disturbing cackling. Each and every one of the people bound by the Queen bursts into manic laughter. It grows louder still when a hand takes my injured ankle and pulls me back.

I scream in pain and roll onto my back. My intent is to cut myself free, but I'm shocked into inactivity once more.

The Queen has modified the merged bodies more than I knew. With Talbot's body missing, there is now an open gap at the core of the creature. Where Diane's stomach should be, there's an opening like a mouth. The flesh inside undulates, as though eager. Hungry.

The Queen doesn't want to kill me.

She wants to consume me.

44

So this is how it ends. Eaten by a giant parasite formed from human bodies and millions of tiny asshole worms. But I won't be killed and digested. At worst, I'll be disassembled and merged to the beast, while my consciousness lives on and my memories are hijacked. At best—well, there is no best. I'm pretty much screwed no matter which way you look at it.

Look at me now, Dad, I think. *Bet you didn't think my life would end like this.* I'm not even sure he'd have any hard-edged advice for me now. Probably would just feel terrified for his daughter. Hard as he was, he still cared, and my fate would probably leave even that man speechless. If he's watching now, I hope he has the good sense to turn away, or maybe put a gun to God's head and tell him to help me out.

There's no more taunting from Diane. No more mocking. Our scintillating back-and-forth has come to an end.

My end.

Or at least, that's the intention.

Still, I'm holding a sword that's sharper and stronger than any parasite or the human body it possesses. *Attagirl*, I hear the Colonel say. "You don't have to go down fighting," he told me once. "Just refuse to go down." If the Colonel is watching, he's not looking away, he's shouting at me to kick some ass.

"No!" I shout. "You can't have me!"

With my foot just inches away from being shoved inside the mouth of the writhing mass like a chunk of steak, I sit up, bring the sword down hard, and sever the arm pulling me. The monster twitches, and somewhere far beyond my vision, one of the trapped bodies shouts in pain.

I fall free, but before I can scramble away, a second arm reaches out and catches my foot.

This time, when I swing, I don't aim for the arm. I aim for the body. I hack and slash, back and forth, weakening Diane's form with wide slices. When the maggot-like parasites start falling from the wounds, screaming erupts. The sound of men, women, and children shouting out with each swing of my sword nearly causes me to stop.

Then I remember what Talbot said. They're not alive. They're in hell. Instead of swinging, I thrust. The blade slides in nearly to the hilt, piercing several bodies.

The monster quivers and shifts away from me. But the hand is still holding fast, and I'm pulled along on my ass. A quick swing remedies the situation, and I'm free once again, staggering to my feet. But only for a moment.

The artificially created mouth, which now oozes blood and parasites, opens wide. Tendrils of what I think are human intestines coated in parasitic goo lunge out and wrap around my legs. One tug and I've toppled onto my back. I land hard. The air is knocked from my lungs and the sword from my hand.

I reach for the blade, but it's just inches out of reach.

I stretch for it. My fingers brush the handle.

"No!" I shout as I'm pulled away from the weapon. With my only means of defense out of reach, I do the only thing I can: turn forward and look my enemy in the eyes.

Diane leans forward so that her body and face are directly above mine. Her arms are free, but she's held aloft by the limbs of the Queen's other victims, which poke out from the core like short, jointed tentacles.

She pauses for a moment, her face just a foot from mine. I think she's going to start talking again, which would be fine by me, but she doesn't. Instead, she snarls and takes hold of my cheek. Her hand squeezes tight. Pain and pressure force my mouth open.

She grins savagely, taps into some part of Diane's memory of me, and says, "I've always wanted to do this."

Her white tongue extends from her mouth. She waggles it seductively over my face. The parasites buried in the pink flesh spasm with excitement, preparing to free themselves and infect me.

She angles her tongue for my open mouth.

At first, I'm rage incarnate, struggling, shouting angrily, punching at her.

But when the first of the small parasites is licked against my upper lip, my tough exterior cracks. Tears bleed from my eyes, and my shout becomes a whimper. I'm having trouble seeing. I try to shake my head to the side, but her strong arms hold me fast.

"Hey!" a voice roars.

Diane's head snaps up.

The tongue recoils as her eyes widen.

A blur passes me, and then I hear a wet crunch.

When I can focus again, I see that Diane's face has been cleaved in half vertically.

Her ruined head folds back, and the mass behind her recoils from me as a chorus of screams fill the hall.

"Jane!" The voice is like a drug. All of my fear fades. Willem is here.

"I can't move!" I shout as I try to tug free from the retreating creature.

He rushes past me and swings down with the ax. The pressure on my legs drops away, and I kick free from the loops of intestine. The creature, experiencing Diane's pain, is in full retreat, thrashing wildly and bucking hard, throwing itself into the walls and ceiling.

Willem takes my hand and pulls me to my feet.

I quickly look him over, searching for wounds, and notice that he's doing the same with me. "I'm fine," I say.

He nods and pulls me behind him. "This way." After picking up my sword, I follow him down the hall.

As we retreat from the defeated monster, I look back. It's shedding Diane's body in the same way it did Talbot's, pulling her limp body from the mass. Strands of red-tinged but clear slime, like viscous dog drool, stretch out between the monster and the corpse. The slick tendrils snap, and the body comes free. Diane is cast aside, her corpse of no further use. As the thing's limbs flail angrily, the sconces illuminating the hallway are smashed. The thing is plunged into shadow once more.

Willem pulls me into the large stairwell. The stairs are carpeted in the same blue and gold pattern and look wide enough to allow eight people passage. Steven stands on the stairs to the left, which lead up. Beside the stairs is a door labeled "Maintenance—*Poseidon Adventure* Crew Only."

The door is closed, and a red light on the keycard shows that it's locked.

"Did you get inside?" I ask, looking at the locked door.

"We did," Willem says. His voice is strangely quiet, but I don't notice at the moment.

"Are we all set?" I ask.

"Fifteen minutes," Steven says. He's halfway up the stairs to the next level, holding an unlit Molotov cocktail in his hand. The keycard belonging to the captain of the *Poseidon Adventure* hangs from a chain around his neck. "We need to get the hell out of here before Jakob blows the ship."

I understand the fifteen minutes part, but not the "before Jakob blows the ship" part. I look at Willem. "The hell is he talking about?"

"My father stayed behind," he says. "To detonate the C4."

What? "C4?"

"He had it with him the whole time," Willem explains. "I didn't know until we got down there. It's not much, but it's enough."

"This is bullshit," I say. "C4 can be remote detonated. We are not leaving your father behind!"

"Jane," Willem says, his voice quiet.

"What!" I shout.

"He was bit."

"No…" I say. "No…" Tears return to my eyes. I point my *katana* at Steven. "Give me the keycard."

Steven looks at Willem.

"Give me the fucking keycard, or you won't make it to the top of the staircase."

Steven removes the keycard from his neck. "Geez." He tosses the card toward me, but Willem snatches it out of the air.

"You can't," he says.

I give him a shove. "The hell I can't."

"The C4 is on a timer. It was set for twenty minutes when we left."

"And if he turns before the time is up?" I say. "They'll know about the explosives. They'll know how to stop it."

Jakob would have thought of that. Something doesn't add up.

Willem shakes his head. "I put it out of reach. They can't stop it. Jane, we don't have much time."

I hold out my hand. "I didn't get to say good-bye to my father. I'll be damned if I'm not going to say good-bye to yours."

Willem's eyes tear up.

Whatever Jakob is up to, Willem is definitely not trying to trick me. He's barely holding it together. But I don't want to just say good-bye to Jakob, I want to know the truth. Plus there is another small problem. "Did he give you the key?"

"The what?"

"To the *Raven*," I say, trying not to get angry. Willem is shaken by the loss of his father, and I'm not quite as harsh as mine. "The key. Boats work like cars. Without it, we're stuck here." I'm sure there's a spare on the ship, but I'm not sure where, and Willem's frown suggests that he doesn't, either.

A communal groan echoes from the hallway, as though giving voice to the pained expression on Willem's face.

"Guys," Steven says, his voice a warning. "I think whatever is out there is coming this way."

"When it gets close, use the Molotov to hold it off," I say with a shake of my open hand.

Willem deposits the card in my hand and follows it up with a brief kiss. "Hurry," he says. "I can't lose both of you."

I give him a Viking nod. It's all I can manage without bursting into tears. Then I jam the keycard into the locking mechanism and open the door.

45

The maintenance tunnel is cramped, filled with long white pipes that branch out in every direction. I hurry forward, glancing into a room on the left as I pass. The room contains lockers full of equipment and an array of breaker boxes. Water and shit aren't the only things contained in these pipes.

"Third door on the left," Willem says from behind. "There's a hatch. He's on the next level down."

"If I'm not back in three minutes," I say, "leave without me."

"Not a chance," he replies.

The knowledge that my slow return could cost Willem his stubborn life spurs me on. The smell of gasoline strikes me when I pass the halfway mark. It grows stronger the farther I go. By the time I reach the third doorway, a headache blooms. I've always had this problem with gasoline. Even when I was a kid. Waiting in the backseat of my father's Impala while he filled the tank was something of a torturous experience. I complained about the resulting headache just once, though. To confess discomfort from something as intangible as the scent of fuel—something the Colonel's nose delighted in—was basically asking for a lecture on what the human body can endure when the spirit has the will to endure pain.

As I push through the noxious vapor in search of Jakob, I realize my father was right. Again.

Bastard.

The room contains more pipes, panels, and cables, but none of it matters. There's an open hatch in the floor at the center of the room. A ladder leads two levels down.

Jakob is nowhere to be seen.

When I reach the bottom floor, I turn around, and there's Jakob just five feet away, his back turned toward me. The white walls are metal and featureless. These are the fuel tanks, one to either side of the ship, each containing roughly twenty million gallons of highly explosive fuel. Mounted on one of the walls is a brick of C4 about the size of my fist. It's primed, wired, and ready to blow. The gasoline scent comes from a horizontal geyser of gasoline spraying into the hallway beyond Jakob, where a single hole has been drilled. The powerful drill, its bit a ruined mess, lies on the floor at Jakob's feet.

I take a breath, intent on saying his name, but the fumes tickle my throat and I cough instead.

Jakob whirls around, swinging his sword with a battle cry.

I duck and feel the blade pass over my messy hair. It strikes the ladder with a clang.

Jakob's eyes go wide when he recognizes me. "Raven! What are you doing here?"

Before replying, or taking another breath, I pull my sweater collar up over my mouth and cup my hand over it. I take a breath, lower the collar, and speak. "I think I should ask you the same thing."

"Did Willem find you?" he asks.

"He told me you were infected."

Jakob puts his hand over a wound on his neck, covering it, but not before I can see the clean slice. "Yes," he says.

"You were bit?" I ask.

"We were ambushed," he explains. "There were five of them. It was a silly mistake."

"It's bullshit, is what it is," I say. "If you had a parasite inside you, we wouldn't be having this conversation. You weren't bit. You cut yourself on purpose."

He doesn't reply verbally, but he does remove his hand from the wound, which is clearly superficial, but would have bled a lot when it was fresh.

"Why?" I ask.

Jakob holds up a detonator switch. "The range is poor. There are too many metal walls."

I let go of my sweater collar. That Jakob is willing to blow himself to bits keeps my attention far from my personal discomfort. "There is no timer, is there?"

"I am the timer," he says. "The timer on the explosive is a digital watch. Willem is a smart boy, but he knows nothing about modern weaponry."

"And you do?" I ask.

"I spent the past months with Klein and Talbot," he says. "I was educated."

"You never planned to return, did you?" I ask.

"The Draugar are my family's respons—"

"Shut up!" I shout and punch his shoulder. "I don't want to hear about your stupid family. I don't want your excuses. Or reasoning."

Jakob looks disappointed. "What do you want, Raven?"

"Jane," I say.

"What do you want, Jane?"

What do I want? That's a good question. Part of me wants to chew him out. To tell him he's a fool. That his martyrdom is the most idiotic thing I've ever heard of. But I know the man. He won't be moved. He's committed. He'll see this through to the end. And I respect him for it. And I'm grateful because he's helped me understand my own father more fully. Having experienced what I think is one of the worst scenarios any human being could live through, I now know that there is not only a place in the world for people like my father, but a need for them. And soon there will be one less old codger around to protect us.

A vision of Jakob and the Colonel causing hell at the pearly gates, demanding entrance, lightens my despair a touch. Of course, I'm not sure either of them believes in God, or even if I do, but if that damns them to the abyss, heaven help the devil if the two of them find each other.

With a pained smile, I step forward and wrap my arms around him. "To say good-bye." I try to control my tears and quivering lips but fail pitifully.

He wraps his big arms around me and squeezes.

"I understand," I say. "I understand everything."

He squeezes me one last time before pushing me away. He wipes the tears from his own eyes. "Go. Take care of my son."

"Also," I say, extending a shaking hand, "the keys."

He looks confused for a moment, and then his eyes light up and he's shaking his head, grumbling Greenlandic insults at himself. He digs into his pocket and pulls out a set of keys attached to a small yellow float that would keep them from sinking. A seaman's keychain. He plucks a large, worn silver key from the bunch. "It's this one."

I take the keys. We share a final smile, and I back away to the ladder.

"I'll wait twenty minutes," he says. "But if they find me down here—"

"You do it," I say. "Even if it's five minutes from now. You do it."

"Good-bye, Jane," he says.

I take hold of the ladder. "Good-bye, Jakob."

"Iluatitsilluarina ukuaa," he says.

"Iluatitsilluarina," I reply. *Good luck.* I don't recognize the second word he used, but if I stop to ask, I might not leave. Or have time to leave.

Before I break down and weep like a nancy, I set my jaw, give Jakob a look that says, *See you in the next life,* and climb the ladder as fast as I can. When I reach the top, I look back down. Jakob's not there. He's not just staying, he's leaving. His son. Helena. And me. If I saw him again, I might just decide to stay. Or he might decide to leave. And if that happens, they win.

I close the hatch and lock it.

The sprint back to the stairwell hatch feels agonizingly slow, but it's only thirty seconds before I reach fresh air again, and another ten before I reach the door and swing it open.

Shouting voices greet my return.

"Light it!" Willem shouts.

"I'm trying!" Steven says. He's flicking a half-size translucent red lighter and having little luck with it.

I step between them, take the lighter from his hand.

"It's almost here!" Steven shouts.

I can hear the thumps of the monster's hands and feet on the floor, walls, and ceiling. It's definitely approaching, but after getting stabbed, sliced, and axed, the Queen is being a little more cautious.

They have no idea, I realize. While we've got a ticking clock motivating us, the Draugar believe we're simply trapped and are in no rush to kill, capture, or devour us.

I look at the lighter and see that there's no fluid left. While that'd be the end of it for most people, I've spent an inordinate amount of time around pot smokers and know all the tricks. I place the metal shield in my mouth and bite down hard on it with my molars. The metal bends and snaps free. I spit it out and hold the lighter up. "Get ready," I say.

Steven brings the Molotov close.

I hold the button for just a second, then give the wheel a firm twist with my thumb. With the metal shield gone, the last of the lighter gas is allowed to escape. At a centimeter tall and the width of a pencil lead, the flame is insignificant, but it's enough. The alcohol-soaked rag lights quickly.

Steven moves to the hallway.

Then he steps into it.

"I can't see it," he says. "It's too dark."

I can still hear the army of footsteps. It's close. "Just throw it," I say, moving to the ascending staircase with Willem.

"Steven?" The voice is feminine. Sweet.

Fuck.

"Shamaya?"

"It's not her!" Willem shouts. "Throw it!"

"Steven, I missed you—"

Something about this statement snaps Steven back to reality.

The living train rushes forward.

Steven throws the bottle. It crashes on the floor, setting the hallway ablaze and lighting the living train rushing toward him. Shamaya leads the way, arms outstretched. She shrieks as the flames set her ablaze, but the monster doesn't stop. It slams into Steven and continues past. His horrified screams make me cringe, but they're quickly drowned out by the anguished wail of the now burning bodies rushing through the fire.

Willem and I watch the mash of bodies flow past for just a fraction of a second before turning and bolting up the stairs.

Two flights later brings us to the main deck. A group of three Draugar spots us and head our way, but we never even slow down to look at them. We charge down the first hallway we find and head starboard. Rushing. Panting. Slamming into walls. Our retreat is anything but quiet. But at this point, we don't really care.

Willem crashes into a door, fights with the handle, and then throws it open. Cold air rushes over us. We head out into it.

"Do you see it?" Willem asks, looking to his left.

I turn the other way. "Here!"

The harpoon fired from the *Raven* is still embedded in the wall, pinning the Draugr woman to it. She's alive but unable to move. That doesn't keep her from reaching for us or from transmitting our location to the hive.

With a grunt, Willem swings his ax and removes the woman's head. The collective knows we're here, but they won't know what we're doing. Or where we're going.

I step onto the rail, take hold of the wire, and prepare to wrap my legs around it.

"Hold on," Willem says, looking over the rail, toward the *Raven*.

My view is upside down, but I can still clearly see what he's seeing.

Nothing. There is a pile of bodies at the front of the ship, lit by the fleet's array of halogen bulbs and spotlights, but Klein and Helena are nowhere in sight.

The *Raven* has been abandoned, or worse, overrun.

46

I look back at the empty forward deck of the *Raven*. Helena and Klein are missing, but I don't see any active Draugar, either. There could be a mob of living dead waiting for us belowdecks, but there's no way to find out. The sound of approaching feet reaches my ears. *Doesn't matter*, I decide. *If the Raven is lost, we'll take it back and bug out before—oh my God, I've become my father.*

I swing my feet up and lock my legs around the wire. Willem quickly undoes my belt. I'm about to complain when he wraps it around the wire and buckles it again.

"Thanks," I say, and then pull myself along the wire. The cable is strong but thin and freezing cold. My hands burn from cold after just a few pulls. But the downward angle of the taut wire also makes the going easy, and I'm quickly a quarter of the way across.

The cable suddenly bounces. I'm tossed back and forth, up and down. I squeeze my hands tight and clench my legs together. But I'm tired and beaten. My fingers spring loose from the cable and I fall back. My back arches painfully as my descent is quickly arrested by my secured belt.

Willem saved my life. Again.

"Sorry," Willem says.

With a grunt, I pull myself back up and grip the cable. I look toward my feet and see Willem sliding toward me. The cable shook when he climbed on.

Okay, so he nearly killed me, too.

Not that he had much choice. There are three Draugar standing by the cable. They're just staring at us right now, but that will soon change. The horde knows where we are and where we're heading.

I redouble my effort and make decent time. Before I reach the bottom, the cable starts wobbling and shaking. I glance back, wondering if Willem is having trouble, but he's almost caught up to me. It's the Draugar. All three of them have taken to the cable and are clumsily pulling themselves along.

Ignoring our pursuers, and that my hands feel like they've been dipped in gasoline and set alight, I complete the journey and stop just before the harpoon gun to which the cable is attached. I unbuckle my belt and fall to the deck a few feet below. I pull myself aside in time to miss Willem's drop to the deck. He frees himself from the cable so fast that I realize he didn't bother buckling himself to the cable. He could have fallen at any time.

My body protests as I stand, but we're far from safe. The Draugar giving chase have only covered half the distance, but they seem to have gotten the hang of it. They'll be here soon. I draw my sword and swing it at the cable. A loud metallic *twang* rises up the wire, but the blade can't cut it. My arms vibrate from the impact, and I nearly drop the sword.

My body is rebelling against me. I won't be able to stay on my feet much longer. We need to get the hell out of here.

"Jane," Willem says, and he actually grins. He takes his ax from his back and gently whacks a metal pin where the cable connects to the harpoon gun. The cable shoots free, springing away like it was fired from the cannon. The three Draugar fall without a sound.

With the cable detached, the *Raven* starts to drift backward, away from the conjoined fleet. "You know how to reverse out of the prop foul?"

I take the key from my pocket and toss it to Willem. He heads for the bridge. "My father taught me."

Mention of his father sours my stomach. Jakob is still alive, hidden within the bowels of an infested cruise liner and perhaps just moments away from sacrificing his life to save ours. *Not just our lives*, I think. *He's saving everyone on the damn planet.* That's what I understood. That's why I let him do it. Because if he hadn't, I would've.

"C'mon," Willem says when he reaches the stairs.

"Can't," I say, pointing my sword to the nearest ship, still within leaping distance. "We have company."

Draugar approach from every direction.

Willem charges up the stairs without a word. If we don't get out of reach, there's no way I can stop that many, not even if I didn't feel like I'd spent the day playing Roller Derby with a bunch of roid-raged women.

The *Raven*'s engines roar from beneath. The ship slowly inches backward. Willem needs to gently unravel the prop fouler line so that it falls away instead of just rewrapping around the prop in the other direction. It makes for slow going, but we *are* going.

Five Draugar, some of the healthiest looking I've seen thus far, reach the nearest ship. They leap out, arms outstretched, and smack into the side of the *Raven*. There are four splashes as the failed long jumpers drop into the ocean.

Four splashes.

I step closer and see the fifth zombie's hands clinging to the lower rung of the forward rail. I lean over the rail and look down at the man. He's athletic and strong and dressed in tight exercise clothes. Must have been working out when all hell broke loose. He looks up at me with fluid white eyes but doesn't bother trying to climb up. He knows it's no use. So he just stares. She's watching me. The Queen is watching me.

"I know you can see me," I say. "I know you can hear me."

No reply. Just an angry scowl.

"I hope you like barbecue," I say.

A hint of confusion emerges on the twisted face. When I grin, the scowl becomes a sneer. The man opens his mouth to retort on behalf of the networked Queen, but before a word can escape, I jab my sword into his skull. The hands go slack, and the Draugr falls into the dark ocean.

"And the last word goes to Jane Harper," I say. The ship shakes from an impact. "Or not."

Free of the prop-foul line, the *Raven* moves away from the glowing island of ships. Draugar gather along the outer fringe, staring at me. I'm tempted to flip them off, or perform Willem's classic "cocksucker" gesture, but the ship is struck hard again.

The *Raven*'s exterior lights, including several spotlights aimed at the surrounding water, turn on. I run to the port bow harpoon and look over the rail. A passing humpback fin is caught in the glow of a spotlight. I turn the harpoon down and pull the trigger. The explosion of the firing harpoon and its exploding head shake the air just seconds apart. I duck away from the edge as water and whale meat slap against the hull. When I look again, the whale is gone, but chunks of flesh and a severed pectoral fin swirl in the bloodied water.

As Willem brings the ship about, I rush to the harpoon on the other side, searching for a target. I'm surprised when I find none. Where are the sperm whales? The blues? Their combined might could be enough to sink the *Raven*, and I've given the Queen every possible reason to unload the big guns without mercy.

The *buzz-whump, buzz-whump* sound of a small speedboat cutting through the waves tickles my ears. There's another boat moving out here. Wondering if the Draugar are giving chase, I search for the boat and find it on a collision course with the *Raven*.

I position the harpoon gun toward the ship and place my finger on the trigger. The motor is in the back, which I can't see, or shoot, but the explosive-tipped spear should reduce the small craft to splinters.

The speedboat comes off a wave. The prop buzzes as it cycles faster in the open air. I aim for where it will land and nearly pull the trigger. A rising humpback causes me to hold my fire. The breaching whale just misses the boat's aft. A barrage of automatic gunfire draws my attention to the front of the boat as it lands again.

Helena crouches atop the forward deck, holding one of the automatic weapons, but she tosses it away. Klein stands behind the wheel, steering the fast-moving craft, angling it toward the *Raven*. *They're alive!*

My small measure of relief is short-lived. A blur of white pulls my eyes down. Two ghostly white forms lit by spotlights surge out from beneath the *Raven*'s hull and rocket toward the approaching speedboat. I recognize them immediately. Narwhals. Their sixteen-foot-long, two-ton bodies will make short work of the small craft, which appears to be just fifteen feet long and a small fraction of the weight. But the danger is increased dramatically thanks to the ten-foot-long tusk jutting out of the whale's head like a unicorn's horn. That the creatures are now Draugar is almost fitting; their name comes from *nár*, the Old Norse word for corpse.

As the white blurs close in on their target, I aim the harpoon just ahead of the whales, which also happens to be just ahead of the speedboat, and fire.

47

The harpoon launches. Coils of cable unravel as it travels the distance. The tip pierces the ocean, slips through a foot of water, and comes to rest a foot inside the head of one of the two narwhals. Then it explodes and reduces the front half of the creature to something resembling pink-slime beef filler.

But despite my lucky shot, the second narwhal continues forward unscathed.

Klein reacts to the sudden appearance of the whales, and the explosive fate of one of them, by turning the wheel. But the effort is too late. Almost four thousand pounds of fast-moving whale strike the bottom of the fifteen-hundred-pound motorboat, and Einstein's laws of action and reaction take over.

The ten-foot tusk pierces the hull first, slipping through the fiberglass like a needle through skin. The lance stabs up, emerges from the deck, and punches through Klein's chest, lifting him high into the air like a speared fish.

The whale's head strikes next. The ship's forward momentum is arrested in an instant. Helena, however, continues moving. She's launched out over the ocean. Halfway through the arc of her flight, she takes control of her body, twisting until she's facing forward. The chaotic fall becomes a well-formed dive.

God, I like this girl.

She enters the water like a torpedo and surfaces just ten feet from the *Raven*'s hull. I toss a few more loops of cable into the water so that it goes slack. In my current condition, I couldn't possibly climb up the frigid metal cable, but Helena is strong and wearing gloves, which do nothing to thaw her out—she's soaked to the core—but help her grip the line.

When she nears the main deck, I reach over the rail, take her coat, and help haul her up. We fall to the deck, cold, wet, and exhausted.

Willem must have seen all this because once Helena is safe on deck, the *Raven*'s engines roar. We pull away from the island at full speed.

"What about Klein?" Helena asks, pushing herself up. Her lips are blue, and her body is starting to shake.

I shake my head. "He didn't make it."

She clenches her fists and whispers a curse. The anger gripping her face is suddenly replaced by concern. She looks around the deck. "Where are the others?"

"Willem is in the bridge," I say. "Talbot is dead."

My silence about Jakob is deliberate but quickly noticed. Helena grips the arm of my sweater, twisting the fabric. "Where is Jakob?" she asks.

I look at the glowing island of ships, but I can't bring myself to speak.

Helena twists her fist. The sleeve constricts my arm. "Where is my father?"

"Doing what needs to be done," I say, never taking my eyes off the cruise ship.

Helena follows my gaze and looks at the ship. "No…"

A muffled *whump* makes me jump. The sound is so deep and powerful that it shakes my body. A sharp crack tears through the air and is followed by a fireball like something out of a sci-fi apocalyptic film. The orange glow, traveling at the speed of light, illuminates everything for a mile. The boom, traveling at the speed of sound, arrives next. It knocks Helena and me to the deck, which is good, because a hot pressure wave follows.

The ship is lifted up and tilted at a sharp angle. Helena and I slide across the deck on a collision course with the port rail. The ship rights itself a moment before we hit, sparing us further pain. While the ship cants back and forth, finding its equilibrium, Helena and I clutch each other, ducking our heads beneath our arms as glass from the shattered bridge windows rains down from above.

When the sound fades, the glass stops falling, and the ship is no longer wobbling like a Weeble, Helena and I separate and get our first look at the aftermath of the explosion.

The gates of hell have been opened in the North Atlantic. The cruise liner—what little hasn't been reduced to confetti or already sunk—is burning with flames that reach hundreds of feet into the air. The surrounding ships are shredded, sinking, and burning as well. It's the world's biggest bonfire. If there are any astronauts looking down at this part of the world tonight, I have no doubt they'll see the orange glow as easily as I do. We're a half mile from the burning fleet, but I can still feel the heat. Helena's soaked clothes are actually steaming.

"He did this?" Helena asks.

I look up at her. She's even more beautiful in the orange glow. I nod. "He died well."

Despite the tears threatening to spill from her eyes, she smiles. "He died amazing."

"Yes," I say as one of the large ships overturns and slips beneath the waves. A series of secondary explosions rips through the night as fuel tanks erupt and add to the column of fire. Even the water surrounding the ruined fleet is burning. "He did."

An impact rocks the ship.

"Fucking serious!" I shout, annoyed that this fight is not yet over. The fleet is destroyed. The Queen is dead. And they're still taking potshots at the *Raven*? Unless… "What happened to the blue whales?"

"They left an hour ago," Helena says. "Most of the whales did."

"Where?"

Helena looks straight ahead and points. "North."

As I stare into the darkness to the north, I see something large faintly glowing in the light cast by the massive fire. "What the hell…"

The ship is struck again. I feel the jolt, but it's nothing compared to the impacts delivered by the sperm whales that attacked before. A juvenile humpback breeches and slams itself onto the deck. It doesn't come close to landing on us, but we back away as it flops back into the ocean.

"I think they're pissed," Helena says.

She's right. They're not going to let us leave without a fight. "Where's the grenade launch—"

"Jane!" Willem shouts from the bridge.

I look up and see him leaning out one of the shattered windows. His face is covered with bloody cuts, probably from flying glass, but he appears to be okay, that is, if you ignore wide-eyed worry.

He thrusts a finger north, pointing toward the faintly lit object. "Take cover!" he shouts.

Take cover?

He shouts again. "It's a destroy—"

A sound like the world's largest chain saw revving up pulls my attention north. In the distance, I see twin spikes of fire. The light illuminates the giant ship that I quickly recognize as a US destroyer. Bright orange tracer rounds flow toward us like twin laser beams, chewing a path through the water, straight toward us. The buzz of the twin chain guns is joined by the slower but louder boom of two 57mm close-in guns. The big gun fires two rounds every second.

The barrage is enough to tear the *Raven* to pieces, so I don't bother taking cover. If the Draugar have a destroyer, we're like Spock in the *Enterprise*'s reactor room—dead—except without the being-reborn Project Genesis stuff.

So I watch.

As the powerful rounds rain down, I'm struck by a realization—this destroyer has really shitty aim. They're chewing up the water all around us, but not a single round has struck the ship. Not one.

Then the world goes silent, and the destroyer disappears into the darkness once more.

"Are you crazy?" Willem shouts from above as he reappears in the window.

Helena stands up next to me—she'd dived to the deck.

I shrug. "I didn't think it would matter."

He shakes his head, exasperated.

I hear a voice. It's small and garbled by static. "Come—this is— Is everyone—" The voice is coming from the radio.

"This is the *Raven*," I hear Willem say. "Say again. I repeat, say again."

The destroyer wasn't trying to kill us, they were saving us!

I rush up the stairs, pushing my sore legs to the limit, and enter the bridge as the voice replies. "This is the USS *Bainbridge*. Are you okay? Did we get the sonsabitches? Over."

Willem turns to me and extends the radio in his hand.

Helena enters behind me. "What are you waiting for?" she asks.

At first I think she's talking to Willem, but then I notice she's looking at me.

"Why me?" I ask.

"My father made you first mate," Willem says. He doesn't need to explain any further, but he does. "You're the captain now."

"But—"

"I've seen his will," Willem says. "The *Raven* is yours. It was always intended to be."

Something about the way he says this triggers a realization. "You knew," I say. "You knew he wasn't bit."

He nods. "I figured it out." He holds the radio out. "Captain."

I take the radio from him slowly, the surreal moment dragging out. I push the call button and speak. "This is Jane Harper, captain of the whaling vessel *Raven*. We're in bad shape but alive. Thanks for your assistance. Over."

"Copy that, Harper," the man says. "Maintain your heading, but be ready to power down. We'll come alongside. Or medics are standing by to receive you. Over."

"Roger that," I say with a grin, hearing my father's voice in my own. "Will do. Over."

"Sounds like you've done this before, Harper. You have a military background?" the man asks.

I think of all the time spent with the Colonel, being taught the same lessons as the men he trained, learning the lingo, and taking more hard knocks than the average recruit.

"Yeah," I say. "I do."

EPILOGUE

Two hours later, our wounds have been tended to and we're enjoying bowls of beef stew in the *Bainbridge*'s mess. We're warm, bandaged, and safe but feeling a little bit in the dark, since no one has said a word to us in the past thirty minutes. I'm pretty close to pulling a "Harper," which is the moment my father, or I, lose our patience and tear some unfortunate soul a new asshole until answers are forthcoming. If not for my physical and mental exhaustion, I'd have already started my one-woman war for answers. For now, the stew has bought the crew some time.

While being patched up, we were gently interrogated by the ship's captain, Kane Gilmour, who looks a little like Richard Gere but with a scruffy beard. He spoke to us one at a time, asking about our encounters with the whales, what happened on the island of ships, the parasites (after I brought them up), and why the *Raven* was outfitted like a "whale slayer." He started with Willem and finished with me. When I completed my description of the *Raven*'s weapons and their intended purpose, he gave a nod, said, "Awesome sauce," and left.

We were escorted to the galley a short time later and offered a choice between fish fillets and beef stew. We all took the stew and were pleased when large cubes of corn bread arrived with it.

With my stomach near bursting, I lean back in my chair, stretch, and let out an old-fashioned military-style burp that relieves some of the pressure on my stomach.

Willem chuckles and polishes off his meal.

Helena, however, has only eaten half her food. She sits across the table from Willem and me, looking back and forth at the two of us. "How did you do it?"

"Do what?" I ask, thinking she's talking about some aspect of our time inside the *Poseidon Adventure*.

"Deal with all this," she replies. "The first time, I mean. After the island. Our friends are dead. My father. Not to mention all of the people just living their lives on all those ships. They're *all* dead, and we're eating beef stew and laughing at burps."

By *we*, she means Willem and me. She's definitely not laughing.

I look to Willem. "Some of us did better than others." It's an admission that doesn't agree with me, but it's the truth. "I hid. Drank. Got in fights. Watched TV. You know, real womanly stuff. Mostly I tried not to think about what happened, but that's impossible."

I shift in my seat, battling my physical and emotional discomfort. "Your brother did it right, though. Focused on his family. Forged strong bonds."

"But," Helena says. "Your father…"

I know what she's trying to say. I don't have a family. But she's wrong. I hold my hand out to Willem, and he takes it. "Families can be made," I say and hold out my other hand to her.

She smiles and wraps her fingers around mine.

"We'll get through it together," I say. Thinking of family brings my thoughts back to Jakob and his final words to me. "Before I left him—your father—he said something that I didn't fully understand."

They both look at me with eager eyes, clearly curious about the last words their father spoke on this earth. "Iluatitsilluarina ukuaa," I say.

The response is immediate and not at all what I expected.

Both of the somber Vikings break out laughing. Willem's laugh is subdued, but his face is turning beet red. Helena cups her hands over her mouth in an attempt to mute her laugh, but to no avail.

"What, did he call me a bad word or something?" I ask.

"Depends on your perspective," Willem says, laughing a little harder now.

Helena opens her mouth to speak, and it's clear by her expression that she's about to let me in on the joke. But Willem raises his hand at her. "Wait! Don't!"

"Willem," I growl, "I swear if you don't—"

"Daughter-in-law," Helena blurts out with a guffaw. "He said, 'Good luck, daughter-in-law!'"

That wily SOB. I try to fight it, but a smile creeps onto my face, which is likely growing as red as Willem's. When the door to the mess bangs open, I'm grateful for the distraction. That is, until I hear the tone of our visitor's voice.

"Harper!" Gilmour shouts. He enters with two other officers and a few sailors.

"What's going on?" I say, sounding a little defensive because it looks like I'm about to be thrown in the brig.

But Gilmour pounds straight past our table and heads for the flat-screen TV mounted in the back corner of the mess.

I stand and follow him. Tight wraps on my legs, coupled with some military-grade painkillers, dull the pain from my injuries, but the ache seems to have grown worse, or maybe I'm just noticing it without zombies or whales trying to eat me.

"What's going on?" Willem asks.

Gilmour turns on the TV and steps back with a remote in his hand.

"Three fifty," one of the other men says.

Gilmour changes the channel, punching in the numbers with enough force that the remote makes a crunching sound with each push. The screen goes black while the satellite TV connects to the selected channel. Gilmour looks back at us. "Nuuk has been quarantined."

Helena pushes past some of the men blocking her view of the TV. "What!"

"Came through ten minutes ago," the captain says.

The channel connects, and an image is displayed on the screen. It's a helicopter view, Nuuk. The patchwork of islands filling the harbor and the brightly colored homes, not to mention my towering apartment building, are easy to identify.

I notice the lack of channel logo or graphics and ask, "What channel is this?"

"It's a secure military channel," Gilmour says. "This is a live feed from a recon Comanche."

The aerial view sweeps down toward the harbor. Lines of docked ships stretch along the dock…which is covered in corpses.

"What happened?" Willem asks.

When the view shifts from the dock to the long, pebbly beach just beyond, I know the answer to that question. Thirty now empty lifeboats line the shore. They didn't carry survivors. They carried Draugar. That's why only injured, immobile, and weak Draugar remained behind. The rest—thousands of them—were sent to Nuuk.

The camera pans up, revealing a city in ruins. Smoke billows from several fires. I can see people running. And more chasing them. Cars race down streets, careening into everything and everyone.

"No!" I shout. "God damnit!"

Willem puts his hand on my shoulder and squeezes. He calms me and reassures me all at once.

"You know, I thought you all might be suffering from some kind of delusion," Gilmour admits. "Whales are one thing. They were attacking us all day."

"They weren't attacking you," I growl. "They were distracting you." I point to the screen. "From them."

Gilmour frowns. "Parasitic zombies are a little hard to swallow. But now…" He motions to the TV. "I mean, there it is. Reports coming out of the city support everything you've said."

"What are you doing about it?" Helena asks.

"Right now?" Gilmour says with a shrug. "Nothing. We're waiting for—"

"Take us there," I say.

"What?"

"The three of us," I say. "Give us weapons or not. But take us there."

"There is an army of those things running around the city." Gilmour shakes his head. "Even if you weren't torn to bits—which you are—the three of you aren't going to take back the city on your own."

"I'm not interested in Nuuk," I say.

"You're not?" he says.

"You're not?" Helena repeats.

"They're just passing through. They'll head for the mountains."

"How could you know that?" Gilmour asks.

"Because she knows what they're looking for," Willem says, understanding filling his eyes.

Gilmour crosses his arms. "And what might that be?"

I look up at the screen and the ruined city that was my home for the past few months and Willem's home for most of his life. I clench my fists, doing my best to contain my anger. We've come so far and sacrificed so much. We thought we'd won. And Jakob...he gave his life—for nothing.

Not nothing. He killed a Queen. And that means there is only one left, trapped somewhere in the mountains of Greenland. But she's not alone. There's something else out there that the Draugar want just as much.

I set my eyes on Gilmour and give him a look that says I'll rip his nuts off if he doubts what I say next. When he gives a slight nod of agreement, I tell him.

"The host."

"What's the host?" he asks.

I'm about to shout, "How the fuck should I know!" when I remember some of Talbot's last words and lower my head.

I was right. I was right about everything.

"It's an alien," I say. "A fucking alien."

ACKNOWLEDGMENTS

Most of my acknowledgments over the years have featured long lists of people who contributed to the initial writing effort in some way, whether it is research, advance reading, brainstorming, etc. But for this book, I just sort of disappeared into my imagination, lost in the voice of Jane Harper, which is to say, I had a lot of fun writing this book! There are, however, plenty of people to thank in getting this book into readers' hands.

To Scott Miller, my agent at Trident Media Group, thank you for your resolve, commitment, and hard work. At 47North, I must thank Alex Carr, who saw potential in a wise-cracking, foul-mouthed, kick-ass heroine. Also at 47North, thanks to Katy Ball, Patrick Magee, and Justin Golenbock. Your support means a lot, and I'm looking forward to knocking this one out of the park with your help. I must also thank Jeff VanderMeer, whose supreme edits greatly improved this book.

And finally, my dear family. Hilaree, my wife, and Aquila, Solomon, and Norah, my wildly creative and fun children—I love you guys and am thrilled to be sharing the adventure of life with you.

ABOUT THE AUTHOR

Jeremy Bishop began his career as an artist and comic book illustrator, before turning to screenwriting, and eventually fiction. His first novel, the post-apocalyptic zombie epic *Torment*—a #1 Horror bestseller on Amazon.com, was a self-publishing success story. In addition, as bestselling author Jeremy Robinson, he has written more than thirty sci-fi, thriller, and action/adventure novels and novellas, five of which are published by Thomas Dunne Books/St. Martin's Press. His novels have been translated into eleven languages. He lives in New Hampshire with his family.

Printed in Great Britain
by Amazon.co.uk, Ltd.,
Marston Gate.